I0659857

Death is Overrated

By

Jeffrey Perren

Deep Read Press
Lafayette, Tennessee
www.deepreadpress.com

Copyright © 2021 by Jeffrey Perren

All Rights Reserved. No part of this book may be reproduced, stored in a retrieval system, or transmitted in any form or by any means without permission of the publisher, except by a reviewer who may quote brief passages in a review to be printed in a newspaper, magazine, or journal.

First Deep Read Press edition

Printed in the United States of America

ISBN: 978-1-954989-02-3
Cover Design by: Kim Gammon
Edited by: Brenda Seaberg
Published by:
Deep Read Press
Lafayette, Tennessee
www.deepreadpress.com

Para Aydé, mi alma gemela

"I love the man that can smile in trouble, that can gather strength from distress, and grow brave by reflection." – Thomas Paine

1

THOMAS didn't plan to end up dead on his vacation. To the contrary, he kept insisting the man lying lifeless on the ground was not Thomas Payne. Couldn't be, since he was. It was just bad luck that the Brecon detective on the scene was as dense as a Welsh peat bog.

Detective Inspector Bedwyr knelt on the moss outside Dan-yr-Ogof Cave and leaned over the dead body. He rifled through its backpack, barely still attached, and culled a passport from an inside sleeve. After inspecting the document then the body again, he declared that the stiff was indeed Thomas Payne, like it or not.

The animated Dr. Payne didn't like it at all. He argued at length, but nothing moved the copper. He gave his home address in the United States. He described his Cardiff laboratory an hour south of Brecon. He even leaned over and held out his thumbs for comparison to the passport print.

Bedwyr eyed the thumbs suspiciously, then transferred his gaze to the eyes of the man holding them out. "U.S. passports have no thumb prints, sir."

Thomas, his gut clenched from a suspicion-inducing error, said nothing.

The inspector closed one eye and clamped his mouth, his lips forming two lines devoid of nuance, like his thinking.

After all, why should he doubt? He had Thomas Payne's passport in hand, taken right off the body. And the victim's face — the half still intact after an apparent fall from the cliff above — matched the photo pretty well. He'd even bet his partner that the lab would say the thumb prints matched.

He laid the passport on the body and leaned over. "Do you mind?" he asked, snatching one of Thomas's still-proffered thumbs. He pressed the digit to his ancient field-issue ink pad then pushed it onto a small, white card. It pays to be sure, he always said.

He didn't offer an alcohol wipe as he closed the pad and put it back in his pocket along with the card. He ignored his partner's sneer as the junior inspector wagged the biometric tablet like a fan. "Never trust 'em," Bedwyr growled.

Thomas looked aghast at his purple thumb then back down at the detective, as if the man had stolen his soul. Branded like a criminal. Like his father. He tensed to keep from shaking, but it only made his tremors worse.

The DI made another close examination of the body. He was a careful sort who rarely made mistakes, or so he'd swear.

By contrast, Detective Sergeant Bevan, now taking down accounts from the milling spelunkers nearby, swore often, in both senses. Profanity passed his lips as often as Welsh whiskey. He'd swear in court too, if necessary. To anything. Anything for the pleasure of seeing men he despised put away, and he loathed this lot on sight. Jammy university gits. Privileged pansies, in his view.

Even though the cops had been on the scene for only minutes, both were firmly convinced already they had the facts right. The possibility that a man would kill someone then plant his own passport on the body was absurd, like a balmy trick out of a comic film. The dead man was Dr. Thomas Payne all right. There could be no mistake.

Thomas complained someone *had* made a mistake. He was standing upright and the body was definitely horizontal. It just couldn't be him. To think otherwise was to embrace the most elementary contradiction in geometry, not to mention biology.

He tried again to reason with the senior detective. "Look, Inspector. I'm alive. You can plainly see that. And I *am* Dr. Thomas Payne, I assure you."

Bedwyr, busy examining the body, said without looking up, "We can't go by assurances, sir." His words were polite but his tone was dismissive. He knew his job and no bloody tourist from America was going to mock his investigation.

Finally, he turned to face Thomas squarely. "Have you any identification?" he asked for the second time, his voice stern. He picked up the passport again with a latex-gloved hand and tapped it in his other palm, effectively smearing any prints it might have.

"You're holding it," Thomas protested, jabbing a finger at the document.

The kneeling hulk dropped the booklet into a plastic evidence bag. "We'll see." He put the bag in his coat pocket and aimed a grimace at Thomas. "Can anyone here vouch for you?" He waved his arm toward the clot of cavers talking to his partner.

"I've never met them in person before yesterday. But I've worked with all of them for over a year on a research project I'm head—"

Bedwyr silenced Thomas with a snort. The inspector didn't think he needed to point out that anyone could claim to be the person who sent them emails. "Ever chatted with them by video?" he asked, his voice smug. No one was going to suggest he didn't know the latest technology.

"No, we never felt the need."

"Well, there you go. No one to vouch for you." The inspector turned away before Thomas could answer and focused his attention on the rocky outcropping above the cave entrance to his right. He scanned the rim, searching for loose stones. Any he found might suggest the young man at his knee died by accident.

Possible, not likely, he concluded after another examination of the victim's face. He'd have to take a closer look from the top later.

Sergeant Bevan, done taking statements, ordered the cavers to stay put and went to examine the ground around the body. The surface was soft from a thick covering of low vegetation and he reached the same conclusion as his partner. Even if the body had simply fallen from above, the impact couldn't account for the bloody pulp that was now one side of the corpse's face.

He'd seen plenty of bashings in his ten-year career. Brass knuckles, tire irons, cricket bats. Once, even from the arm of an ice sculpture that melted before he arrived on the scene. The lot. They all made a hell of a mess, but nothing compared to this. A twelve-foot fall onto heather just couldn't do that to a human face.

To the sergeant's practiced eye, the damage appeared more like a hammer blow. His cousin's crazy wife had taken the same to her husband's cat one day, ticked off by the tabby's chronic meowing.

Bevan walked close to the body. "Look," he announced to Bedwyr, nudging the victim's head with his toe, "there ain't no bruisin' 'round the neck. Not even broke."

The DS sauntered a few yards over to the base of the cliff, then looked repeatedly at the ledge above, over to the body, and back again. The body was barely close enough to the rock face for somebody to have pushed him off, much less the man falling by accident. "This monkey'd have to fly to get that far on his own. And monkeys don't fly."

"Some do," Thomas said, his voice genial. "The Colugo of Singapore, for example. Technically a dermopterans — a flying lemur — not a monkey, but close enough. And they don't really fly, they glide using skin flaps. Still—" He shut up when at last he noticed Bevan's scowl.

Bedwyr ignored him. "What about suicide from a running jump?" he challenged Bevan, less to needle him than simply to cover all bases. "This Payne fellow might have come to Dan-yr-Ogof for just that purpose."

He stood up and put his hands on his hips, drawing his coat open to reveal the DI badge on his belt. It was a show of authority that he knew irritated his junior partner, who had failed the exam and gained his job through political connections. "Stranger things have happened."

Bevan twisted his face into a comic frown and walked away without a word. He hated strange things. Give him a clear-cut case anytime. Suicide or murder, all the same to him. But puzzling out which was which mandated sleuthing, and he had better things to do — like chatting up the chief inspector's dishy daughter when she came by the station.

Thomas tapped Bedwyr on the shoulder. The detective whirled around and stumbled backward a step, glaring at him, livid at being touched.

Thomas' vocal cords wobbled, "Ask my lab manager." He pointed to a tall, good-looking Welshman leaning against the rim of the cave entrance, his arms crossed.

Rhys ambled over and said, "Yeah, he owes me money. If he were dead, I'd be the first to scream bloody murder."

Bedwyr leaped forward like a bolt from a crossbow. He glowered up at Rhys, his nose almost touching the younger man's chin. "Are you tryin' to be funny? Murder is still a pretty big muck in Wales, even if you lot take it small in America."

Rhys blinked twice and wiped the spittle off his neck, barely annoyed. "I'm Welsh."

"Don't be smart, prat."

He considered trying to argue that he couldn't be an idiot and smart at the same time. But it would only worsen Thomas's jam. Instead, he tried to distract him. "How do you know he was murdered?"

Bevan wagged, "He sure as hell didn't have no heart attack."

Thomas caught the looks they exchanged. "I told you," he said as he circled his arm to encompass the knot of people nearby. "We were all on a caving expedition."

"Spelunking, you mean," Bevan said, trying to appear 'in the know'.

"Uh, that word is usually reserved for amateurs. We've taken a trip together every summer for the past four years." Thomas knew there were two exceptions to that: himself and the man on the ground, a stranger and last minute replacement for a regular member.

Inspector Bedwyr caught the discrepancy. "You said you'd never met this lot before in person."

"I meant to say, they have taken a trip every summer together. It was an innocent slip of the tongue."

Bevan said, "Right. Just like that guy on the ground had an innocent slip of the foot."

Thomas rolled his eyes, then closed them, then took two deep breaths.

Bevan had collected the personal data of all those present. All of them were physicists. That alone annoyed him. He hated eggheads instinctively – more so when he wasn't sure what type they were, and he was vague on the word "physicist."

He asked Thomas, already knowing the answer since he'd grilled the club president, "Why'd you call your club: 'Force'?"

He inched in close to make his witness more nervous, his body odor doing half the job for him. "You geeks like to do a bit of bashing in the caves once a year? Pick out the weakest link, maybe. Do him harm for jollies?"

Thomas stood his ground, trying hard not to sound patronizing, not so easy for him. "It's not 'force' like 'violence'. The club name is 'F-o-u-r C', the Cardiff and Cambridge Cavers Club. We just thought it was clever because force is a basic concept in physics and—"

Bedwyr interrupted, waving his hand. "I just want to know how and why this one," he wiggled the bag with the passport, "ended up on the ground with his face bashed in."

"I keep telling you," Thomas croaked, "that's *my* passport." He could tell they weren't buying it and his body deflated. He shook his head, his chin hanging down to his chest. He closed both eyes when his view fell on the dead body.

His mind raced ahead. Without his passport he couldn't return home 'til he got another, which could take weeks. The contract with Vestry Tech hung in the balance. And that didn't account for the woe that would dawn if the coroner decided it was murder and he was involved.

He felt a familiar stomach churn. He often despaired of squeezing logic into someone abusing his power.

He said flatly, "Considering the condition of his face, the amount of torn flesh, I don't see how you could say it was anybody, much less me." It came out sounding more clinical than he intended.

"Are you a morgue doctor or something?" asked Bedwyr sarcastically.

"No. I'm a kind of doctor. I'm a physicist."

"Well, this guy ain't your patient," Bevan said, smirking at his own joke. "He ain't anybody's patient ever again."

Thomas sighed involuntarily. "No, not a physician, a physicist. I've invented a special power system for—"

"We're not interested," Bedwyr said, flipping his hand skyward.

Thomas was about to respond when Sergeant Bevan hushed him as his phone buzzed. The cop grunted for a few seconds, then snapped at Thomas, "You should think yourself lucky, mate. If you was Thomas Payne, I'd have to arrest you." He turned to his partner. "This bloke," he said, pointing to the body, "was wanted for stealing military secrets."

Bedwyr glared at his suspect, the skin between his brows pinching together like a dog's anus. "I think you'd best come with us to the station. We'll be having a lot more questions for you."

Thomas groaned.

2

*J*AMES Paine limped along the highway near Worcester, still feeling the effects of his struggle that morning. A greasy weasel had contradicted him on a point of Quaker canon. He put up a better fight than expected, but there was now one less dumb son of a bitch in the world.

James stuck out his thumb when he heard the sound of an approaching car, but it kept going with no change in speed. He didn't frown. In his view, no one owed him anything until he made a promise. His actions often contradicted this view but that didn't bother him. A foolish consistency was the hobgoblin of little minds. What did bother him was the thing that sent him on this trip.

He had come to Wales to fetch his son Thomas to wed a lass he'd picked out. She would breed him a fine grandson, something he had need of now.

Nothing on Earth would stop him seeing his bloodline continue. His Aase Syndrome was catching up with him, and he was determined to ensure his immortality before he died. Fortunately, it wouldn't take long now to find Thomas... if he could just get a ride.

The next car flashed past while he was occupied with his thoughts.

He'd learned from a plonker who'd been at Dan-yr-Ogof about Thomas going to jail. That was no problem for him. He could pop open that 19th century box at Brecon before they knew what was what. But he had to get there before Thomas was out on bail or risk losing his trail again.

It was slow going for a man with no funds and no opportunity — yet — to steal a car. If someone would just stop for a minute. He turned around as the sound of tires swished on the wet road. The driver wouldn't so much as look at him. He walked on.

The trip had already taken far longer than he planned and he was becoming impatient. Stowing away on a freighter had been easy, but he'd been kicked off the train. The bus ride had taken the last of his money, and a forty-mile walk was taking its toll.

At the sight of another car, he stuck out his thumb again and it slowed, then zoomed past when the driver got a closer view of him. This time he frowned and thrust his hands on his hips as the car sped off. "Fine, if you're all a bunch of fancy boys, I'll clean up."

He saw an old farmhouse a mile off the road. Tired as he was, it took only fifteen minutes to reach. His eyes scoured the property, seeing no one but a man on his tractor at the far end of a barley field. He assumed the wife would be in the kitchen, where she belonged.

As he drew close the sight of the primitive farm, virtually unchanged for a century, made him smile. Then he noticed several cages holding a number of minks and pursed his lips. Slaughter for the sake of vanity. And against the law, too. Evil twice compounded. Might have to delay long enough to chastise the wicked.

He took off his shirt and washed himself in a horse trough. When he finished, he stole some of the man's clothing off the line. He noticed a woman caught him doing it. She looked on blankly through the window, the lines on her face matching the grain of the wooden frame, both the same shade of gray.

The sight of her worried expression through the glass gave him pleasure. He noted she made no move to alert her husband, which pleased him even more. Her eyes told him she understood what would happen. She disappeared from the window but didn't appear at the doorway. James wondered if she'd gone to call the police.

"Be thankful I'm in flight to a serious purpose, woman," he mumbled to himself.

He finished dressing quickly and headed back toward the road. He supposed the local sheriff just might look the other way at their mink farm, but happily nab a stranger for the fine. Hypocrites, all. They live to punish the righteous.

He was already off the property before he glanced back and saw the woman holding up high a paper sack and waving it in his direction. He guessed it contained food, a gesture of charity toward a needy passerby who had to steal clothes. He ignored her, moseying on, as indifferent to kindness as he would've been to hostility.

He lifted his eyes skyward for a moment and marked the sun's position, judging he had another six hours to reach Brecon before nightfall. They might transfer Thomas to Cardiff in preparation for the coroner's inquest, and he would never be able to free him from that jail. He'd been in it enough to know.

He looked anxiously down the long road. There were more than sixty miles to go yet and he would never be able to walk it in time. If no one stopped, he was sunk.

Providentially, an ancient truck rattled past him and pulled over. A woman stuck her head out the driver's side, revealing the same dry face he'd seen through the farmhouse window.

James smiled.

The whole thing was absurd, Thomas thought, sitting in his cell at Brecon Station. The guy on the ground was a total stranger. They met for the first time early that morning. Owen called the president of the club complaining of stomach cramps, and Perry emailed the group that someone called Carl Tuppenny would be filling in.

Normally, the group vetoed strangers on a trip. They were all serious cavers, scooping grunt sites exclusively. An unknown had to be assumed a spelunker 'til proved otherwise, and amateurs slowed them down.

They were willing to make an exception for Thomas who, after all, wasn't really a stranger. They'd chatted with him many times about caving. Anyway, Rhys vouched for his expertise and they knew Spiderman wouldn't lie just to suck up to his supervisor.

"In fact," Rhys had told Perry, "you'll have a hard time keeping up with him." He enjoyed rubbing it in because he knew how jealous the club president was of anyone with superior ability. Needling him to puncture his puffer fish ego was one of Rhys' favorite pastimes.

Thomas argued in the chat room that same morning they really didn't need a replacement, but Perry pushed back. The others, more easy going, thought it okay this once. He let it go. As long as he wasn't asked to babysit the newcomer he couldn't grouse. He and Rhys could still travel ahead to the area he planned to explore.

The group gathered at the entrance at five, just as the sun was coming up. They were late starting, in part because of having to wait for Carl. It wasn't actually his fault. Perry had delayed him with incessant instructions.

Perry made his usual pompous speech before entering the cave, the president first. Thomas was indifferent to the self-appointed privilege. He chuckled as the vain cock made a show of it, as if he were Joan of Arc's rooster leading her troops to glory.

Rhys followed Thomas at the rear of the group and they straight away veered right, according to plan. Perry would be peeved they hadn't all stuck together but, provided each member had a buddy for safety, the club had no rule they had to explore together.

Thomas had a special reason this time for wanting to separate. He'd long suspected that the system still held virgin spaces, despite being well explored for a century. After studying the topography in his spare time for a year, he found a promising formation. If he was right, he could write an article for Descent magazine announcing a bonny new scoop. That privilege he was not willing to cede to Perry.

"EarthQuaker Tom" as Rhys called him — a hated nickname born of his Quaker ancestry and unpredictable temper, which only he could get away with using — was just the man you wanted to explore the unknown with.

Thomas led the way down a main corridor. After an eighth of a mile it branched off to the right into a smaller one. They stoop-walked through a narrow passage, soon forced to crawl. Far from entering reluctantly, the actions of getting down in the muck and scrabbling through a tiny tunnel was one of the most joyful parts of the process.

The natural light from the entrance had faded right away, the glow from the main tunnel fluorescents not long after. It was practically dark now and the pair switched on their headlamps as they trudged ahead. Their huff and wheeze rose higher with every hard yard.

Despite the ample illumination, Thomas felt the walls close in on him. He felt the dank terror of small spaces rise, as it always did. It swelled inversely to the tunnel diameter, growing larger as the tunnel narrowed. He'd taken up caving deliberately in order to conquer his fear, the product of childhood experiences. The phlegm in his throat matched the muck he crawled over. He swallowed hard.

"That which does not kill us makes us stronger," he murmured jokingly, quoting Nietzsche to himself. He only half-believed it; no one had ever said anything about scar tissue. He forced himself onward through the pipe, spurning his weakness as just uncollected debris from juvenile nightmares.

It took another half hour to reach the dead end. The tunnel opened up a few feet before the wall straight ahead, allowing them finally to stand upright. Rhys's head nearly touched the limestone ceiling; Thomas' topped out a few inches below.

"Now what?" Rhys asked.

Thomas grinned, his fear sponged away by the thrill of what he was sure lay just ahead. He pulled a hammer out of his kit bag along with a spike. He raised his arms to strike the rock directly in front of him at shoulder height.

Rhys frowned and touched his friend's forearm. "Uh, you know that's not kosher. Take nothing but pictures; leave nothing but footprints." He'd never known Thomas even to bend a valid rule, much less willfully breach it. Something was up, something hammer-and-tongs huge. "You need a special permit."

"And alert every caver in Wales to the biggest discovery in decades? Not yet." He ignored the finger wagging and went to work.

Thomas chipped away, opening a hole the size of his face. He turned and beamed a pride-filled face at Rhys. He said, the pitch of his voice rising from adrenalin, "I wound up here a few years ago, curious to see what everyone insisted wasn't worth seeing."

"I thought this was your first time in the UK?"

"No, second." The moment he said it, it sounded wrong. He wanted to say "third," but he couldn't remember another. Dismissing the swimming memory before it could gel, he rushed on. "I didn't have time to investigate then. But I thought I noticed something about the geology."

"What?"

"I'll show you. Look here." He pointed above the hole. "See this bacon speleogen?"

Rhys nodded and Thomas smacked his chisel hard against a small section that stood out from the rest. Some calcite chunks crumbled down to his feet, exposing a larger hole. Thomas peered in for a long moment while holding his breath, then invited Rhys to take his place.

Rhys said, "Son of a—"

"Ain't it grand?"

The small opening revealed a huge cavern. Rhys aimed his helmet lamp downward, but saw no bottom. He gazed upward for a long time, speechless, taking in a dome above the shaft that was covered with breathtaking structures.

Cave pearls — tiny half-spheres of calcium carbonate — lined the walls, shining like their namesakes in the light from his lamp. Anthodites, formed from aragonite crystals, blossomed around them like orange flowers, sparkling like petals freshly dewed.

"What do you see?" Thomas asked.

Rhys was too stunned to describe the sight.

"Step aside. I want to open it up far enough for us to get inside," Thomas said, his voice as shaky with glee as his hands.

It took him an hour to succeed, with Rhys helping to clear. He put his tools down at last. He stepped into Rhys's cupped hands, which then boosted him into the hole. He crawled through and jumped down onto a small ledge several feet below, grateful it didn't collapse beneath him. He was too excited to test it first, as he knew he should have. He stomped on it now to ensure it would hold two then turned to offer a helping hand to Rhys.

Rhys stepped onto it and suddenly the pair were alone inside a space that no human eyes, probably no eyes of any kind, had ever seen. Rhys whistled as he scanned his headlamp around the multi-colored walls. "Wow. Just wow."

His lamp illuminated a larger variety of speleothems than he'd seen through the hole, most of them radically unlike those of the main complex. The stalactites were shaped like gargoyles and colored an eerie red-orange, like million-year-old blood. The bottlebrushes — delicate hanging structures resembling the plants that gave them the name — was enormous. Dozens ran along the top as far as his light let him see, lining it with inverted orange and white mushroom clouds.

"EarthQuaker, you are going to be famous," Rhys declared, his face flush with awe.

Thomas frowned, deep shadows forming under his eyebrows, and not from the nickname. He anticipated a big thrill from announcing the find in a major publication. He'd never considered that it would make him well known. The thought didn't sit well.

Because of his specialty, his papers attracted little notice outside a small group of physicists. And it was too soon for the newspapers to take an interest in his upcoming invention.

That's just the way he wanted it. Fame could alert his father to where he lived – and that would not do.

"Well, I can publish under another name, I guess," he muttered, not realizing he'd said it aloud.

Rhys shook his head, smiling. They'd worked together almost two years and his boss's behavior constantly surprised him. One thing never changed, though. For a man with such a strong will, he had none of the usual ego. He was totally disinterested in credit for his work.

They spent a long time surveying the walls from their small perch, the cave reaching back further then their lights could show. No path appeared that would allow them to scout it now. They'd have to come back with climbing gear to cross the chasm to a narrow trail on the opposite side.

Thomas crawled back up into the small tunnel using a pair of heel-sized limestone ledges. Rhys followed him, inadvertently knocking off first the lower one then the upper as he climbed.

Glancing back inside the cavern, Thomas' worry about the notoriety returned. *Rhys was right*, he thought, as he repacked his tools. It would be deemed the biggest discovery in caving in 50 years. Anybody who announced it would be famous overnight.

He could see the caption now. "Secluded scientist spends years slaving over data, crawling underground for weeks to make new find," with his picture splashed all over.

He mulled over that prospect and mumbled, "No, that wouldn't do at all."

He came out of his stupor when Rhys tapped him on the shoulder. He blinked a few times, then said, "Let's go before someone comes looking for us. I'll decide later how to let the world know."

The pair picked up some large stones from the tunnel floor and fitted them back into the hole, leaving a small gap at the top. The space was too high for anyone casually passing to see, on the odd chance they'd bother to come down the long, narrow tunnel at all.

They made their way back, reaching within a dozen yards of the main tunnel section in ten minutes.

Without warning, Perry's face appeared out of the darkness as he rounded a bend, illuminated by Rhys' beam. The club leader asked with phony good cheer, "Where have you lunkers been? The group is ready to eat."

Thomas said quickly, "You lead the way." The sop to Perry's vanity was enough to close off the question of their absence, at least for now.

A few yards further on, Thomas felt a slight tug on his backpack. He peered over his shoulder and noticed that Perry was no longer beside him. He turned around but didn't see him right behind either. Did he go back to check where they'd been?

He decided there was no scant of his finding the new cavern. Going after him would just make him suspicious. "Let's keep going," he said to Rhys, who hadn't even noticed Perry's absence. "He'll catch up."

They waited near the main entrance for many long minutes. Rhys grew ravenous. Thomas checked his watch for the fourth time. It had been more than a quarter-hour since they arrived at the opening. He swiveled his head around and barked, "Where in hell did he go?"

Rhys was about to make a rude remark when Perry appeared at his shoulder. Perry said, "Right here, and I'm starved. Let's go, mates." He rushed ahead to forestall any questions.

They joined the others outside, settling down quickly to a mix of trail bars, sports drinks, and — in Rhys's case — a foot-long sandwich with six different meats. He heated it to oven temperature with a portable mirror device of his own design, then tore off half for Thomas.

Perry sniffed at the elaborate dish. He pointed to the fog still clinging to the hillside and said, "You're lucky there's sun down here. Otherwise, you'd have lugged that thing for nothing."

Rhys ignored him. Always rooting for rain on someone's parade. Putz.

Half an hour later, three men and a woman standing atop the cave opening heard a scream a few yards away, followed by a loud thud below their feet. Thomas wasn't among them; he'd been far away from the group when the body fell.

The quartet rushed down to see what happened, and the woman identified the dead man. His looks had registered because he was "cute, like Thomas."

Perry called the police, pointlessly ordering everyone to stand clear of the body; no one wanted to be near it anyway. They formed a subtle ring facing outward to keep the tourists at bay. The police arrived in twenty minutes.

An hour later everyone was free to go except Thomas, hauled off to Brecon Gaol, suspected of killing himself.

3

$\mathcal{N}$OT for the first time in her life, Terri Mawr wished she had no ears, like the snakes she loved to play with as a child. Her nerves were raw from listening to her father bark at breakfast for the past half hour. For the first time in her life, she envied Arwel his hearing aids. She wondered if he had them turned off just now. He didn't appear pleased to be listening to her either.

She glowered across the kitchen at him as he sat bolt upright in the dining-table chair, his hairy arms crossed and his face as clean-shaven as one of her marble sculptures. She turned away to get control of herself, chopping cherries at a fever pitch. "Da, you promised if I moved back home you wouldn't be a nag." It was the third time in a year she had reminded him.

"And you promised, girl, to cease your wild ways. How do you think it looks for my daughter to be coming in at five in the a.m., singing at the top of her lungs?"

She flung the knife into the sink and turned on him. "I wasn't drunk, so what's it matter?" She gripped the countertop behind her to keep her hands from making rude gestures. "And it wasn't the top of my lungs. I can yell much louder." She waited for him to agree. When he didn't, she said, "Anyway, since when is it a crime to be happy any time of the day?"

That brought the bickering pair to a temporary stalemate.

Arwel was a stubborn curmudgeon but he definitely favored being happy. She knew he just wished for a less boisterous form.

Terri secretly sympathized with him, convinced he couldn't help himself. Her father seemed stuck in the '50s, despite not being born 'til they were over by two years. His morals were like his car — grand, dignified, but old-fashioned, probably obsolete.

They traded tight-lipped stares for a solid minute, each unable to fathom a reasonable compromise, both unwilling to back down.

Inflated by a second wind, they were about to start up again when Terri received a text message. Arwel opened his mouth to voice the devastating comeback that had just popped into his head. She held up a hand to silence him, then turned away as she tapped on her phone.

"Rude, rude girl," Arwel muttered, and loped out of the kitchen. He plunked down in the chair in Terri's sculpting studio at the back of the cottage, aware of invading her private territory. He still took care not to knock over her latest creation. Property was property and he was no vandal, no matter how miffed he might be.

He pored over the small statue with a mixture of pride and contempt. Some kind of indecipherable, half-formed human it was. The body's pose suggested a hopeless struggle to escape its stone bonds, the face ecstatic at the effort. He had no idea what it meant. But the girl had a talent; that, he could not deny.

Carved from two feet of rock dragged from a cave near their cottage in Brecon. Lord knows how she managed to get the thing home. Probably charmed one of her thuggish admirers to lug it all the way with a promise of who knows what reward afterward.

The instant the thought formed he felt ashamed. He knew Terri was no more promiscuous than a Victorian spinet player. She had her drives, no doubt, as any young woman must. But indiscriminate she was not.

There had not been above three young men in the house in the past year and none stayed long past suppertime.

One had been particularly prime, too. He might have had a chance, Arwel had thought at the time. No dice as it turned out. He came for one more dinner a few days later and never again. Whether that was his choice or Terri's, Arwel never learned.

He couldn't understand it. She wasn't Kate the Shrew by any means. Just...well, just Terri. A perfectionist about her men, same as she was about those damn statues that spread stone dust all over his antique piano.

"Someone with no hidden cracks," she'd say whenever he asked what she was holding out for. "Otherwise, the whole man breaks in pieces the minute you give him a hard whack."

"With that attitude, I'll never get you married off," he grumbled to the empty room.

Terri ignored the faint sounds of her father's harping and tapped a final reply into her phone. She promised to be at the Brecon police station within an hour. "Less if I can get Da off my back sooner."

"Please hurry. Wait. They want me," Rhys typed back.

But there was no further message, and he didn't respond when she sent a single question mark.

She wandered into the studio, announcing, "The nickers probably took his phone away."

Arwel didn't know why she was saying it but said, "Terri, how many times have I asked you not to refer to the police as 'nickers'. It's undignified."

She sighed, knowing it was useless to explain. "Da, I've got to go. I'll be overjoyed to fight with you some more when I get back." She beamed the wicked smile that always warmed his heart against his will.

"Which will be when?"

"When I get back." With that, she left, careful not to slam the studio door for fear of knocking off one of her smaller pieces from the rickety shelf beside it.

She made the sound of a loud kiss and then her steps receded, the tap, flop, tap of her sandals echoing off the wood floor.

Arwel was secretly relieved at her abrupt departure. He hated arguing with her, appearances to the contrary notwithstanding. He persisted in thinking it his duty to keep her on the straight and narrow in a world gone mad. He congratulated himself on at least partial success as he pulled on his uniform shirt.

It was true, she hadn't come home drunk, he thought as he plucked his badge off the dresser. In fact, he couldn't remember seeing her take more than a single pint any night of her life.

And she'd never tried a drug stronger than cold medicine. "Who wants to be fuzzy minded?" she would explain to her peers when they tried to push them on her. "Hard enough to think straight in the best of times."

Come down to it, she might not be a good girl by his antique standards. But she was a good woman, of that he was sure. That ought to be enough for any pater, he concluded.

That dilemma neatly tucked away, he finished dressing and headed out to work. He was equally careful not to slam the front door, since he hadn't taken time yet to fix the shelf there either.

He was particularly fond of one piece lying on it: the little bust she'd done of him. He especially liked the jaunty cap on its oversized head.

Detective Chief Inspector Arwel Mawr entered the Brecon police station he ruled with a velvet hand in an iron glove, reversing Napoleon's advice. He found more than the usual chaos.

The explanation was quick in coming when he discovered his hellion progeny had preceded him there. He listened to the desk sergeant just long enough to get the basic facts. He couldn't stand to hear more this particular morning.

Terri had entered the station and insisted on seeing Rhys Anarawd, a young man trying to get his friend Thomas Payne released. Because Sergeant Bevan could refuse her nothing, he allowed the Chief Inspector's daughter to enter the cell area, against the rules.

The chaos commenced when the prisoners made rude comments of a personal nature, particularly about her... upper body parts, the consensus being that they were— "Skip that," Arwel commanded. "Go on."

Bevan explained that the mayhem spread when he sent a man in to quiet them, which only inflamed the situation more. He wanted to bash their heads together but that was a bigger rule infraction than letting Terri near the cells. He was about to take action of some kind when the DCI entered the station, demanding an explanation for "the devilish din."

Arwel thought it his duty to expel the wildcat and quell the clamor personally. Doing his duty would normally have been all the motivation he needed, but after his row with her at breakfast, he just didn't have the will. He gave Sergeant Bevan orders to take care of the problem by any means necessary, so long as it wouldn't leave any marks.

Luckily for Terri, and Thomas as it turned out, Arwel didn't tell him how he had to do that. The sergeant chose to interpret it as not necessarily requiring that he eject her.

It was clear he intended it as a first step, but Bevan was reluctant to do that. He liked having her around. More important than his preference, he knew well what happened when a man insisted she do anything she preferred not. When that someone was an authority figure, the effects were magnified.

Instead, he scraped across the rowdies' cell bars with a nightstick, rapping in one sweep the six knuckles poking outside the bars. "And if you don't stay quiet, it'll be your heads that feel it next," he said.

That restored quiet. The three men in jail knew it was no idle threat. They had the scars to show for it as prior guests of Brecon Gaol.

Bevan swaggered over to Terri who stood next to Rhys in front of Thomas's cell. He smiled, the gap between his two frontmost incisors forming a measurable percentage of his open mouth. "Let me know if they bother you any more, Miss Mawr."

Terri returned a wispy smile, a little embarassed at Bevan's open-faced adoration, a feeling she knew would never be reciprocated. "Thank you," she said, and stalled politely while he walked out like a robot with defective hip hinges. She turned back to Rhys. "So, again, why are you both here?"

Rhys said, "Thomas was arrested. For nothing."

Terri suspected that was more than a slight exaggeration. She knew how her father ran his station and no one would ever be arrested for nothing. He would have considered it a crime against the Magna Carta, a document as sacred to him as Terri's birth certificate.

"Well, what do you think I can do about it?" she asked. "I don't have any influence with my father when it comes to the law. He'd sooner jail me than violate a rule."

"I saw the way that sergeant looked at you. Can't you get him to recommend a solicitor? I don't know a single one in Wales and I'm sure you don't."

Terri laughed with a touch of cynicism. "Don't be too sure."

The whole time, she stared at Thomas, fascinated by his sharp features and disturbed by their dour expression. He looked to be the last man to wind up in a cage, and he was visibly desolate about it. There was something feral in his tension, like an animal who didn't know what cages were for but instinctively hated them.

Still, she had to admit, her father's men rarely made big mistakes. "Why should I want to help your friend if he killed someone? Da and I wrangle about a lot of things, but I think bludgers should be caged, just like he does."

Rhys shook his head. "The Quaker kill a man? He couldn't if he was inclined to, since he was with me when it happened."

She ignored what she took to be a reference to the man's religion. Her father had told her enough stories to know it made little difference in a murder case. She said, "Why don't you tell them where he was?"

"I tried. They said I could 'tell it to the magistrate at the proper time'." He pitched his voice like shoes over gravel, making Terri chuckle. "When I insisted, they threatened to lock me up with him if I didn't shut it."

Terri appraised Thomas again. He was sitting with his back to the wall, staring forward intently. She had expected him to look pitiful on being reminded of his charge. Most men would. Instead, he seemed to be concentrating very hard, on what she couldn't guess.

She prided herself on being able to read a face, a skill developed over years of sculpting. His didn't strike her as a criminal's, and she believed in judging people by their looks – if one combed them fine enough to get the judgment right.

She'd seen many troublemakers in her life, even in little Brecon. Thugs who thrilled at mayhem. She'd watched this man when the others laughed at her and he lacked any hint of the usual furtive snigger. He also showed no sign of the standard self-pitying pout such men wore when they were nicked.

Quite the contrary. This one had a heightened clarity in the eyes. His expression struck her as odd under the circumstances. He had a lot to be troubled about just now.

"Thomas..." she cooed. When he didn't move, she raised her volume a notch. "Dr. Payne?... Hello?" When he still didn't respond, she tapped the bars with a knuckle. Nothing changed. He sat as if posing, or catatonic. "Is he autistic?" she asked Rhys.

Rhys chortled. "No, just strange. When he's thinking, it's very hard to get his attention." He stood in Thomas's line of sight, kneeled down, and tapped on the bars in Morse code.

Thomas blinked then focused on Rhys's eyes. "Yes?"

"What are you thinking about? How to get released?"

"I was trying to figure out how the hell Carl got my passport." His voice tapered off as he retreated to his thoughts again.

Terri said, "He doesn't talk much like a Quaker, does he? And what's that about a passport?"

Rhys laughed. "'Quaker' is a nickname I made up," he explained. "The detectives think the victim is Thomas. They wouldn't believe me about that either."

"Won't they be able to confirm that very soon by fingerprints? Then they'll let him go."

Thomas looked at her for the first time. Struck dumb by pitch black eyes in a lovely square face framed by silken brown hair, it took him a few seconds to speak.

Finally, he said, "Or, they'll conclude that the dead man was someone else and I'm the killer. Trying to cover up my crime by planting my passport on him."

"My, aren't we the pessimist?"

Thomas's mouth stretched into a pair of razor blades stacked together. He sighed at the ceiling. "Why does everyone say that?"

Bevan walked in just then and slapped a set of papers down on the table outside the cell.

Terri looked down at the top document, familiar from seeing many like it over the years. "The report says the victim is Dr. Thomas Payne, employee of the University of Virginia. They have no idea who's the guy being held. His prints aren't on file in the UK or the United States. We ain't tried Interpol yet."

Thomas sucked in a deep breath, steeling himself for what he suspected would happen now. They would dig around, pass his photo from one agency to the next, and eventually find out who his parents were. Then he would rot in a British prison for god knows how long, awaiting extradition. All for something having nothing to do with the morning's tragedy.

"Shite," Thomas swore aloud.

Rhys scowled at Bevan's departing back. He had a special distaste for Schadenfreude, especially from pit bulls who liked to abuse their authority. He asked Terri, "Will you help us now?"

Terri tried to read Thomas's expression again but failed. She was intrigued by the rarity of that failure. That feeling was enough to decide her. "I'll help him. I like his looks."

Thomas' eyes went wider starting from the pupils outward. If the situation didn't make it so absurd, he'd ask her for a date. He forced himself to concentrate. "*Can* you help?"

Terri snaked her hand between the bars and grazed his cheek with one smooth sweep. "I think I can. Give me a few minutes."

Thomas watched her go, relishing the sensation on his face — like a cool, wet cloth on a red raw scrape.

Arwel stood squarely in front of DI Bedwyr and DS Bevan, his arms dangling, holding a clipboard in one hand. By his expression, anyone else would've concluded he was not happy. That would not have been obvious to the two men. They'd known him half their lives and still could never be certain from his face alone when he was displeased. He often had that same expression when he was delighted.

"So, tell me why we have this American — if he is an American — locked up?"

He waited for a reply, long in coming. Both men knew that the first one who spoke up would be obligated to give a legal rationale. "My gut told me he was involved" would carry no weight with Mawr.

Bevan braved the first response. "I got a message from a stooge that the victim was involved in nicking military secrets."

Arwel replied, "Even if true, what's that to do with the young man who is locked up? Do we have evidence he's involved in that?"

Bedwyr came to his rescue. "He kept claiming to be the victim. That is, that he was Dr. Thomas Payne."

"So?" Arwel flopped the clipboard onto his desk and then sat down behind it, waiting for a reply that didn't come. "If he is, you should return his passport and let him go. If he's not, he's not the man accused of stealing classified material."

He leaned back in his chair, crossing his arms, his feet solidly on the ground. "Anyway, you know we'd have to turn that over to Cardiff without delay, who'd probably pass it to London." His eyes shifted from one face to the other like an angry metronome. "I still don't have a reason he's being held here."

"The man is hiding something," Bedwyr insisted.

"Aren't we all," Arwel shot back, a weary statement, not a question. "Is that something germane to this murder investigation? And, while I'm on it, is he supposed to be a suspect or a material witness?"

Bevan puffed up his chest. "Terri thinks he's innocent. That ought to tell you something."

"Leave her out of this, as you should have the second she entered the station." Bevan shrank back. "On second thought, since you brought it up, does she have any evidence? She talked with him, yes?"

Bevan and Bedwyr exchanged nervous looks. Both of them knew they were on boggy ground and sinking fast. Neither wanted to back down, sure the detainee was withholding something relevant. But they couldn't say what it was, and Terri either didn't know or wouldn't tell them. They shrugged in unison.

Arwel saw the gesture and said, "Fine. Release him. But don't give him the passport. If he's not Dr. Payne, and so far there's no evidence in favor, there's no reason. If he is, he can't leave the country without it and we've got a misidentified dead man."

Bedwyr added, "And we can always ask the Immigration gents to tug his chain."

Bevan chimed in. "Yeah, they can save us a lot of useless traipsing around."

Arwel tsk-tsked at them, displeased, and this time unmistakably so. He had no truck with bullies who used the law to pervert justice. But in Brecon he had to make do with what he could find. Thank god they didn't have a murder to solve every day. He had half a mind to turn the whole thing over to Cardiff at once, anyway.

"Get him out of here. Now." They started to turn and he added, "But tail him for forty-eight hours. I'll make the decision later about whether to call in Immigration."

The pair shuffled out, glad the grilling was over.

Arwel watched them go, shoulders sagging. "Cheer up, men. If he is guilty, he'll sooner lead us to evidence being free than locked up here."

Bevan mugged at Bedwyr, thinking Arwel was being cynical, which cheered him. He muscled his way through the door first.

Bedwyr caught the smile and thought Bevan was simply hopeless. He'd never understand how a man like Inspector Mawr reasoned. Cynical or no, though, the DCI was right. This egghead was going to lead them to something. Bet on that. The guy who claimed to be Thomas Payne knew a lot more about this business than he was willing to tell them.

Ten minutes later, Terri returned to Thomas's cell with Sergeant Bevan in tow. She snuck Thomas a mocking grin.

Bevan unlocked the cell, handed Thomas a business card and said, "Don't leave the area, spit. They'll have more questions for you at the coroner's inquest."

Thomas followed Rhys and Terri out of the station in a daze. Outside, he still said nothing, a combination of surprise at his freedom and shyness from still feeling her caress.

None of them noticed a man following them at a casual distance. Had they looked, they might have recognized him behind a thin disguise that seemed put on by an amateur make-up artist.

Once in the sunshine, Rhys asked Terri, "How did you do that?"

She beamed a wry smile. "I'll never tell."

Thomas said, "What's more interesting is *why* you did it?"

As they walked, Terri scoped out Thomas for a long time without answering, wondering about his motive for asking. It was obvious he liked her; she'd seen the look many times. But there was something else, something she couldn't quite ferret.

The best thing was to set him down hard, and let the bounce show her what he was made of. "Let's just say it amused me to tweak my father's nose."

Thomas looked puzzled. There was something arresting about her beyond her looks. That damned wicked smile, maybe. It seemed to challenge him to rise to the occasion.

He elected to plunge ahead, heedless of Rhys's presence or her teasing. "I'll be in the UK for another two weeks, and I'd like to see you while I'm here—"

He stopped short when he registered her pained expression, as if he'd hit her in the stomach. He was used to women looking at him without interest. This had a special quality, as if she were offended by his clumsy approach.

Terri ignored him and took a sharp left at the street corner, heading back toward her home. She waved a hand above her head, wiggling her fingers.

The man following them glanced her way as her figure receded, but stayed behind Rhys and Thomas. He drew in close enough to hear what they were saying, hoping they would talk about the morning's events.

Thomas was too steamed to have any hope of noticing his stalker.

Rhys walked off in the direction of the train station to catch the 12:05 to Cardiff.

The man following kept walking straight when Thomas turned into the entrance to his hotel to check out from his room.

4

*T*HOMAS rode Rhys' motorcycle through Brecon Beacons National Park, heading to the American Consulate in Cardiff. He was grateful for the time alone. The hour-long trip would give him time to think.

The first task was to get a passport; without it, he couldn't get home. If he somehow snuck past security at Heathrow, the Feds would surely stop him in New York. He wasn't sure which place would be worse to be locked up.

He was equally unsure how to persuade the Consulate to give him a duplicate passport. Living a mile from the university, he seldom drove in Virginia and stupidly forgot to put his driver's license in his wallet for the trip to Wales. Well, cross that bridge when you're drowning, as his mother used to say.

"Mother," he snorted through his helmet. There was a piece of work. Her and father both. Second cousins born into a large Quaker family, they rebelled in their late teens and fled the tribe. By the time Thomas was two, they were heavily involved with a violent anarchist group. He fled the two of them at fourteen and never looked back.

But they were looking back at him. He had hints from time to time of their efforts to find him. Later, he heard she had died from a drug overdose. His father continued the search alone.

Thomas hoped he had given up. Being found could only cause him grief at the university, since he was not tenured. Worse, with this trouble over Carl's death, locating him now would be a complete disaster. Associations like that always made the police look twice as hard at a suspect.

He felt a splash of road spray on his helmet visor and it shook him back to the present. As he had so many times, he stuffed the thoughts of his parents down and returned to his immediate problem.

The sergeant had told him not to leave the area. Luckily, Wales was a small country and "the area" might reasonably be interpreted to include Cardiff. If the police felt otherwise and, on finding him missing, alerted the Consulate, his first task would be his last as a free man.

He shook off his dour mood when dark clouds hovering over him began to pour. He noticed the sign for the A4161 and prepared to turn for the final leg into the city.

Ten minutes later he pulled into the American Consulate parking lot. Inside there was no line to speak of, but he still expected to wait an hour before reaching anyone who could help him.

He approached the window after the hippie chick in front of him left, girding himself for a dose of apathy. He gave the briefest possible explanation to the agent, omitting who had his passport. He said he'd lost it while caving, a true statement so far as it went.

The functionary expressed no interest, no emotion of any kind. He seemed the kind who would indifferently direct a man to the gallows, if handed the right document.

The pencil pusher pushed him onto a second gray man in a gray office. The nearly bare walls held nothing but a photo of the British Ambassador who'd retired ten years earlier. The man listened with faked interest to his sad story, then shrugged his shoulders a centimeter.

"Without some kind of identification, I'm afraid there's little we can do in a hurry. Replacing your passport will take about six weeks at best. When did you say you had to return to the United States?" His tone said the answer would alter nothing, no matter what it was.

Knowing what was at stake, Thomas held his temper, never his strong suit. Apparently, the man had never heard of computers, able to transmit photographs in seconds with a few taps. That gave him an idea. "I'll be back in a few minutes," he declared, then excused himself and went outside.

A man following him, dressed more discretely than the one in Brecon and sans any disguise, sat on the stone bench just outside the Consulate entrance. He thumbed through his men's magazine as Thomas passed him.

Thomas pressed the needed entries on his phone and was soon connected to an information operator in the U.S. "Department of Motor Vehicles in Charlottesville, Virginia, please." The number rang.

He waited a few seconds until the computer-voice menu droned out the first selection. He stabbed the keypad's zero a few times, hoping they hadn't disabled the default option for reaching a live person. After a short delay, he was rewarded with a close facsimile.

"Department of Motor Vehicles. How may I help you?"

"Hello, my name is Thomas Payne and I'm calling from Cardiff, Wales. I'm really hoping you *can* help me."

"I can't imagine how if you're out of the country."

Bureaucrat dullness or subtle sarcasm? He couldn't tell, but he took the fact that she knew Wales was outside the U.S. as a good sign. He could always reason with a person with a brain, even if she was wired to obstruct.

"I've lost my passport and to get another from the Consulate here I need a photo id. I'm sure it's an unusual request, but is there anyway you could email an image of my driver's license to the—"

"That would be against the rules, sir."

"Sure, sure, I understand. But, under the circumstances..." When there was no response from the other end, he added, "I'm not asking you to email it to me. I can see why that would be a security problem. But if you email it to the American Consulate, then—"

"No, I'm sorry I can't do that either. There's no way for me to know that the address is really the American Consulate, is there?" Her tone was so muted that any intended sarcasm was no more than a shade of Hades.

Uncooperative, but still showing some IQ, he concluded, believing there was hope. "Sure, you can. The government domain, that is the last part of the address after the little 'at' symbol in this case, tells you that. No one can fake that."

There was a pause; Thomas hoped that meant she was thinking it over. After a second, a heavy sigh came through the speaker. "I'm sorry, sir. If you come into the office, we might be able to help."

Thomas felt his anger rise. He forced it down. It took a huge effort not to point out that he could hardly come into the office if he couldn't get home with no passport. Which he couldn't get without a photo id. Saying so seemed pointless.

She had clearly reached the end of her ability to connect facts or feel empathy. Still, somewhere inside her there had to be a human being. He had to reach her, somehow. "I need the ID to get a passport so I can come home. Then I'll be happy to come in and–"

"I'm sorry, sir."

"I really wish you'd stop saying you're sorry you can't help and start helping." His irritation leaked into his voice, against his will. "I'm really in a jam here."

"I'm sorry, sir."

Thomas hung up and exhaled heavily. He gave himself a few minutes to calm down, sucking in air to relax his chest muscles and steady his shaking hands. Then he took another few minutes to think of an alternative. He flipped through his wallet, finding nothing useful. Maybe the Consulate would accept the lab photo id. It's from a public university. The department could email that.

He tapped the phone again.

The man watching him tried to lean over close enough to see what his fingers were pressing without being noticed. When Thomas spun his head around, the tail casually turned away as if continuing a motion already in progress. The spy stayed near enough to hear, pretending to text message someone.

Thomas withdrew to his motorcycle and straddled it, then pressed the number for the administrative assistant of his department. He kept to himself at the lab, letting his postdoc act as liaison. So he knew her to say hello, no more. With luck, though, someone he knew better might be in the lab.

He checked his watch. It was 8:10 a.m. in Virginia. His odds were good.

The admin picked up and Thomas explained what he wanted. "I'm sorry, none of the regular staff are here," she said. "There's a summer replacement in the lab. What did you say your name was?"

Thomas clenched his jaw. "Thomas. Thomas Payne." When that seemed to have no effect, he fell back on something he'd always thought absurd: the medieval class system that universities never grew past. "*Professor* Thomas Payne. I'm the lab director for the Magnet Unit."

This time it didn't help. "I'm sorry, Professor, there's still no one here who might know you. You can understand why I couldn't send that without some authorization."

"Could you at least look up my personnel file? If I describe its contents, that should convince you I'm the real Dr. Payne." It was a long shot, but he was improvising. He waited, his palms growing moist. He told himself it was just the humidity in Cardiff and wiped them on his jeans.

An endless minute later, the secretary's voice came back on the line, as mechanical as a computerized recording. "There's no Dr. Thomas Payne in the database." Her voice morphed from ice to snot in a transatlantic beat. "Nice try. Tell the guys at the frat house you failed. Maybe they'll buy you a consolation beer."

She hung up.

"Damn!" He glared at the phone thinking of several Welsh swear words to describe her. Then he slumped over, resting his forehead on the chill gas tank of his bike, at a loss for what to try next.

Owen Caldicott peeled off his caving gear and threw it into his locker at the Cardiff Lab. He rubbernecked around to see if anyone was watching then put on his street clothes and lab coat. He entered the lab, then stood still and listened for a few seconds to make doubly sure there was no one around.

It was lunchtime and summer on top of that. He'd have no better chance to carry out his plan. It was just icing that everyone who might interfere had been rounded up after Carl's murder. This should be easy.

He sat down at the lone computer that stored the plans he was after.

Making copies to take out of the lab was illegal, but he didn't care. What his contact would pay him was worth plenty for such a small risk. Once he finished there would be no way to know if anyone had made a copy. He'd have to get caught in the act to get in trouble.

He stopped typing long enough to check again for any sounds. All he heard were the soft whirrs of the fans in the computers around the table. He rammed a card into a slot at the side of the laptop, which was bolted to the table. How stupid the grad student slaves who tended them were to leave open such an obvious security hole, he thought.

He navigated to the file he wanted. Too bad he didn't have a photographic memory like that arsehole Payne. If he did, he could just reproduce the plans from memory at home and suffer no risk at all. Well, once he was done it wouldn't matter. He sped up typing.

He tried to drag the file onto the flash drive icon and found it wouldn't go. Weird. He tried again, but his copy just failed to appear. The geeks had disabled that feature in the operating system. Wankers!

Now he would have to hack the system to re-enable it and someone would know the computer had been re-booted at lunchtime. They might wonder why. If he hurried, no one would know he'd been in the lab. They might suspect the purpose of the reboot but could never trace it to him. At best, any of six people could be the culprit. Well, five, since Payne was in jail.

He smiled at the mental image of Thomas behind bars and went about his hack with lightning speed, sure of every keystroke. It was a simple task for a guy with his skill. Making the change and getting his copy took less than a minute. Now, all he had to do was put things back and leave.

The system was still shutting down when he heard the outer door of the lab open.

Shite! He couldn't stop the system going down now and he didn't want to leave his change in place. One of the geeks might notice. But if he waited for the system to restart, whoever had come in would find him in the lab. Puking shite!

He plucked his card out and padded to a corner of the lab to hide behind one of the huge electromagnet housings. Whoever came in would have no reason to wander back there. The question was how long the s-o-b would stay before moving to the office on the other side of the glass. They wouldn't see him leave from there.

He waited until he heard the footsteps grow loud enough to know the person had come into the lab proper. He couldn't resist trying to find out who it was. He poked his head out lightning quick from near the floor then hid again.

A looker, that one. He didn't recognize her, but her expression resembled that idiot cow Brenda, who fawned all over Payne at their team meeting yesterday. This one was stepping around the lab touching stuff like it was some kind of holy frickin' temple of Saint Thomas or something.

He wanted to jump out and order her out of the lab. No visitors were allowed unless accompanied by an authorized person.

The outer door opened and shut again, admitting a second person.

Shite and double shite! Now there's a pair of them. Well, maybe they'll go off somewhere for a shag. There wouldn't be much to do in the lab right now with Payne not there to give assignments.

Owen flicked his head out again to see who was the second entrant.

Rhys? That prick. Payne's pal. Always ready with a reach around for "the boy genius." Boy, my ass, he was pushing thirty. He'd hacked his personnel file. Why wasn't Rhys still in Brecon trying to get his hero out of jail?

Owen checked to see if it was possible to escape without being seen. There was a six-foot open space between pieces of gear. Apart from that, he had a good chance of getting out the back door without them noticing.

He weighed his odds. Getting caught skulking out of the lab was a lot more suspicious than just popping up and acting surprised to see someone there. He could always say he was checking something.

But what? Knowing Rhys, he would ask.

Owen came up empty. He didn't have anything to do with the equipment normally, just because of that one mistake that wasn't even his fault. It would sound thin if he couldn't be specific about what he was doing behind the big coil.

Everyone in the lab knew how valuable Payne's design was to Vestry. If the company found out someone was trying to pinch it, they had deep pockets for solicitors. The legal leeches would be happy to fry the thief, and Rhys was sure to tell them. He'd always had it in for him, the snotty bastard.

Finally, he chose to stay put and take his chances that they'd leave soon. He wiped the sweat off his forehead with his sleeve. He wasn't nervous. The heat from the coil was just making him warm, that's all.

His sweat increased when he heard the door open a third time. Mother of all cockups! He peeked one last time. It was that priss Payne himself. What the hell was he doing here?

Owen crouched, his bulk making it difficult not to fall, which would make a sound. He held himself around the knees to keep from rocking in fear. He could hear the murmuring sounds of voices, but he couldn't make out what they were saying over the hum of the coil. Then he noticed the unit's control panel and had an idea.

Before he could put his plan into action, he heard the voices getting nearer. He put his hands on the floor, ready to rise as if he had been checking the panel's lights. Then he realized it was useless. He had no business being near it.

If that prick Dr. Payne sees me here, he'll know something's up.

Owen was frozen, wracking his brain to come up with a plausible reason to be crouching in a corner of the lab. He could hear footsteps, but he couldn't make out which direction they were headed.

Then he heard the lab door open and close, the light from the outside brightening and dimming three times. Then there was near silence, just the hum of the coil and the blood rushing through his ears.

He flicked his head from behind the device then back again. No one there. He darted out twice more, checking each section of the lab. They were gone!

He rushed over to the computer, sitting there still waiting for his login. He accessed the system, changed the security file back to its original status, then re-booted the computer one more time. He didn't wait for it to come back up again, certain he'd made the change correctly.

On his way out the back door he passed the coil he'd hid behind. He had a deliciously vicious idea. He picked a screwdriver out of the toolbox, hoping he would have at least two minutes before anyone came in again.

He was done in one and fled out the back door, his flash drive securely stored in his shirt pocket.

A few minutes before, when Thomas had walked into the lab to talk to Rhys, he noticed Terri in a heartbeat. She wore ragged jean shorts and a stained blouse with torn sleeves, enticing despite her dishevelment. Looking as if she had just tumbled out of—

Never mind, he thought. He stuffed down the thought, too distracted to question her presence in his lab.

Thomas said to her, "There's nothing you can do but get yourself in trouble."

Terri felt her temper rise, then caught herself. She had seen innocent men caught in desperate situations many times. "Thomas, you know who my father is."

He nodded, conceding her point. He looked around. "No one here. Let's go."

Outside, Thomas noticed Owen Caldicott loping away from the lab's back door. There was no reason he could think of why Owen should hide from them.

No reason but one.

"I'll be back in a minute," he said. He was halfway to the entrance before either could react.

Rhys said to Terri, "Better you than me to ask what he's worried about."

Terri eyed him approvingly.

Inside, she saw him hovering over a computer. She drew closer and saw it was stuck at a portion of the startup sequence. "Is something wrong?"

"I'll know in a minute," he said, not looking up.

Thomas tapped a key to let the sequence complete, then logged on. A few minutes later, he announced, "Somebody's been hacking this system. Owen, I'd bet."

"Is that a big deal?"

Thomas assayed her. He suppressed his automatic response, afraid it would sound too stern. Instead, he said, "Let's rejoin Rhys. He's in charge of the lab and I should let him know about this."

They had almost reached the front door when a high-pitched whine began. At first, it was merely annoying. Within seconds, it was so painful Terri had to cover her ears. Thomas shouted something at her, but she couldn't hear it. He clamped her arm and dragged her toward the exit.

He pushed on the door. It wouldn't budge.

5

THERE was no chance that Thomas could call Rhys over the shrieking. From the picnic table, no one would hear him pounding on the door either. He would have to turn off the noise himself. The first thing was to find out where it coming from.

He turned toward one of the huge electromagnet coils in the corner of the room. Fed enough current, they could create an awful howl. Theory told him this would be the kind of squeal they'd make, but no calculation conveyed how punishing the reality was. A few minutes more and permanent brain damage was not out of the question.

He searched the desk for a pair of noise canceling headphones. Damn. One lone pair. He slapped them onto Terri's head and pointed her toward the control room a few feet away. It looked onto the lab, separated by a piece of soundproof glass. She obeyed but found that door stuck, too.

He staggered toward the coils, knowing the covers housed an emergency shutoff switch. He was right about the source of the wail, though how the safety protocol got overridden he would have to look into later. If he survived.

The intensity increased. If it grew much stronger, he would pass out from the pain. The sensation made it hard to think, but through the haze of hurt he estimated he had two minutes tops to switch them off. After that, it wouldn't matter. Nothing would.

The echo in his head made it impossible to pinpoint the culprit. It could be any one of the four experimental magnets. He went to check the first, found nothing wrong and stumbled to the next. The second looked equally untouched, but he couldn't do better than limp to the third one.

He nearly fainted on his way to the fourth coil as he crawled and slid, keeping his right arm wrapped over his head to block one ear, his hand covering the other. It made little difference. The vibrations pulsed through his flesh like a laser through a cornea, searing his skull.

He reached for the control panel, his fingers inches from the shutoff switch. He stretched up and tapped it. Nothing. He couldn't understand it. There was no reason the strongest magnetic field should disable the safety switch.

He would have to remove the cover to manipulate the wires directly, something requiring a minute at most. He told himself he could surely last that long without his head bursting. His father had hurt him much more than this, many times.

Yet, it was already impossible to think, and if the intensity kept growing his eyeballs would start to bleed. He could feel a thin trickle of blood pooling in his left ear already.

He turned to start the long crawl back to the toolkit in the desk five yards away. God help him if it wasn't there. He pushed the thought away to concentrate as best he could on putting one knee ahead of the other.

He'd gone three scoots when Terri appeared above him, toolkit in hand. She smiled, as if offering a picnic lunch, but her hand was shaking. She was feeling the effects despite wearing the headphones. She mouthed, "Thought you might need this."

He tried to smile in return, to show how unafraid he was, but the pain was too severe and it was a lie anyway. He felt sure they were about to die. Then he saw her look of confidence in him as she reached down to help him up. He stood up, pulled a screwdriver from the box and staggered back to the coil, waving Terri away from the equipment.

He reached the coil and found her right behind him. If she touched the wrong thing.... He couldn't argue now. He turned to the panel and leaned in to put maximum torque on the screws.

He noticed the screws were nearly stripped; that had to be deliberate. He pressed in hard and twisted to take out the first, but his hand shook so much it was taking dangerously long.

Seeing him struggle, Terri snatched the screwdriver and removed the screw in three seconds flat. The other three were out in less than ten. Then she jerked off her headphones and clapped them on him. She winced at the sudden onset of noise.

He accepted the gesture, knowing he would have to concentrate for a moment to have any hope of saving them both. This close to the coil, she was as likely to suffer organ damage as hearing loss, anyway. He nudged her backwards, but she wouldn't go. He turned back to business.

After pulling the panel down, he could see the problem at a glance. Two of the four wires connected to the emergency switch had been pulled loose from their contact points. Several inches of the insulation had been stripped off and two were touching.

There was no chance of soldering them back on before he stroked from a burst blood vessel. He would have to conjoin them with one hand and hit OFF with the other. And hope the juice died before he did.

Seeing what he was about to do, Terri ripped off a sock and thrust it onto his left hand. He pushed the wires and tapped the switch at the same time.

The coil shut down. The noise was gone.

But he'd been too slow and the sock too thin. The shock hurled him across the floor, unconscious before he coasted three feet.

Terri saw him slide and thrust out a hand to catch him, brushing the exposed wires with her knee. Thomas's shoes protected him from a fatal shock, but Terri had bared one foot in giving him the sock. The sweat on her heel lowered her skin's resistance and the massive current drove her down to the floor head first, her leg charred in a line from knee to heel.

Thomas regained consciousness in a few seconds and through a haze noticed Terri lying on the floor. Groggy, he dragged himself over by one hand and one leg, then leaned his head on her breastbone. No sound. He put his hand inside her blouse at the base of her throat. No pulse.

Then he passed out.

Rhys had been banging on the front door for a solid minute. When Thomas still hadn't come out, he went around the back to try the rear exit. When it too wouldn't open and neither of his friends responded, he called the campus police, explained the situation, and took off in the direction Owen had gone.

He'd never liked the junior lab tech. Two years of caving shenanigans was more than enough to convince him the skeeze bucket was untrustworthy. The most recent episode — pretending he would toss Brenda down a shaft inside Llechwedd Caverns, and getting damn close to it — was his worst stunt to date. Even for clowning that was way over the line.

Despite such pranks, Thomas kept him on the team for his computer skills, downplaying Rhys' warnings that he would be real trouble someday. That day seemed to have arrived. Owen had something to do with why the doors wouldn't open, he'd bet. He would take deep satisfaction in finding the slug and then watching the police grill him to charcoal.

It didn't take long to catch up with him. He was at the first place Rhys looked: the faculty dining room. Owen wasn't faculty, not even close, which Rhys knew bothered him. Eating at the club surrounded by professors and postdocs was some kind of ego compensation.

He debated less than five seconds whether to risk making a scene in the dining room. He could get in trouble if he were wrong about Owen's disabling the lab doors, but his desire for revenge won out. Anyway, the old bores around the room would probably get a charge out of having some drama thrust into their lives for once.

Rhys approached Owen's table just as he set down his tray. It was piled high with the most disgusting garbage: six seaweed pancakes slathered in butter. No wonder Owen always fell behind on their caving trips.

Rhys sat down without being invited. "I saw you come out of the lab a few minutes ago," he hissed, following his initial impulse to lean on the little coward. He hoped Owen could be intimidated into offering some useful information before he called the police again.

He watched carefully for any reaction, but there was none. As usual, Owen was expert at controlling his expressions, affecting a long-familiar innocent mien that had never fooled Rhys. He'd seen it countless times after as many screw-ups in the lab.

Owen was too clever to deny the charge outright, opting to bluff his way through. "One of the systems was acting up. I sacrificed my Saturday morning to fix it." He sighed deeply, as if doing his job was a great burden for which he was not properly appreciated. Then he dug into his pancakes, which gave him an excuse to avoid Rhys's eyes.

"Is that why you corked the doors on your way out?" He let his voice rise just enough to attract the attention of several nearby diners.

Owen betrayed not a wisp of guilt, his control perfect. The sole sign of discomfort was a fine mist of sweat starting to spread over his temples. He knew the faculty resented his use of the dining room and he preferred to remain low key.

"They worked fine when I arrived and left. Otherwise, how could I have gotten in and out?" he asked, his voice full of quiet sneer. He didn't add "Stupid jerk," letting his tone do it for him.

Rhys knew he wouldn't get anywhere this way. Owen was too clever at appearing the victim. He rose to leave. The police could handle searching him and his apartment.

In a gesture of faked respect, Owen rose a split-second later, then bowed theatrically. A storage card fell out of his pocket onto the pancakes. He reached for it but Rhys was quicker.

"And what's on this, then?"

Despite his panic, Owen was too well controlled to forcibly reclaim the device. That would confirm he was desperate to keep it out of Rhys's hands. "Can I have that, please? It has personal information."

"I'll bet," Rhys said, and whipped out his tablet. He was about to plug the card in when Owen reached across the table, forcing Rhys to take a step back. He hit his heel on the chair and fell backward onto a professor of mathematics, who had never been fond of him anyway. "I am sorry," he said, struggling to right himself.

In the fall, the card flew out of Rhys' hand and skipped across Owen's table. Owen snapped it up, then pretended that dropping it was a clumsy accident. He then thrust out a hand to make it look as if he was overeager to steady Rhys and crunched the card under his foot at the same time.

"Damn!" they both said simultaneously, one expression of regret a fake, the other genuine.

Owen pivoted his foot aside. Rhys looked down at the pieces, missing Owen's fleeting look of mixed triumph and despair.

Thomas hovered over Terri's hospital bed, ignoring the nurse's insistent reminder that visiting hours were over. Finally, the nurse marched out to fetch the attending physician, huffing audibly, her butt tilted upward at the same angle as her nose. He didn't look around at the sound.

He sat in the visitor's chair, resting his forehead on his palm. Terri was in a coma and he blamed himself for not insisting that she leave the lab. That she could not have if she'd been willing, he completely forgot in the stupor of guilt.

He took some comfort that at least he was able to call the ambulance right away. He'd been unconscious for less than a minute. He also felt some small relief that the power surge had released the door locks. If the emergency med techs had had to wait for the doors to be axed down, Terri would certainly have died.

In another moment, the ambulance had pulled up to the ER entrance and she was being wheeled out before the driver could set the emergency brake. The paramedics nearly knocked down two nurses racing her to the doors.

Inside, the ER physician bellowed at Thomas to stand back from the gurney, then ordered a nurse to wheel her into a room, stat. He spent a few minutes with her, all he needed.

After checking her vital signs and listening to Thomas's explanation, he knew she'd either survive intact or be brain damaged. The EEG didn't settle the question one way or the other. There was no way to know which until she woke up, if she would. Half an hour later they moved her to a room.

As Thomas continued to hold her hand in that room, he heard the sound of footsteps. The angry nurse had returned with the ward physician, who diplomatically but firmly told Thomas he would have to leave. Thomas nodded, then dipped his head to kiss Terri's hand before rising. He was turning toward the door when he heard her moan.

She opened her eyes and said, her voice feeble, "Did you just kiss my hand?"

"Well... I..." He blushed, an expression she hadn't seen on him before. Then he stood erect. "Yes, yes, I did."

She blinked and said, "How charming." She rubbed her chest. "I'm sore."

The doctor said, "The alternative would be much worse, I can assure you." He beamed at Thomas, knowing she had him to thank for saving her life.

The doctor examined her eyes. Then he ran her through a series of short tests to check her memory function. He asked her to squeeze his hand in rhythm and made her ape a few complex finger motions with the other hand. He pronounced her fit to leave in a day or so, patting her shoulder, then turned to leave.

Thomas beamed at her, overjoyed at her returning from the dead. Then his guilt returned, thinking he'd almost killed her.

She noticed his expression and said, "Buck up, Thomas. I'm not dead and you didn't do this. I'm just so damned clumsy."

"Terri, I—" He wouldn't say what he wanted to say.

"Now, about that hand kissing business..."

Thomas blushed again, but was saved by the nurse from having to respond.

"Really time to go, young man." She waved a hand like a stork with a broken neck in a Florida gale. Taking stock of his expression, she added with unexpected compassion, "Not to worry, she'll be fine now."

He bit his upper lip, exposing his lower teeth. Terri laughed at the sight and waved her hand to urge him to lean toward her. She kissed his forehead, her hand caressing the back of his neck. She whispered into his ear, "Thank you for saving my life." Thomas beamed. She gave him a little prod on the shoulder. "Now, go."

Thomas fiddled a second longer, aching to stay. Then he said, "I'll be back during visiting hours this evening."

"I'm looking forward to that," she said.

He grinned and left, feeling elated.

Outside in the hallway, thinking of Owen Caldicott brought him down to Earth. Rhys had been right. He should have fired him a long time ago. He left the building, heading across campus back to the sealed lab. He'd requested security to guard the doors until he returned, lying that there were valuable military secrets inside that someone had tried to steal.

Or was it a lie? Why else would Owen risk murder? The technology was worth a great deal to Vestry, but industrial theft was so common the courts barely slapped a violator's wrist. Some judges seemed to think the companies deserved it just for trying to protect their patents.

Could his invention do something he hadn't imagined, something worth killing for? Was he the intended victim at Dan-yr-Ogof?

Rhys entered Terri's hospital room at the beginning of visitor's hour. "I came as soon as I found out from Thomas where you were," Rhys said.

"What's he doing, do you know?"

Rhys shook his head. Then, seeing her expression, he added, "Don't worry. If he said he'll be back to visit tonight, he'll be here. He's the most boringly reliable guy I know."

"I don't think he's boring at all."

Rhys examined her one-eyed for a moment.

She asked, "Is there something I should know?"

"Nothing it won't be better for you to find out yourself." He squeezed her arm playfully.

He sat on the metal back of the visitor's chair, his feet on the seat, so he could look down at her from on high. He was already having mixed feelings about his decision to leave the field clear for Thomas.

He'd known Terri casually for a year, after meeting her at a caving event. She had attended to get stone for a sculpture. But she'd never looked so beautiful as she did lying helpless on the bed. He took his chance to ogle while she was gazing out the window.

He gripped his knees wondering what had happened to his casual attitude about women, and knowing the answer was right in front of him. Today wasn't the first time he'd wanted to ask her out, but the timing never seemed right. Now he wanted to more than ever and the chance was there.

He couldn't take it. Not yet. Not with a clean conscience. Thomas would be back in American soon enough; then the field really would be clear.

Unable to think of anything casual to say, and not willing to say what was on his mind, he slapped his thighs and jumped down from the chair. "Well, gotta go." He turned for the door, but Terri clutched his hand.

"Can't you visit a little longer? I want to know what you found out about the incident in the lab." Seeing his face, she raised an eyebrow. "I was right. You do know something."

He leaned against the bed and frowned down at her. "You're too much like your Da."

Terri frowned in return. "Never mind that. Give."

Rhys held back, despite his desire to tell her about Owen. He was reluctant to make unfounded accusations, and without the storage card he couldn't prove anything. Still, nothing else made sense. Maybe Terri could talk to her father and get him to pursue it.

"There's a guy who works in the lab. Owen Caldicott. I don't have the evidence because he stepped on it, but I think he copied Thomas's plans for a new invention."

Terri wondered what the invention was, but guessed that Rhys wouldn't want to tell her. Maybe Thomas would when he came back. She felt a novel desire to learn about a man's work, the same feeling she'd had in the lab. It puzzled her; she'd always been mostly indifferent to what others created, even to the work of contemporary sculptors. She checked the clock on the wall, marking how long evening visitor hours lasted.

Rhys interrupted her thoughts. "I thought you might get your Da to look into it. You know, on the quiet-like."

Terri chuckled at the thought of her father doing anything quietly.

Well, there was one time of day. He would come home and look at her deceased mother's portrait for a long time, gazing at it, a glass of his prized Laphroaig scotch still barely touched after an hour.

Terri was jolted back to the present when Rhys received a call.

He looked at the number: Thomas's office at the lab. He picked up and listened for a minute. "Ok, I'll meet you there in forty minutes. When I see you, there are a few things I have to tell you about Owen."

He hung up and turned back to Terri. He laid his hand on her arm. He held it there long enough to soothe his need to touch her, but not enough to let her guess his motive. He bolstered the illusion by saying in a brotherly tone, "You rest. I'll be back later."

"With Thomas?"

She never saw his crestfallen face. He left without responding, almost knocking over a passing nurse on his way down the corridor.

She leaned back against her pillow and appraised her condition. She actually felt fine;

the shock had worn off. Anything else could be attended to at home.

She waited until she heard the nurse was far away then swung her feet onto the floor, testing whether she still felt dizzy. So far, so good. She stood. Wobbly, but far from invalid. A second later she thumped back down onto the bed. The room spun around her head two turns before she fainted.

6

$\mathcal{A}$FTER leaving Terri at the hospital, Thomas made his way to the lab, thinking about Owen Caldicott.

Somebody rigged that coil and Owen headed the list of suspects, a docket of one. But Thomas couldn't go to the police without something solid. They would just lock *him* up again, and this time Terri couldn't come to the rescue.

The solution was to gather what evidence he could, confront Owen with it and somehow get him to confess. Then he could deliver the facts and the culprit to the police and trust them to do the right thing. After he laid it all out logically to himself, he drew one conclusion: impossible.

The police wouldn't assign much weight to computer logs. Exiting the rear door of the lab just before the 'accident' was circumstantial at best. Any defense lawyer would make it seem like Rhys was just out to get Owen fired and duped Thomas into doing it.

No, without proof, it was impossible. Still, there was nothing to do but go through the motions and hope the proof would appear.

He greeted the security guard at the entrance to the lab and let himself in. He switched on the lights and made a beeline for the laptop that he'd started to check out when the emergency popped. He noticed at once that its usual spot was empty, outlined in dust.

Damn.

He spent a few seconds looking around, knowing in advance the search was pointless. There was no reason for someone to relocate it rather than remove it. Owen must have doubled back after he and Terri went to the hospital and before the guard arrived.

His only hope was to find him. With luck, the laptop would be with him. Then he grimaced; all trace of Owen's treason would be erased by then.

He spent a full minute paralyzed, bouncing between despair and hope. Then he shook himself out of it. It was all speculation until he found Owen himself. But how? He went to another computer, accessed the personnel records, and looked up Owen's home address.

He wrote it down, ripped the paper from the pad and thrust it into his pocket.

When he arrived at Owen's apartment there was one light burning in the window, odd since it was still a few hours before dark. Not proof he was home, but a good sign. He looked around to see if he could find any evidence of Owen's vehicle, an Indian Chief motorcycle with leather tassels on the seat.

Thomas didn't notice the man following him, who kept well out of his line of sight. The tail meandered along the other side of the street, mixing in with the small number of pedestrians. When a hive of neighborhood kids buzzed past him, drawing attention to him, he disappeared around the corner of a building.

Thomas was too busy focusing on the apartment building to notice anyone's efforts not to be seen. He walked up the steps and was about to knock on the door when someone tapped him on the shoulder. He jerked around to find Rhys smiling at him.

Rhys said, "You were going to meet me at the lab, no? When you weren't there, I guessed you might come here."

Thomas whispered harshly, "Lower your voice." He pointed to the light in the window.

Thomas tapped on the door and immediately the light inside went out. He rapped again, waited a few seconds, then heard a door slam far to his left, blown shut by a gust of wind. He looked out to the street to see a gray figure running toward a motorcycle parked next to the apartment.

Rhys said, "That guy has a real penchant for back doors."

"Too slender to be Owen. Stay here in case Owen comes out the front." Thomas bolted to catch the figure racing for the bike.

"Right," Rhys said with a huff, then rocketed down the steps after Thomas, catching up in a few strides.

Thomas glanced over his shoulder at the sound of footsteps, then swore. Rhys ignored it and pulled ahead, reaching the man on the bike just as he started the engine.

The figure was about to gun the accelerator when he spied Rhys almost on him. He reached his left hand behind his back and pulled out something too quickly for Rhys to follow, then smacked him in the head with a tire pump.

Rhys went down like a clint on a cave top felled by Thor's hammer. The rider ramped up the rpm and sped off.

He aimed the motorcycle directly at Thomas and poured on the gas, gaining as much speed as he could within a few yards. He stuck out a foot at the level of Thomas's knee, hoping to break it backwards.

Thomas waited until the last second then jumped up on a car parked at the curb. He jumped down as the motorcycle sped away. He rushed over to where Rhys was lying on the ground and knelt down to examine him. "Are you okay?"

Rhys nodded. "He only clipped me." He touched his head, feeling a sticky, wet spot. "Ouch."

"We'd better get you to the hospital."

Rhys snorted. "Bunk. I've had worse scrapes caving."

Thomas was about to argue when a scuff and tinkle sounds coming from behind distracted him. He turned to see a chubby figure waddling toward a Tesla Roadster parked at the curb, dragging a duffel bag along the ground. "Owen!"

Thomas rasped at Rhys, "I told you to watch the front door."

"Wag your finger later. Go get him!"

Thomas wavered, reluctant to leave Rhys. Then he sprinted to catch up with Owen before he could get into the car. He reached the driver's door just as the engine roared. Owen steered away from the curb, running over the tips of Thomas's shoes as he peeled the car's tires on the pavement.

Thomas looked down at his feet, thankful he'd jumped back a foot when Owen whipped the car leftward. He walked over to Rhys, feeling the pinch from his shoes. He stretched out a hand to help him off the ground and said, "Well, so much for getting the lab computer back. I'm sure we'll never see it again."

"What do you mean?"

"I came here to retrieve it, with the slim hope that it might have some evidence left intact." He led Rhys out of the street. "I thought I could use that to get Owen to fess up."

"To confess? He never would," Rhys said, shaking his head. "But not to worry." He smirked. "I've got the laptop. I snagged it before you went to the hospital and took it home."

Thomas looked at him, then slapped his hands together. "Jumping Jehoshaphat! Let's get to your apartment, quick."

"What the hell does 'Jehoshaphat' mean?"

"Never mind. Come on!"

Before Thomas got three more steps, he looked down the street and said over his shoulder, "If that was Owen, who the hell was that guy on the bike who clipped you?"

"His roommate, maybe?"

Thomas hurried on. "Who is that?"

Rhys shrugged, holding his palms up.

As they jogged toward the train station, the detective following Thomas came out of his hiding place and tapped his phone. He waited a few seconds for the line to connect, then relayed the license plate number of the car that had nearly run Thomas down. Then, he ran to catch up with the two men.

Two men walked along a beach on Barry Island, an amusement park fifteen minutes by train from central Cardiff. One was short and chubby, the other tall and muscular. Owen and his roommate.

"Did you have to make such a cock up of everything?" the roommate charged.

"Me?" Owen whined. "You had the chance to run him over and you missed."

That shut up the critic and they walked a few seconds in silence, both stewing. The roommate said finally, "This git has got to be snuffed. And now." Something down the beach caught his eye. He gripped Owen by the upper arm, squeezing hard. "I have an idea."

Owen jerked his arm away and listened for a few minutes. He asked a few questions and then said, "Ok, but I promise just to get them there. I know nothing about what happens after that." He looked up into the gelid eyes of his roommate. "Then I never want to see you again. Get your stuff out of the apartment."

The man had no objections. Once Thomas was out of the way, the police would close the case on the incident at Dan-yr-Ogof. Then he could pursue his original plan.

The pair split up and Owen powered up his phone. It took scant seconds for him to convince Thomas to meet him on Barry Island. He claimed to have another storage card with the plans for the power system. He was willing to exchange it for a promise not to prosecute.

Thomas's voice came across skeptical, but Owen knew that made no difference. His boss couldn't risk the plans being sold. He would come.

Owen hung up, pleased to have put another one over on the man he hated more than anyone. He walked into the restaurant at the top of the steps.

Thomas and Rhys arrived at the bottom of the steps just after dusk, two hours later. They could hear the squeals of revelers at Pleasure Park, a few hundred yards away. Rhys insisted again that coming was a bad idea, that it was a trap.

"Of course it is," Thomas said, zipping up his jacket to block the cool ocean breeze. "How else to find out what he's up to?"

The low-angle moonlight drew his pinched expression into peaks and shadows.

Rhys bobbed his head. "I just don't want you to wind up dead." He bobbed his eyebrows, Groucho Marx style. "Again."

Thomas's expression sharpened, its peaks brighter, the valleys deeper and darker.

Rhys ignored it and continued, "You should leave this to the police."

Thomas shook his head vigorously. Spray from the nearby surf flew off the end of a curl of hair. "They'll lock me away and plod on for god knows how long. I've got three weeks to get back home or lose the Vestry contract." He inspected the beach looking for Owen and said in a distracted tone, "Followed right after by my chair at the university, I'm sure."

"I'm sure Vestry would give you a job, as would a hundred other firms."

"After being suspected of murder in Wales? You've been in academia too long. Company executives are the most timid men on Earth."

Rhys looked around. He had a clear view of the meeting place down the beach a quarter mile. The dark wouldn't prevent him seeing someone on top of the rock, silhouetted against the moonlit sky. The dark oval below was the cave entrance Owen mentioned to Thomas on the phone.

Thomas took his shoes off to relieve the cramp in his toes from the crushed leather tips. He took off his socks. The sand felt good beneath his feet. He passed by a wad of seaweed washing up at the shoreline and stepped around it. "Oww!" he yelped.

"What the hell?" Rhys asked.

Thomas knelt down and saw a small crab near his foot. He walked around it and shivered. "I had nightmares as a child about hundreds of them crawling over my body, tearing my skin off. They're like giant wet spiders with hard bodies."

Rhys chuckled, a grim sound this time. "You had some bitch of a childhood." Thomas nodded, his face impassive. Rhys went on, "You should talk to someone about it. Like Terri. She's very intuitive."

Thomas shook his head violently as they neared the cave entrance. To distract Rhys, he pointed to a path that led to a plateau atop it. "Where's the flashlight?"

"You Americans. We call it a torch for a reason. It stays on. A flashlight would flare and then go out. Like a camera flash."

Just then, a camera flash flared in both their faces, three times in quick succession. Blinded and disoriented, Thomas instinctively stood still. Rhys staggered ahead to see who had done it, hoping to knock him down. In a few feet he was well inside the cave mouth.

Thomas had shot his hand up after the first flash and his sight was already recovering. He saw Rhys get struck on the head from behind and go down on the sand. He ran forward, heedless, and received a twin blow the instant he passed the entrance.

A few seconds later, a huge blast hurled boulders off the plateau, closing off the entrance to a height of fifteen feet. The pile left open only a sliver of sky barely thicker than a boy's torso.

Rhys regained consciousness, followed by Thomas a second later. Both rubbed their heads, feeling lumps already forming.

Rhys looked up at the shaft of light streaming in above the boulders and said, "Tell me again about my great plan for not getting caught in the trap?"

7

TERRI stood in front of the Library of the Religious Society of Friends in London, otherwise known as Friends House, the central Quaker library in the UK. She knew a little about Thomas's past from talking with Rhys, and wanted to learn more.

Nothing she found would exonerate him, she knew. But it might help establish his real identity and give her father some reason to take his story seriously. If she could prove that Thomas was who he said, Da would have to wonder why the dead man had his passport. And once Chief Inspector Mawr began to wonder, he never stopped 'til there was nothing left to wonder about.

She walked inside and felt a cool, dry breeze across her face, a sharp contrast to the humid swelter on the street. She wasn't surprised. Everything about the place whispered gentility. This was a place where no one would dare to shout — and faithfully refused to shout about itself.

Light wood panels, plain and rich at the same time, lent a lovely background for similar tables and chairs, furniture that invited study. The illumination was low but serviceable, and intelligently placed. No medieval monk's cell, this; it offered everything necessary but nothing in excess.

Terri couldn't think of a place in greater contrast to Thomas's lab. That was busy, bold, and full of the latest technology. Both had something in common, though: a dedication to finding what was true. Her confidence rose that she'd come to the right place. She glided to the counter and described briefly what she was seeking.

"Is there nothing you wanted to find available on the web?" the clerk asked.

From his clothing, Terri was a little surprised he'd heard of the Internet. Then she realized it wouldn't do to insult someone she wanted help from. Given his angelic face, it also struck her it would be incredibly bad taste. She said simply, "I've already spent two hours searching from home."

The young man said he really wasn't surprised. What she wanted would be of interest chiefly to Quakers, a quiet tribe whose members were guided by an inner light. That light was aided more often by time-honored texts than modern documents. Few of them had found their way into contemporary computers.

He informed her he would try to help and shuffled off. Within ten minutes, Terri had several tomes to inspect. She spent the next hour skimming for what she wanted, then another reviewing what she'd found. The material was exactly what she'd hoped for.

Thomas's parents, James and Celia Paine, were born in Thetford into a group of Quakers descended from the family of Thomas Paine, the Revolutionary pamphleteer. Their mutual ancestor was a close cousin of his, born in 1737. The family's mores had changed little since and, like Paine, the pair had chafed under those strictures growing up. Both developed a strong streak of skepticism, an outgrowth of the Quaker devotion to seeking truth.

In their case, it led them often to question the basic beliefs of the Friends and one in particular: pacifism. Celia was no more inclined to turn the other cheek than James and they fumed at being unable to respond to a perceived injustice, with force if necessary.

During their late teens, an outsider attended a Friends meeting one Sunday morning and took a shine to Celia. James could subdue his jealousy for the sake of keeping the peace, especially seeing she didn't return his interest. But when the man kept putting his hands on her after the gathering disbanded, he asked him to stop. When he refused, James vised the man's arm and marched him down the street several paces before he broke free.

The records were mixed on what happened next. Some onlookers reported the visitor swung first. Others swore James struck the first blow after the stranger spoke a rude word describing Celia. All agreed the stranger went down in a hail of fists, like boulders hurled from arms made powerful by years of farm labor.

The adults held a 'Friends business meeting' that same day, an unprecedented speed because it had never been necessary before. No one insisted that James should leave, but none could overlook his act of violence, either. James argued he had ample provocation. A man respected by all responded that provocation is what a Friend should rise above. That turned the tide of opinion against him.

In the end, the group voted to allow James to continue as part of the Friends society, but he was to be monitored closely for a year for any hint of an encore. During that twelve months, his contempt grew to new bounds, blending with a growing judgment that all Quaker beliefs were wrongheaded, nay vicious.

James waited with ill-concealed rage for Celia to come of age before leaving the group. He feared the elders would notify the law, men he viewed as more authoritarian than the hated Quaker leaders. The pair rebelled with finality at ages 18 and 19; they married and left town to lead their own lives, unfettered by the suffocating rules of the Society.

They set off with a few dozen pounds in pocket and a single suitcase of clothes between them, their entire stock of possessions but one. The exception was a small kit of science toys containing magnets, a compass, and assorted other educational gear that James had stolen and hidden long ago.

The pair sailed to Rhode Island after spending two more weeks in Britain, just long enough to find a cruise ship to stow away on. Not daring to be seen among the passengers, they sometimes ate rats raw to avoid starvation, supplemented by a few pilfered apple cores from the galley's trash can. By the time they arrived in America, each had lost twenty pounds of flesh.

Both tried hard to fit into the society of their new country, but they were misfits from the start. Unwilling to seek out a Society of Friends, they were equally unable to bond with the mainstream. Both viewed their well-to-do employers with suspicion. Yet, their impoverished neighbors struck them as crude and ill-educated, and so prompted equal contempt.

The self-induced degradation led them within a few years into a militia group where they felt at home for the first time. Soon, they were engaged in violent bank robberies that tapered off when Celia became pregnant with Thomas's younger brother. The baby died before age two and the parents went back at it full bore, more bitter than ever.

By the age of eight Thomas knew something was morally wrong with his parents, though he couldn't name what it was. He understood down to the root by twelve. He ran across the words he'd felt but hadn't previously found when he read them in a popular book on philosophy. When he spoke them that evening to his father, James banned him from going to the library ever again.

Thomas's rebellion against that order launched a war between them that was to last another two years. It took him that long to devise a practical plan of escape that would let him survive on his own.

The day he left he hid behind some boxes in the cellar of his home. He waited for his father to search him out at the library in town and drag him back, as he had so many times before. His mother was away from home cutting a deal for new guns.

Two minutes after James left, enough time to make sure he'd really gone, Thomas hefted his small canvas sack holding a shirt, three pairs of socks, and the science kit. He ran away as fast and as far as his burgeoning legs and mind could carry him.

In the fifteen years since, his father had not stopped looking for him, but never got close. Thomas had outwitted him by the simple act of hiding in plain sight, doing not so much as changing his name, but being careful never to have his photo or biography on the web.

Terri finished reading and returned the books to the clerk, still open to the passage she'd read from one of them. She described part of it and asked, "Can you give me any idea how the author would know all this subsequent history about the Paines if James and Celia left the Society? Especially any detailed portions about Thomas Payne's escape?"

The clerk speculated that someone who knew them might have learned their tale after the pair were imprisoned, but he admitted it was just a guess. He told her that Friends were eager to record as much of their history as possible, even — one might say, especially — when it was unsavory. It provided valuable life lessons for others.

Terri thanked him and turned to go.

She didn't notice a second clerk talking to the helpful one as she was leaving. His Puritanical stare fixated on the door closing softly behind her, then he went to make a call.

Terri understood better now why Thomas was so closed off, so reluctant to talk about his past. More to her purpose, she now had photocopied evidence to support Thomas's claim about his identity. There were no photographs of any use, but few outsiders would know the book's contents. She was confident Thomas could relate the incident of his escape like it happened the day before.

It would be enough to get her Da to reconsider. She thought of taking it to him directly, then decided it would be better for Thomas to do that himself. She set off to find him, unaware that the second Quaker clerk had just hung up the phone.

"Don't panic," Thomas said to Rhys. "We've been trapped in caves plenty of times and always gotten out, right?"

Rhys looked at him in the glow of the torch. "Uh, not with ten tons of rock in front of us and no one knowing we were there." He noticed Thomas's frown. "Not to sound the pessimist, you understand."

Thomas took the flashlight and shined it along the rim of the boulders. "There might be enough room for someone to crawl through that. One of us gets up there, squeezes out, and goes for help, that's all."

"That's all, eh? Up that rock face? Without gear? I'm a caver, not a rock climber." He held up a hand to forestall another protest. "Ok, ok, I know they're similar. Far be it from me to yield to despair." He held out his cupped hands and stooped over to give Thomas a boost. He said, under his breath, "Still, it is pretty smooth..."

Thomas stood the flashlight on end to shine on the rocks, then put his bare foot into the stirrup and started to climb. He reached two strides up, still a full three feet from the top, when he ran out of obvious handholds. "Shine the light around my hands. I can't see any place to grasp."

The illumination made clear what Thomas had feared. The rocks curved backwards toward the interior of the cave. To keep rising he would need a better hold than the ones used for a straight vertical climb. He saw none. Two solid minutes more of exploring with his hands and feet confirmed it.

"It's hopeless," Thomas said.

"Now who's the pessimist?"

"Don't be contrary. It's just a fact." He climbed part way down, then jumped onto the wet sand. "That doesn't mean there isn't another way out." He picked up the flashlight and shined it further into the cave. It ended six feet behind them without so much as a trickle of water through the stone. "Not that way, unfortunately."

"Well, look on the bright side," Rhys said. "With the opening at the top we won't run out of air." Thomas scowled. Rhys grinned back. "Just trying to be optimistic." He sat down and leaned back on his hands, feeling the moist sand between his fingers.

Thomas said, "Maybe you could stop evaluating your feelings and focus instead on devising a way out of here."

"Wow, what a crab." Observing Thomas's pinched lips, Rhys howled at his own joke. Just then, he felt a pinch on one finger. "Ouch!" He jerked up his hand and stood. "Shine the light down here."

Thomas waved the flashlight around Rhys' feet. He tensed and swirled it in a slow, widening spiral. There were a dozen small creatures crawling toward them. The one that pinched Rhys was just the point man. Thomas lowered the light near the sand to silhouette them. "Great. Crabs. Why did it have to be crabs?"

"Very funny. Now is no time for your film nostalgia." He took the light from Thomas and waved it all around the cave floor, focusing on the space behind them. There were at least another hundred crawlers further back in the cave, slowly making their way toward the two men.

To Thomas, they looked hungry.

8

"YOU lost him?" Arwel barked at Sergeant Bevan. "Need I ask why? Or should I just speak a single name that explains it."

Bevan stood at the best imitation of attention he could muster. It wasn't very good, thanks to his paunch. He knew he deserved the chewing out and secretly he was glad. Punishment relieved him from his sense of guilt.

Arwel asked, "I don't suppose you have a clue how to find him again, eh?"

Bevan shrugged. He had a strong suspicion where Thomas would be sometime tonight: visiting Terri. He didn't want to think about that, and anyway he promised not to mention her injury to the Chief Inspector. He could never break a promise to her, and so he waffled. "I'm sure he'll be in the area, sir."

"An American with no ties to Brecon? Why, Sergeant?"

Bevan was the fastest liar in Wales. "He has a lab at Cardiff University, sir. And he's got no passport. He can't leave."

Arwel shook his head. "He has no passport — if you believe his story. If you don't, he may have one in another name. Did you consider that?"

"You think he's some kind of spy, sir?"

"I think he's a material witness in a murder case who may very well become a suspect. If, that is, you and DI Bedwyr start doing your jobs better than you have today and get some actual evidence."

Bevan deflated. He could bear any bashing for Terri, but he hated having his professional competence questioned. He thought fast to redeem himself. "There's something else."

Arwel looked at him but didn't ask what, not sure he wanted to know. His curiosity finally got the better of him. "Well?"

"I think he's sweet on Terri." He hated to say it out loud, but he added, "There's some reason to think she returns the yearnin'."

In his thirty-two years, Bevan had never seen Iron Heart Mawr with quite that expression. It wasn't anger exactly. More the look of a man under a toppled statue crushing his foot, and no prospect of it being removed anytime soon.

"You'll keep that belief to yourself. That's an order. Arwel waved him out of his office without asking anything more. His forehead furrowed to the point that his eyebrows touched. He took deep breaths to remove the tightness in his chest.

Finally calm, he thought the problem over logically. The best thing to do was track down Thomas himself, through his daughter. He lived in a small village where everyone knew everybody's business. He didn't want it whispered about that Terri was involved with the Professor, if that's what the man was.

On his way out of the station, he ignored Sergeant Bevan's question about when he might return and closed the door behind him. He paused on the steps to talk to Bedwyr, who was returning from dinner. He asked him to look into a few things, then he got into his immaculate 1948 Bentley Mark VI and drove off.

His lifetime savings had been nowhere near enough to purchase the classic luxury car. It was a gift from a wealthy relative who never liked him. Arwel suspected he willed it to him because there'd been thousands in repairs needed to get it to run. The old man was fond of the car and probably the thought of junking it pained him too much.

Arwel had spent the better part of three years restoring it himself, using all his spare income just to buy parts. The pride he felt driving it away reminded him once again that the effort and expense had all been worth it.

His first intended stop was home. He had little hope of finding Terri there, given it was Saturday night. Still, he had to start somewhere. Where to look next would be the real problem. God alone knew where she'd go for enjoyment. She would never frequent the usual low spots around Brecon, and Cardiff was too big to search.

He sighed aloud and wondered for the hundredth time how a piece of clockwork like himself ever produced such an iconoclast. He might have blamed her free-spirited mother, but she hadn't survived the birth long enough to have a parenting effect, and he didn't believe in inherited personality. It would have to remain one of his few unsolved mysteries.

He pulled into his driveway then went into the house. He headed straight for Terri's studio.

As expected, she wasn't there. But she seemed to have been recently. A half-empty glass of scotch near her sculpting stand still held two floating ice shavings, not fully melted. At the current temperature, that put her in the room within the past forty minutes or so.

Her, or someone, he said to himself. Careful of assumptions. Then he remembered she never drank anything stronger than beer. So, who was her guest? The fellow who called himself Thomas? Arwel frowned, his eyebrows touching again.

He violated his standing rule about respecting her privacy and checked out her bedroom, convinced the situation warranted the exception. The room was a whirlwind, as usual. But amid the chaos something unexpected popped out from the middle of her bed.

The clothes on it were in two neat piles, rather than the normal random pattern, as if she'd been sorting them. Odd, as she hadn't done her own laundry since moving back home a year ago, after they'd patched up their biggest fight to date. As penance, he'd agreed to have a woman in once a week to give Terri more time to work on her art. This was not the day for her to come.

He checked her closet. Her suitcase was gone. It made no sense. Nothing they had argued about at breakfast was serious enough to make her move out again. And even at her most irate she'd never leave without telling him.

He searched the room, then the rest of the house. If she'd been abducted at gunpoint, there might be no signs of a struggle. But there were no signs of forced break-in either. Terri at her wildest would never invite someone in who was the type to kidnap her.

He was tempted to abandon his search for Thomas and look for her, but he had a feeling the two disappearances were linked. Bevan had said the man was fond of her. If she returned his feelings, she might go off with him. But without leaving him a note? Not like her.

He checked her bedroom one more time. On the dresser lay her usual personal items: a pearl and ruby ring her mother had owned, a postcard of a Frank Lloyd Wright house never built, and an old photo of himself in the Army. Along the mirror was an array of small stone figurines she had sculpted as a teen, each a perfect replica of one of her heroes: sculptors Barrias, Frishmuth, and — mystifying to Arwel — the mathematician Carl Friedrich Gauss. They were flanked by her trophies earned from teen cliff diving competitions.

And, one thing that definitely did not belong: a matchbook.

Terri had never smoked, there were no candles around, and she used nothing in her work that involved fire. He inspected the logo and address, a fancy restaurant south of Cardiff. To a lesser detective, it would seem like a clue to where she'd gone. But he realized that if she had gone there, the matches wouldn't be on her dresser until she returned.

More, it made no sense for her to have the matches in the first place. They must belong to whomever she was with. He tried to remember if there was any evidence — a smell, finger staining, cigarette packages — that this self-alleged Thomas Payne was a smoker. He couldn't remember. Now he wished he had examined the man himself.

It wasn't much, but it was all he had to go on at present. He left the house, his expression grimmer than when he'd left the station.

From within the cave, Thomas and Rhys yelled for several minutes in the direction of the boardwalk above the beach. It proved useless. The sound of the surf drowned out their cries more than those from the carnival.

Thomas remained standing on the rock face, one of two places the crabs couldn't reach. A few tried to scale the wall but never rose more than an inch or two.

He pulled the flashlight from his jacket and examined the cave floor again. It was now covered with them, spaced at about six-inch intervals, radiating outward all the way to a boulder at the back. He shut the light off and growled.

Rhys stood on the sand and tried flinging a few crabs away with his foot, but they were too persistent. Ultimately, he retreated to another boulder. After alternately sitting and standing for fifteen minutes, uncomfortable on the peaked platform either way, he noticed something during one of his upright periods. "Toss me the torch," he said to Thomas.

"No, if you miss it, we'll never get it back from the crabs."

"I won't miss."

Curious what Rhys had in mind next, Thomas readied his toss by turning on the light. Careful to keep the beam tilted upward to avoid blinding him, he flung the flashlight. He missed his friend's outstretched hand by a full foot.

"Great control, Sandy."

"Sandy?"

"Koufax." Not hearing an acknowledging grunt, Rhys added, "The Dodgers pitcher from 1955 to 1966? Your head is in the past so often I thought sure you'd get it." Ignoring Thomas's "oh," he looked down at the torch. When it landed, a few crabs had scurried away, but others quickly moved to take their place. "Here goes."

He jumped down onto the sand before the crabs could completely close the gap around the flashlight. He heard a sickening crack when he landed on one with his left foot. He snapped up the light and jumped back onto the boulder. On his way, he dragged a crab with him that had clamped onto his pants leg. He shook it off, hearing it bounce against the stone a few feet away.

"What are you up to?" Thomas asked.

"Just playing crab toss, a native game we enjoy in Wales. Children here don't grow up with Sony game units in each hand, you know."

"What a crock. You certainly did."

Rhys laughed, then wiggled the beam through the cave opening. "I think I can signal someone at the restaurant."

"At that angle? Not a chance. A passing plane, maybe."

"Boy, are you a crab, pun intended, ever since you got arrested." He shined the light through the slit again. "But you're right about the angle." He calculated the beam's height at the position of the restaurant, a hundred feet from the shoreline. "The solution is simple trigonometry. If I elevate myself another four feet that should do it."

Rhys worked the torch down the front of his pants, aiming the light upward at his face. He started to climb the wall near the boulder, having to feel his way around for handholds since the light shined more in his face than onto the rock. He managed to increase his elevation by a yard. He pulled out the torch and wiggled the beam through the opening for a few minutes.

"They'll pay attention quicker if you use Morse code."

"How many people read Morse code today?" Rhys objected.

"On the south shore of Wales, where fishing is an ancient practice? Probably quite a few." He changed his tone from annoyed to conciliatory. "Anyway, even if they don't know what it means, they'll interpret it as a signal, not just some kids playing a game."

That made sense to Rhys, always amenable to sound reasoning. He steadied himself against the rock and tried to signal. The torch wouldn't cooperate. The button wouldn't flick off the beam. "Your bad toss broke the on-off switch."

"Wave your hand in front of it to interrupt the beam."

It was precarious to use one hand to hold the torch and the other to block the light. He might well end up falling onto the crabs. So, with his back to the cave wall, he bent his leg and jammed one foot into a crack as far as it would go. He had to rely on his toes to keep him from falling forward. "What's the code for S-O-S?"

Thomas reminded him — three dits, three dashes, three dits again — and Rhys flashed it out. He repeated the signal five times then paused for five seconds, then repeated another five volleys, keeping it up for half an hour. "I have to rest." He spidered down the wall and sat on the boulder for a few minutes to ease his aching legs. Rested, he picked up again, keeping it up for another half hour.

Thomas grew discouraged. The cave was a two minute walk from the restaurant. If someone had seen the signal, they should have come over to investigate by now.

The idea of ending his days in a such a simple cave struck him as the worst kind of irony. He had explored some of the world's finest caverns and to die in such a plain little nothing, to be eaten afterwards by crabs, seemed ridiculous. A man should never have to die an absurd death, he thought.

He was also getting very tired of standing on the rock face. It occurred to him that if someone did come, it would still take hours to enlarge the cat's eye space at the front wall. He could never stand there that long.

He searched by the dim light to see if there were any other boulders like the one Rhys stood on. There were none. "Damn," he mumbled. Fighting the crabs looked inevitable.

Rhys was tiring of flashing the signal. Worse, the beam was getting weak. He could keep it up only a few minutes more before the battery died completely. If no one saw the light by then, they were doomed.

The odds of someone passing outside the cave by chance were nearly nil. It was too far from the path frequented by lovers taking a stroll on the beach.

Rhys lowered the light and climbed back down to his perch. Jumping down the last foot, he pummeled Thomas, who had climbed up on his boulder while he was signaling.

Thomas landed on his back and shouted up from the sand, "Ouch!"

"Sorry!"

"Not you. It's the damn crabs." He shook one off his bare foot and scooted back onto the rock, squeezing next to Rhys to share the small platform.

"We're in dire straits, boss."

"Dire straits? When did you start talking like a 19th century novel?" Thomas asked.

Rhys didn't register the question. He was too distracted by imagining their fate. They could eat the crabs for weeks, but it would take them only about four days to die of dehydration, maybe six or eight tops. There was plenty of moisture in the sand, but the salt water would ruin their kidneys, making it useless for fluid. "Yup, we're dead alright," he concluded.

He knelt down next to Thomas, taking care not to knock him off the boulder again. "I'm afraid we've had it this time, friend."

Thomas took the flashlight from Rhys and stood up. "I'm not ready to die, yet, damn it. I'm going to have at least one date with Terri Mawr before I go." He tapped Rhys on the shoulder. "Give me a boost," he said, and started to climb the wall.

Rhys was too tired to do more than provide a weak push. It helped, just enough.

Thomas stretched his arm up the cave wall to a handhold that had been just out of Rhys's reach, gaining an elevation a few inches higher than Rhys had achieved. He signaled furiously, an endless repetition of S-O-S, alternating with their location.

He was on his tenth go, the beam almost gone, when a voice boomed out, "Get that damned light out of my eyes!"

Rhys cheered and Thomas tipped the beam down to the cave floor, brushing it over an undulating surface of shining backs. "Careful of the crabs all over the floor when you come in," Thomas said.

"I'm not coming in. You're coming out," the voice said. Its owner tossed a rope ladder through the opening. It unfurled nearly to the sand. "A couple of cavers should find it not too challenging to climb a ladder, I presume."

Thomas thought he recognized the voice and waved the flashlight beam by the slit to confirm his belief. It was Inspector Mawr. He wasn't sure whether to be relieved or not.

He shined the light down at the cave floor again, looking for a path to the rope that wasn't occupied by crabs. There was none. "Here," he said to Rhys, "hold the torch so the beam makes a straight line from this boulder to the rope ladder, along the ground."

Rhys did and Thomas jumped down. He bounded to the rope ladder at top speed, hearing a crack then a squish, then another and another as he ran. "Yuck," he said, feeling crab meat squish between his toes. "Ok, toss the light over."

Rhys did, then ran across. The pair scrambled up to the slit, just as two big rocks were yanked off the top. Inspector Mawr's face disappeared from the opening. They peered down, seeing him standing at the side of a regular ladder, one hand firmly gripping it. Rhys said, "You came well equipped."

"Policemen are trained to think ahead." He added, his tone harsh, "Unlike scientists, apparently."

Thomas scooched himself through the slender crack, then stood on the ladder outside. He peered inside, exchanging a look with Rhys. They both knew the crack was too small for him to crawl through. "We'll go for help," Thomas said. "Just hang stand on the rope ladder."

He wasn't at all sure Rhys had enough strength left to do that. If not, he hoped he had enough to get back to the boulder, otherwise the crabs would chew him before they could return with a bulldozer. Then he had an idea. "Put your back to the rock face and thread your legs and arms through the ladder's rungs." If Rhys passed out he wouldn't slip to the cave floor.

Arwel shouted from the bottom of the ladder. "What's the hold up?"

Thomas looked down. "He's too large to get through the space. We need to get equipment to clear the top boulders."

Arwel put his hands on his hips and snarled, "Nonsense. Clear off the ladder." He waved impatiently for Thomas to come down.

Thomas did as he was told and watched as Arwel scrambled up, nimble as a veteran climber, which he was.

Arwel said, looking down at Thomas, "Step away from the ladder. I'm going to pull more rocks off and it would pain me to kill you. Much more satisfying to have you back in my jail instead."

Thomas gulped and hotfooted a few yards away, then paused. He pondered running for it while Inspector Mawr was busy. He thought for less than a second, deciding he couldn't abandon his friend until he was free. Anything could happen. Arwel might fall and crack his skull. Rhys might collapse inside and the two of them would be needed to haul him out. He had to stay.

Arwel thrust his arm inside the crack, wrapping his fingers around as much of the top rock as he could grasp. He yanked, his huge biceps stretching his sleeve to near bursting. The rock moved an inch. He threaded his legs through the ladder, gaining the right angle to push away and latched onto the boulder with both hands.

He knew moving it would be awkward and worried that the falling rock might break his knees on its way down. But he could see Rhys's face in the moonlight and guessed he wouldn't last much longer standing on the rope ladder. It was act now or face having to haul him up from the cave floor.

Arwel prepared for one last mighty heave.

As he pulled the top rock, he pushed off the one below it, then swung his legs out of the way as the boulder went crashing to the sand below. The ladder wobbled upright in midair for a tentative second before Thomas caught it and eased it back into position against the rocks. Arwel stood up again and said to Rhys, "Come along now."

Rhys dragged himself through the hole and rested on the top boulders just long enough to give Arwel time to walk down the ladder. He looked down at the sand inside the cave, seeing a few crabs silhouetted by the torch for a moment before the light winked out for good. "Well, the EarthQuaker does like to squeeze every last volt out of his equipment."

The trio walked toward the parking lot beside the restaurant.

Arwel returned to detective mode. "How in the world did you get trapped in there, with the hole not big enough even to crawl through?"

Thomas answered, "The boulders weren't there when we went into the cave. They came after. After we were thunked on the head."

Arwel hmmmed, his bass rumbling. "We'll talk about that on the way. I assume you won't mind riding in my car after being stuck in there?" He pointed to the Bentley.

In the light from the parking lot lamps, Thomas could make out what it was. He whistled. Not so bad to be a detective inspector in a small Welsh town, after all. Probably on the take, he ventured silently. "We have our rented motorcycles, sir."

"You can leave them here. I'll phone the dealer in the morning." He waited a moment to see if they would offer any more excuses. Getting none, he went on. "I want to talk to both of you."

He leaned his hand against the car's door handle, careful not to touch the paint. The shadows formed by the parking lot lights exaggerated his already stern expression. "Terri is missing," he said, his voice too flat, evidence of a tense effort to keep emotion out of it.

Thomas puzzled over the familiar way the Chief Inspector referred to her, and more at his worried tone. But he was more concerned about the revelation than the mystery of Arwel's emotions. "Missing?" he asked, forcing his own voice calm. He didn't volunteer where he'd last seen her.

"Yes, my daughter is nowhere I know. And I had reason to believe you were the cause. That's why I came looking for you."

Thomas groaned, unable to hold back. "Terri is your daughter?"

Arwel ignored the question. Before he could ask one of his own, Rhys interjected, "How did you find us, anyway?"

"That's a trade secret." He opened the passenger doors to encourage the two men to get inside. When they hung back, he said, "Well?"

Thomas asked, "Are we under arrest, sir?"

Arwel harrumphed. "You were legally released pending the coroner's inquest by my order, and I'm not going to rescind it..." Thomas stepped into the front passenger seat. "...unless you give me a reason." Arwel latched the door behind him.

After Arwel slid into the driver's seat, Thomas asked, "Tell me all you know about Terri's disappearance, please, sir."

9

*J*AMES Paine pinned Owen with a black look. He'd always had the ability to see a man's thoughts by the expression on his face. It was one of the things the Quaker elders had disliked about him most. Right now, he was seeing Owen's thoughts and the chubby computer geek did not like it one bit.

James said, "Your roommate promised me you'd help. But each man's got to choose to follow the devil of his own accord." He counted to five to give him time to decide. When Owen didn't, he prompted, "So?"

James could tell that Owen had an extreme dislike of being pressured. He watched the gears turn as the furtive hog looked for an easy way out of his pen. He was not about to provide him one. Reclaiming Thomas meant too much to him. He grew impatient when Owen stalled by lighting up another cigarette, a habit of which he mightily disapproved. "Decide," he growled.

"B-b-but... I could get in real trouble with the law." He turned away, unable to withstand James's scowl any longer. "I don't know how I could help you anyway." He hoped James wouldn't explain.

"Think about it. It's obvious."

Owen didn't know what to make of that. He wondered what thirty pieces of silver James had offered his roommate. But he felt he was much better at that game. "What's in it for me?" he sniffed, trying to put courage into his voice that was absent from his soul.

James delayed answering, by design. Negotiation with little men always favored the man who took his time. He sat in the plush chair in Owen's apartment in front of the television. He sensed it was the lad's favorite spot, a possession he treated as sacrosanct and forbad others to use.

"What do you want?" James finally asked, already suspecting the answer.

A leer oozed over Owen's face. "Thomas's girlfriend, Terri Mawr. I saw her the other day and she's hot." Finding her hidden photos during his stealth visit to her house had amplified his desire. He could tell from the clay sculpture she'd begun that she liked Thomas, and that sealed his determination to have her. "Bring her to me and I'll help you any way you want."

James let loose a barking laugh, a cross between a hyena's cackle and a crocodile's hiss. He could easily guess that Owen cared less for possessing this woman than taking something of Thomas'. That Owen felt he needed his help with that just increased his contempt.

No matter. It was enough they were enough alike to do business, and the chosen form of payment carried a decisive advantage for him. Taking her would force Thomas to come to him, eliminating the need to track down his elusive son.

He handed Owen five 20-pound counterfeit notes and a slip of paper with an address on it. "She'll be taken here. No danger of the police finding you there." He exposed his teeth in the facsimile of a smile, the sort an Arab slave trader would show when sending a virgin to a seraglio.

"You can do what you like with her for a day. Then, get word to Thomas where to find her."

He stood up and pushed his sleeves above his elbows, displaying tattoos that fascinated and frightened Owen. One depicted a demon eating the flesh of an innocent young girl. The look of terror on the girl's face was drawn by James himself. A paired one on the other arm showed her soul fornicating with the demon's twin.

James said, "I'll be waiting for him there."

Arwel kept his temper under control as the trio exited his car in front of his home, but just barely. What he'd asked wasn't unreasonable, and these two were plainly uncooperative. Refusing to help the police always set him on edge, no matter the circumstances, and the present ones were not designed to help him curb his anger.

He tried one more time, forcing a calm he didn't feel, going so far as to plead. "All I'm asking is that you two try to locate my daughter." Since begging was foreign to his nature, his tone made the request seem vaguely threatening.

He leaned against the fender of the Bentley, his arms crossed. "I got the impression at the station you wouldn't mind finding her."

Thomas had been relieved on the ride to learn that Terri hadn't really gone missing; she just hadn't told Arwel about the accident. He'd shared a brief look with Rhys, both silently acknowledging the wisdom of keeping Terri's location to themselves. If she didn't want to let him know she was in the hospital, she must have a good reason.

When Arwel noticed Rhys about to lean against the car, he regained his presence of mind and stopped him with a look. He ambled toward the porch and stood on the raised platform, towering over them like Moses before the throng, about to deliver commandments.

Before he could issue any, Rhys said, "You misunderstood me, sir. I'd love— I'd like to find her. But if we don't find the man who killed Carl soon, Thomas is going to get locked up for who knows how long." He diplomatically refrained from saying who would do the locking up. "We think that's Owen Caldicott, and we need time to prove it."

Arwel mentally dismissed Rhys' reference to the dead caver by another name, still not convinced of Thomas' story. But he wouldn't lie about this one's prospects. The man was in serious trouble unless someone found evidence before the coroner's inquest to exonerate him.

So far, that pointed to this American being in it up to his chin. His location at the time of the murder had been exposed as a lie during questioning, and he refused to say where he'd been. The American Consulate refused his request for a replacement passport when he'd been unable to present identification. It didn't help his case when he never returned.

He saw a way to solve his problem of finding Terri, and to give this fellow enough rope to shape his own noose. He stepped down one level to draw close to them, trying to create the intimate atmosphere of solving a mutual problem. "Mr. Payne," he said, using his alleged name to make him relax, "consider. Finding this thief and locating Terri might be one and the same goal."

Knowing Thomas would be reluctant to argue, Rhys said for him, "But, Inspector, why can't you do that? We're not detectives." He was running out of excuses to avoid doing what *he* knew didn't need to be done.

"You were eager enough to play one to pin this one's troubles on Owen Caldicott." He waved a hand in Thomas's direction.

Thomas objected. "Sir, if your daughter is missing, isn't that a genuine police matter?"

Arwel gave a sardonic laugh. "If you knew my daughter, sir, you wouldn't ask." He walked down the two steps to look down on Thomas from a few inches away, his pleading expression genuine now. "No, it's got to be done on the quiet, son."

Thomas felt a little chill on being called "son" but he couldn't decide whether it was from joy or fear. Mr. Mawr was about as far from his father as he could imagine a man reaching.

He said, "Well, I would like to be with Terri. I won't lie about that." He could at least talk to her at the hospital, encourage her to call her father. He turned to Rhys, asking him with a look what he thought.

Rhys nodded, playing along. "It shouldn't take long. I might know a bloke who'd know where she was right now."

Thomas tapped Rhys's ankle with his foot, afraid his sense of mischief toward authority would give the game away. "I'm not sure—"

Arwel sweetened the deal. "I'll lend you my car." He held up the keys. "And, be honest. You want to, don't you?" In the half-light of early morning, he could read Thomas's face like a mug shot. "She's a beaut, ain't she?"

Thomas blurted, "Like your daughter." He gulped, sensing his candor had re-opened Arwel's hot water tap. "If you don't mind my saying so, sir."

Arwel smiled at him benevolently for the first time. "I don't. You're not the first to say so." He puffed on his pipe with a faraway look. "Gets that from her mother."

This man's naïve honesty appealed to him, despite his professional judgment. It softened his nagging questions about his real identity. If anyone could sit on Terri without squashing her spirit, it might just be this fellow.

The young man seemed to have both a strong will and a gentle manner. All the more remarkable, despite being troubled about something more basic — Arwel couldn't tell what — than being in the spotlight over the caver's death.

His thoughts were interrupted when Thomas held out his hand. Arwel handed him the keys.

Thomas said, "Sir, I meant to shake your hand. As a thank you for the vote of confidence."

Arwel's stern expression returned, but now less severe. "I'm not giving you any such vote, young man. Harm my car *or* my daughter and

I'll bury you someplace even *I* couldn't find you."

Thomas's frowned. Getting involved with Terri meant risking Inspector Mawr learning about his own father.

Rhys tensed as well, mistakenly believing that the reason for his friend's worried look was the same as his own. If Arwel found out they'd known all along Terri was in the hospital, the DCI would suddenly get a lot less friendly.

Terri was not in the hospital. She was having an early breakfast with Owen Caldicott.

After recovering from her faint enough to get dressed, she left without notifying anyone. Then she took the train home, called Owen, and dressed to the nines. Before leaving, she mused for a second over the clothing on her bed, wondering why Clara would leave the laundry unfinished. She vowed to call her later to make sure she wasn't ill. Then she drove to Chepstow.

She met Owen at a restaurant near Tintern Abbey. Ten minutes chatting him up had yielded nothing helpful to Thomas so far. But she was used to men saying more than they wanted her to know, sooner or later.

She surveyed the Wye Valley below. In the distance lay the 19th century train trestle and the tips of the abbey's Gothic arches that rose above the hill obscuring the ruins. Purple heather in full bloom covered the valley floor and much of the area. The morning light bounced off it and onto Terri's face, giving her skin a surreal cast.

She artfully turned sideways, as if leisurely viewing the valley, to show Owen her profile. She knew the effect it would have on him.

Owen ogled her, fascinated against his will. Beautiful girls just didn't ask him out, and he knew it was some kind of trap. But watching her face he didn't care, so he let pass her thin excuse for the meeting. The delicious irony of her calling him, when he was supposed to trap her, added to his evil delight.

He leaned forward and picked up his juice cup like it was a martini glass, trying to look suave.

Terri said, "Have you ever seen a sculpture made from a stalagmite, Owen?"

He shook his head, lying. He'd seen several of hers in her studio and bedroom. He tried not to think of her bedroom, determined to act casual. He shifted in his seat to relieve a pinch in his trousers.

Terri went on, "It starts out looking like a giant erect penis. Then you shape it into something lovely." She beamed her most wide-eyed innocent gaze, resting her hand on her chin. She looked at him adoringly, laughing softly at his open mouth. She almost felt sorry for him.

Owen was not fooled. He knew what he was, and her transparent attempt to arouse him went against all his experience. *She must want something pretty bad to put on this show*, he thought. Maybe she was shagging Thomas and wanted to help him out with the coppers.

That thought made him mad. Then he thought of the cave explosion on Barry Island

and felt his sense of satisfaction mushroom all over again.

"No, I've never seen a statue like that." He wobbled his head, looking cocky and ridiculous. "You should show me sometime."

Terri set down her orange juice and said, "Well, no time like the present, eh?"

They left the restaurant and walked toward Terri's vintage Austin Healey Sprite, a gift to herself after her first commission. "Shall we put the top down? It's a lovely day."

Owen helped her into the car, all the time wondering when she was going to get around to what she wanted. He didn't mind waiting, satisfied to let the charade play out. He tugged his sweater down over his pants.

Just as he plopped into the car, his phone buzzed. "Excuse me," he said. He noticed the number and shielded the display from Terri's prying look. He thought about her hearing his half of the conversation and hit the End button without answering, then turned the phone off.

Terri wondered how she might get her hands on the phone long enough to see who called.

She pulled up in her driveway an hour later, relieved to find her father wasn't home. She led Owen inside and offered him something to drink, which he declined. She said, "I meant something like orange juice or tea. Didn't think I needed to get you sloshed."

She knew she was spreading it on with a trowel. In her experience, it didn't matter. Men were lemmings when it came to sex, the tragic creatures. Her conscience bothered her but Thomas's freedom was at stake, so she stifled it.

Owen thought: *She's really pouring it on.* Could she really be in love with Payne after just a few days? Never will understand slits. They just don't think rationally.

He followed her into the studio where he saw a half-sculpted stalagmite about two feet high standing on a low, sturdy support. It was the beginning of the bust of Thomas that he'd seen yesterday. "Is that your work?" he asked, knowing the answer.

Terri nodded.

"Interesting. Where did you get the stone?"

"Dan-yr-Ogof." She saw his face calcify. Interesting. She was on the right track.

He turned away faster than he intended. He wandered around, examining some of the pieces lined along the wall. Some were finished, others still raw. He ran a hand over a raw one, feeling the rough, familiar stone, thinking back to yesterday morning's events. It felt just like the wall near where Carl—

He yanked his hand away and turned to a finished piece. "I've seen something like this before. I didn't know it was yours, though."

"That's the problem. Few do."

"Still trying to get the recognition you deserve, huh?" His voice dropped. "I know the feeling."

Terri looked at him as if one good whack had just revealed part of the face under the stone. Put the chisel point at the right place and a few more blows should make everything plain.

She sat on a stool and put her hands between her thighs, squeezing her breasts together. The act revolted her to the core; she had always despised women who used their charms to get what they want, but she plunged ahead. She had to find out what he knew, and in a few more minutes, she was sure he would tell her. What might happen then, she hadn't considered.

"Do you go caving often?" she asked.

"Nah. Once a year when the club gets together during summer." He added, not sure why, "This year Dr. Payne came along."

"You don't like him, do you?" Tap. She watched the planes on his face shift, showing a little more of what lay under the surface.

"He thinks he's smarter than everybody else."

"Isn't he?" Chip, chip.

"Yeah. Probably." Dangerous ground, he knew, but he couldn't resist moving closer to the edge. "That doesn't make him better."

Terri pursed her lips and shook her head with a girlish wiggle. "No, it doesn't." Chisel. "What does, do you think?" Polish.

Owen sat down, tired of carrying his bulk around the room. He shrugged. He knew there was some kind of cat-and-mouse game going on. He couldn't make out who was the pussy and who the rat. "Probably easier to say what makes somebody worse."

Terri nodded in genuine understanding. There was a human being under there, after all. If she could just reach him before he retreated back into his shell... She jumped off the stool in frustration. She wasn't about to sleep with him to pry his lips loose, but she needed to find some lead to give her father.

She tried to remember what he had shared with her about interrogation techniques. So far, establishing rapport hadn't taken her very far. She couldn't think how to intimidate him. Bribery hadn't worked, and there was a limit to what she would trade. She chuckled nervously.

"What's so funny?" Owen asked, his voice defensive. He mulled slapping her around. She wouldn't expect that. Playing the scene in his mind made him hard.

"I wasn't laughing at you." she said. She noted his skeptical look. "I wasn't. Really. I was laughing at me."

"Why, because you're here with me? A guy you'd never be seen dead with normally?"

Wow, is he weak, she thought. There must be something in that to exploit. "Owen, you don't really know what kind of guy I'd date. You're just assuming I might go out with Thomas Payne, for example." Wham. She could see the blow echo in his head, shattering his facade.

Owen's lips went thin and white. He crept closer to her, near enough to seize her if she tried to flee. He saw that made her nervous. His pants bulged near the left pocket. He said, his voice mocking and ugly, "It's time you took off your blouse."

She shot back, "It's time you took a chill pill. That ain't gonna happen."

She pressed her hands on her lower back, as much to hide their shaking as to appear in control. It had the unfortunate side effect of tightening her blouse over her breasts.

Owen reacted to it as if she were taunting him, daring him to act. "Why, because I'm ugly? If you'd date Thomas, that doesn't matter to you."

She wondered what the hell he could be talking about? Thomas was the best-looking man she'd ever seen. Just the sort of intense, odd-looking, hawk-faced guy who intrigued her.

Seeing Owen's scowl, she forced herself to appear calm, realizing how careful she would have to be about defending Thomas. Getting information was one thing; sending this loony over the edge could get her raped. She hadn't signed up for that.

She said, "Just calm down, okay? I'll give you a peek if that's so important. But that's all. Right?"

It was a dangerous gambit. It might satisfy him, or it might inflame him more. Guys like this were unpredictable. Her father had told her once that rapists of a certain type as often as not couldn't go through with it. What type was he?

She decided it didn't matter. If he couldn't do it, he was the sort who'd get so ashamed he would hurt her anyway. She scanned the room, her view landing on her hammer and chisel. They lay on the table a foot past his left elbow.

She crept to her right. "Look, I'm sorry if I teased you. That was wrong. Let's just forget it and go for a walk, okay?" She circled a few inches closer to the tools.

He compensated. He didn't know what she was after, but there was no way she was getting past him. Not 'til he had what he wanted. "Not a chance, Terri. Not until I see the goods."

Now the whacks were on her. "Please, Owen," she said sincerely. "Don't do this." Pleading only made his expression more dangerous. Try a threat. "Don't forget my father is the Chief Inspector."

"Your word against mine. A slut like you? Who they gonna believe at a trial?"

That made her mad. "Owen, you don't know me or my father. Trust me when I tell you I'm not a slut." She locked onto his eyes. "And there wouldn't be a trial."

"Bold claims. Let's test your theory." He lunged at her, tearing her blouse.

She bolted past him, reaching for the hammer. He hooked the crook of her elbow when she was six inches from the tool. "Come on back, little dove." He dragged her directly in front of him and reached up with the other hand to complete the work on her shirt.

She realized he still didn't know what she was after. She had a chance. She lifted her face, putting one hand on his shoulder and reaching past him with the other hand.

"Owen, calm down, alright? They're just fat cells covered with skin. If it means that much to you..." She started to unbutton her blouse with the hand that had been on his shoulder while she reached toward the hammer with the other.

He blocked her reaching arm, then slid his hand down to her wrist, forcing her hand below his buckle. "Let's have a little of this while the show's on, eh?" He drew her in and wrapped a leg around her thigh as he leaned back against the studio table behind him.

"Oww!" she yelped at the pressure on her burned knee.

"Hey, I barely touched you."

"I had an accident. At the lab in Cardiff." She watched his face. That wasn't intended as a whack, but it looked like a shattering blow. "The one you work at." His face told her Rhys was right. Now, confess, damn it.

He said nothing.

She stifled a frown and leaned in, appearing to relax. "Go easy."

He loosened his grip for a second and lessened the pressure on her leg. It was all she needed. She snatched the hammer and smacked him hard across the jaw. He flew back, staggering like a drunk on the edge of a pier.

He was still conscious, though, and angrier than ever. He drew upright and poised to spring at her, hammer or no hammer, preparing to force her head down. He heard a door slam against the wall behind him and froze.

"Owen Caldicott, you're under arrest!" Arwel bellowed.

10

OWEN turned to look at who was yelling and saw a tall, stout man flashing a badge. His face fell.

Then Terri hit him again on the jaw from the other direction, this time with twice the force of the first blow. He rocketed backward and his head bounced off the floor with a melon-on-marble thumping sound.

"Thanks, Da. Excellent timing, as always. I'm just about to get intimate with a guy and you come bursting through the door." Her rueful smile blended with an expression of relief as she melted into her father's arms.

Arwel held her for a long time, keeping an eye on Owen on the floor. Finally, he said, "Terri, I didn't know where you were."

Normally that statement, one she'd heard countless times, would have started a fight. This time his tone made everything alright. "I've been in hospital, Da." She looked up to catch his expression. "Nothing serious, really. Just a minor electrocution." She stretched up on her tiptoes to kiss his face.

Arwel finessed himself loose from her embrace, damming his habitual reaction. After what he'd witnessed through the front window, he wanted nothing at that moment more than to kill Owen Caldicott.

To get his temper under control, he walked over to where Owen was lying unconscious. He bent down, rolled him over, tugged his arms behind, and slapped a pair of handcuffs onto his wrists. Then he dragged him over to a wrought iron railing and tied the cuff chain to it with a plastic tie wrap.

He used the phone in Terri's studio to call the station, ordering Detective Sergeant Bevan to come pick up the perp. Business completed, he turned back to his daughter, convinced he could now talk to her calmly. "Ok, tell me all about it." Just to be sure of her cooperation he added, "Please."

Terri related the events at the lab and added in a rush, "But there was no reason to stay in hospital because I'm really okay." She gestured to the hammer she'd set on the table, "As you saw," then continued the wave of her hand to end in the direction of Owen's unconscious form. She plopped onto a stool, her head thrown back in laughter. "Strong as a Mawr, we like to say in this house."

Arwel didn't find it amusing, but held to his vow not to start an argument, especially since she was right. Anyway, he could call the hospital later and find out everything.

"Well, I'm glad to see I sent your boyfriends off in my car to look for you for nothing. That's a relief, believe it or—"

"You loaned Rhys and Thomas your car?" she asked, aghast. Then it dawned on her what else he'd said. "Hey, what do you mean, boyfriends, plural? Rhys and I aren't—" She stopped herself cold. Truthfully, she couldn't say Thomas was her boyfriend, either.

She pointed to Owen. "What are you going to do with him?"

"Arrest him for theft of military technology, then turn him over to the lads in Cardiff."

"Not for attempted rape?" She regretted asking the moment the question was out of her mouth. Arwel said nothing. But when he glowered menacingly at the form on the floor, she added, "I take it back, Da. Nothing happened."

She wouldn't mind Owen getting buried in Brecon Beacons; he probably deserved it. But she couldn't bear what it would do to her father and his sense of justice if he killed a prisoner.

"Well, if you won't press charges, there's little I can do... officially."

They looked at one another for a moment, then broke off at the knock at the door. Arwel opened it and saw DS. Bevan. He pointed to Owen. "Mind taking out my garbage this once, Sergeant?"

Terri tensed, hoping he wouldn't mention anything about the attempted rape to Bevan. There was no way he would exercise the same restraint as her father.

Bevan snipped the plastic tie from the railing just as Owen was coming to. He lifted him by the armpit with one hand as easily as he would a beer keg by its spout. He marched Owen toward the door, half-dragging him after he stumbled across the wood floor, still dizzy from the hammer blows.

When they'd left, Arwel asked, "Are you sure you're alright?" Terri nodded. He gave her one more long hug, then marched toward the door. Terri clung to his arm on the way. He said, "I'll be home in a couple of hours. Maybe we could have a nice quiet supper together."

"I'd like that." She slid her hand down to hold his for a moment.

"Fine." He freed his hand and turned to go. He said over his shoulder, "I'll be back after I've arrested Thomas."

Thomas and Rhys stood outside Owen's apartment, pausing to see if anyone could spy them standing at the door. It was beginning to rain. Droplets splashed down in ones and twos onto their heads and over the stoop at the top of the steps. Seeing no one watching, Thomas removed from his pocket a burglar's pick he'd found in Arwel's car. He went to work on the door lock.

"Thomas this is not a great idea," Rhys volunteered.

A click and Thomas had it. He walked in, expecting Rhys to follow. "Are you coming or not?" Rhys stepped in and Thomas walked further into the apartment. "I can't think of any better way to find a clue about where he took Terri."

"It's sheer speculation that anyone took her anywhere. You should know better not to make wild guesses without evidence."

Thomas argued, "She wasn't at the hospital or at home. Owen wouldn't answer my calls. You told her about him and I know she wants to help me."

"That's exactly what I'm talking about. Wild leaps across what are probably unconnected facts." He stopped in the middle of the floor. "Say, how do you know she wants to help you?"

Thomas brushed off the question and responded to Rhys's earlier accusation. "It's a reasonable hypothesis, and I'm testing it."

Rhys misunderstood. "That she likes you? What's reasonable about that?" He laughed.

Thomas frowned. He advanced into the apartment but soon stopped. Within a few steps he'd reached the limits of the combined living room and bedroom. He noted the separate twin beds, both disheveled. "So, Mr. Caldicott does have a roommate."

"The guy who tried to run you over, maybe?"

"Maybe. And he may know where Owen took Terri."

Rhys shrugged, unwilling to argue the point about unfounded speculation again.

Thomas hunted for a notepad, a laptop, a phone, anything that would be used to record a meeting time and place. He continued his search into the small kitchenette anyway.

Rhys raised his voice to make himself heard from the living area. "You know this is breaking and entering, right?"

Thomas called back from the kitchen, "In Britain, you're more apt to get arrested for throwing chewing gum into a pond."

Just then, Thomas noticed a large Mynah bird caged in the corner, near the window. It started to squawk as he approached. "Murder! Murder!"

Rhys said, "Paranoid bird, just like Owen. He thinks you're going to kill him."

"Murder at the cave! Murder at the cave!"

Rhys and Thomas stood stock still. Thomas whispered, "Would it be a wild leap of logic to claim that's not a coincidence?" He inched closer, looking for some birdseed to placate the squawking bird. He felt he was onto something and didn't want a neighbor to call the police.

He scattered some seed from a cup on the windowsill into its feed bowl. "Nice birdie. Tell me everything you know. Tell me about Terri. Terri? Terri Mawr," he repeated, tossing in more seed.

"You're nuts. It's a bird."

"Terri Mawr! Awwkk! Great tits! Great tits!"

"A bird that repeats things it hears," Thomas said.

"Rude things."

"Maybe it heard something more useful." Thomas picked the cage off its hook and headed for the door.

"Where are you going with that?" Rhys asked.

"To Brecon Station. This bird just became evidence."

Rhys rolled his eyes, mildly surprised that even Thomas could be this strange. He walked over to the single closet, still looking for a computer. "I wonder if they cleaned this place out before—" He stopped when he saw Thomas going through with his plan to take the bird. "Boss, don't. You'll just get in trouble."

Thomas continued for the door, holding the cage above his hip. The Mynah bird continued to squawk in his ear. He set the cage down to check the street outside through the front window. He saw no pedestrians and stood there long enough to get an average of how many cars drove by per minute. He estimated they had about thirty seconds to dash down the steps and into the Bentley before anyone spotted them.

"You realize we're supposed to be looking for Terri, right?" Rhys asked, leaning into the closet. Not hearing an answer, he straightened and noticed Thomas at the window. "What are you doing?"

"Trying to make sure we're not caught stealing the bird. Once I turn him over to Terri's father, we can resume looking for her. It won't take more than an hour or so."

Rhys shut the closet door. He looked at Thomas standing with the bird cage in his hand and said, "You really have gone 'round the bend now, friend."

"Please go outside and take a look around. Then get in the driver's side of the Bentley. Signal if all's clear and I'll follow with the cage." He stepped away from the door and waved Rhys ahead.

Rhys shuffled forward. Still skeptical, he was just glad to be leaving Owen's apartment. He'd almost reached the door when he noticed it was open a crack.

Thomas saw it at the same time. He was about to say something when it swung open, knocking Rhys backward.

"Damn!" Rhys said, falling back onto the couch.

Through the open doorway walked a policeman. He planted himself in front of it and raised an eyebrow at Thomas holding the bird cage. He knew all the residents of the neighborhood by sight and neither man was an occupant of this particular flat. He thrust his hands on his hips and growled, "What goes on here, mates?"

While the constable wondered what to do with the Mynah, another one escorted Thomas and Rhys to the lock-up. The patrolman had considered leaving the bird in the apartment, but since it was taken in the commission of a crime it was properly regarded as evidence. The rules required he take it into custody, to be returned to the rightful owner, on proof of ownership.

The sergeant told Arwel on the phone, "He had the keys to a very nice looking car, not his. Turn's out it's yours, Chief Inspector. What d'ya want done with it?"

"Keep it there. I'll have my daughter drive me down later today to pick it up."

They chatted briefly about the Dan-yr-Ogof murder case and then hung up.

The bobby complained about having to deal with "that damn squawkin' parakeet." The sergeant walked over to a table just outside the holding cell where the birdcage sat. "That's not a parakeet, you git. It's a Mynah bird."

The Mynah repeated, "Pushed a cliff! Pushed a cliff! Ogof! Ogof!" The sergeant looked startled for a moment. Thinking it over, he concluded the bird might be a material witness in the Brecon case. He called Inspector Mawr back as a professional courtesy. Arwel said he'd be there in an hour, his voice excited.

When Arwel arrived to collect his car he said casually, in answer to the sergeant's question about the case, "Under investigation." He wasn't eager to have it taken over by Cardiff, and offered no further detail. He put on his best poker face and said, "I'd like to take the bird with me, if that's all right."

Sick of listening to it, the sergeant was only too happy to oblige. After signing an evidence removal slip, Arwel transported the Mynah home, to Terri's puzzlement.

"Da, you can't think this is going to help Thomas? I mean, a bird's testimony isn't admissible evidence, is it?"

"No barrister would put him in the witness box, that's certain. But he seems to know something useful. If we can get him to spit it up, it might lead somewhere."

Terri noted her father had just used the word "we" and smiled. "So if you think he's innocent, why did you have them detain Thomas?"

"Innocent?" he asked in a distracted voice. He sat in his favorite chair, fixated on the bird. He wondered how to prompt it to say more than the few teasing but inadequate phrases squawked so far. "I'm just trying to solve a case," he said, and lit his pipe.

"You know he's innocent."

"Thomas? How do I know that? Because you're fond of him?"

"That's a start. Can you imagine me being attracted to a killer?"

Arwel saw no reason to say aloud something obvious to both of them. He turned his attention instead to the bird. He rose and walked up to the cage. He reached down into a small bowl in which he'd placed a few biscuits, then crumbled one up. He held up a piece and said, "Dan-yr-Ogof." The bird repeated it back automatically. Arwel gave him the food anyway.

Terri noticed her father's frown. "Da, you can't get him to do what you want if you reward him for doing what you don't."

"You try," he said gruffly.

Terri drew the curtains. The day was brightening and sunlight suffused onto the birdcage. She held out a cracker and said, "Who is Thomas Payne? Who is Thomas Payne?"

Arwel pursed his lips, about to announce it was ridiculous to expect the bird to answer her question. He stopped short when the bird yelped, "James Paine son. James Paine son. Awwk!"

He gawked at the bird, astonished. "What did he say? *James Paine*?" He looked out the window, deep in thought. "And who in the name of Lord Denning is *James* Paine?" he asked himself.

She said, "The bird said Thomas was his son. If you can believe a bird. Why would he say that?"

Arwel smiled, tapping his pipe stem on his lip. "You're missing the point, my girl." He put his pipe down and swished his arms through his coat sleeves. "The question isn't whether it's true or not. The question is: why would a bird owned by Owen Caldicott know who was Thomas Payne's father?"

He glanced over at the table, hooked his keyring with a thumb, then sped out the door for the station. Terri watched him go, thrilled that she'd found some way to help Thomas, maybe.

To Thomas' surprise, his cell was opened an hour after Arwel left. To his misfortune, he was faced straight away with a man whose dour expression was less pleasant even than Inspector Mawr's.

Rhys looked at the man as he would someone fresh off the set of a zombie movie.

The ghoul's identity made him still more frightening. He presented a plastic card showing himself to be an HM Immigration Inspector of the UK immigration department. His official work was to chase down persons in Britain illegally and escort them out of the country. His methods were sometimes overlooked by his superiors because of his results. He took special joy in his job when it involved Yanks, whom he loathed for reasons he was happy to expound on at his local pub. He was eager to nab this yob, put him on a plane, and get back there straight away.

"Arthur Pancost-Swinton," he announced to Thomas with a gruesome smile of brown teeth.

If the introduction was meant to put Thomas at ease, it had the opposite effect. He looked at Arthur as if the man were Mephistopheles' from a Renaissance morality play. "Where are we going?" he asked.

"*You* are going home."

For the first time since the caving incident, Thomas felt real hope. He babbled, "So, you know I'm Thomas Payne. Great. Someone at the American Consulate must've told you about losing my passport. The Brecon police are holding it and—"

Arthur slapped one half of a pair of handcuffs on his own wrist, the other half on

Thomas', silencing him. "I know no such thing. But I'm convinced you are a U.S. citizen and I intend to let you be their problem, rather than ours."

He shot a black look at Rhys to stay put when he started to rise. He stepped outside the cell with Thomas and closed it again.

Thomas thought of Terri, and Owen's theft of his plans, and the unsolved death that was still being laid at his feet. "But I don't want to leave now."

Arthur yanked on the chain, nearly toppling Thomas off his feet. "We don't usually ask deportees what they want. Like all bad boys, we *tell* them what they're going to do." He led Thomas outside to a black car with no official markings.

Thomas pulled back, stopping Arthur's forward motion and inciting an expression he never wanted to see again. "Er, are you sure you're from the immigration authority?"

Arthur tugged Thomas forward with surprising strength and opened the driver's side car door. He pushed him in roughly and elbowed in beside him, then started the car. "If I wasn't, do you think I would answer you honestly?"

He whipped the steering wheel, pulling Thomas over to his side. He shoved his prisoner upright again and honked as he nearly collided with an oncoming car.

Once in traffic, he unlocked his half of the cuffs, confident his prisoner wouldn't leap out of the moving car. Then he had second thoughts and clapped the open half onto a metal bar on the dash.

Arthur asked, "Maybe you'd like to tell me why you're so nervous?" When Thomas didn't answer, he said, "Suit yourself," and let it drop. He didn't really care. He knew a bit of this one's story, but the bobs hadn't scratched his back lately. No reason to scratch theirs if it took any effort.

Just another crocodile out fishing, Thomas thought. But he had no one to turn to, and the more officials who knew about his trouble, the better chance someone might look into it. He explained what had happened at the cave.

He didn't mention Owen stealing his plans. He thought it relevant but didn't trust Arthur that far. His father taught him that men lacking scruples are unpredictable. It was the one thing they had ever agreed on.

Thomas finished providing the last details of recent events, and Arthur turned the mirror to see his face. As much out of boredom as curiosity, he asked, "So what's this about stealing a Mynah bird? Why would an innocent man do that?"

Thomas was about to answer when he noticed a sign that said "Rhoose, 1 mile." Something about that name sounded familiar. Just then an Airbus jet lifting off in the distance crossed his line of sight. They were nearing the Cardiff Airport.

"Haven't you heard a word I've said?" Thomas yawped. His voice rose involuntarily when Arthur met his question with a stony stare. "I can't leave the country now!"

"That's not your choice," Arthur said flatly.

He slowed the car to take a curve and Thomas flipped his feet up to his chest. In the next clock tick, he thrust his legs out again, shoving his shoes against Arthur's ribs to pin him against the side of the car and prevent him from pulling a gun.

He reached his free hand behind his head and pulled the door lock up, then flipped the handle. As he opened the door he pushed hard, not caring whether he cracked Arthur's ribs. His caver's thigh muscles gave him a rocket boost out of the moving vehicle, breaking the bar off the dash.

He landed just where he planned, on a soft section of heather growing alongside the road. He rolled down the small hill and jumped up the second he reached bottom, then took off running. He sprinted across half the field before looking back.

"God, I hope he doesn't have a gun," he puffed. It was wide open ground and a crack shot could take him down even at that distance. Arthur seemed just the sort to spend a lot of time practicing on the range.

His more serious problem was whether Arthur's car had a radio. If he contacted the police directly, Thomas would be picked up before he could get a few miles. If Arthur had to use his mobile phone and deal with a dispatcher, he might get halfway to Terri's house before a search started. He tried to visualize the car dash to remember if there'd been a police radio, but he couldn't.

He crouched behind a hedge for a few seconds to catch his breath and check out the area. He looked for alternative roads he could use to hitch a ride. The main highway was out of the question with Arthur still up there somewhere.

Nothing looked promising so he watched until he saw the car take off in the direction from which they'd come. If he knew his bureaucrats, Arthur would pass the buck to the police and go back to the office, dreaming up excuses along the way to avoid any paperwork.

Thomas hid for another ten minutes then trotted back along the hedgerow toward the highway. His immediate problem now was less the chance of Arthur returning than how to get a ride to Terri's house. No one who saw him wearing handcuffs on one wrist would stop, and his short-sleeve shirt exposed them clearly.

He ducked behind a bush and wiggled off his outer shirt, then contorted his body to remove his undershirt. He wrapped his T-shirt into a sling and put his hand through it. He pushed the handcuffs as high on his arm as possible and tucked them inside a fold. Then he donned his outer shirt.

It was awkward trying to thumb a ride with the wrong arm, but at least his sling provided answers to any unwanted questions about hitchhiking. Before long, he was hoping for a chance to be asked some. No one seemed eager to pick him up. Finally, after forty minutes, a young redheaded woman pulled over in a shiny Mercedes Roadster that cost more than his summer house in New Hampshire.

"You look harmless enough," she announced, and waved him into the car. "Not too harmless, though, I hope." She winked into the rearview mirror tilted his way. "A man who isn't a mite dangerous is just a bore, and I'm in the mood for a good gab." She smiled over at him, ignoring the road ahead. "So, start talking, eh, sweetie?"

He never had the chance. She yakked every second of the way to the other side of Cardiff. "Sorry, I can't take you all the way to Brecon, love. I've got to meet a very cute guy, and if I'm late, he beats me." After he stepped out, she zoomed away, grinding the gears.

The sun was high up now and there were no clouds anywhere in sight. He trudged on, trying to develop his next steps. He hoped he wasn't wrong about Terri wanting to help him. Otherwise, he was walking right into hell again. "And, please, Lucifer, cooperate just once," he said to the earth below his feet. "Let her father not be home."

11

OWEN whined into the phone located a few feet down the hall from his jail cell, "You've got to help me out here. You know what they do to guys like me here."

The voice on the other end said, "Can't help you, Owen. Got yourself in. Get yourself out."

The line went dead.

The jailer escorted Owen back to his cell, not bothering to smother a cackle. He limped down the hall behind his prisoner, then waved to the man in the control booth to open the holding cell. He stood aside as the bludger waddled back in.

Owen looked misty-eyed at the robotic guard as the door closed in front of him again. He pouted as he watched the guard walk away, feeling as he had at age ten when his mother sent him to his room for hacking her email account.

So much for his one phone call. Now what was he going to do? He sat back down on the bench, careful not to touch his cellmate. He avoided looking at him, hoping the giggling thug would not try to talk to him.

"Hey, chubs, want a cigarette?"

Owen debated whether to ignore him. He figured that might make him mad and said, curtly, "No, thanks," hoping that would end the conversation.

"You're kind of cute," the man volunteered. He smiled when he heard Owen moan, and scooted over to his side of the bench. "What'd they nick you for?"

When he didn't answer, the man squeezed closer, so close Owen could feel his breath on the back of his neck. It stank. He was pinned against the wall with nowhere to go.

He felt a hand slither over his neck just as the cell block door opened down the hall and a custody sergeant yelled, "Caldicott! Visitor!" Owen edged past the creep and rushed to the bars, grateful for the reprieve. The guard stepped to the cell door and looked in to make sure the other prisoner was nowhere near the front, then waved to the control room. "Let's go," he said to Owen, and flipped a hand outward twice.

Owen followed the guard to a visiting area, so relieved he could barely walk straight. He didn't dare think ahead to what would happen when the visit was over. "Please, please, let it be him with bail money," he whimpered.

He was about to sit down when he saw who was on the opposite side of the glass: Rhys. His heart sank. Come to gloat, likely as not. Or maybe... maybe he wanted something. He put on his wounded look and said, "Thank you for coming."

"You don't deserve it, but helping you might help Thomas, so here I am."

"I really am sorry, Rhys. Honestly." He sat down and let his shoulders sag.

Rhys wasn't buying it. Owen saying "honestly" was a sure sign a lie was present. He'd seen that same look many times when the prat screwed up an experiment that had taken weeks to build. And all because he was desperate to show he was as smart as anyone else.

Rhys had zero patience for all that, and it showed in his tone. "I'll help you if you agree to help Thomas."

"How?"

"You've got to confess to stealing the plans for the power system. And you've got to tell them anything you know about Carl's death at Dan-yr-Ogof."

"But I don't know anything about that, I swear!"

Rhys wasn't convinced, but he was willing to let it go for now. "Ok, maybe not. But you copied those plans and you know it. If you want to get out of here, even temporarily, you'd better say so."

"I don't see how that will help Thomas."

"You don't have to see it. Just do it." When Rhys saw him totter, he sweetened the deal. "You don't have to say what you planned to do with them. Now you haven't got them, it doesn't matter."

Owen trembled. A confession of theft seemed better than going back to that cell. But if he spilled, they would send him where there would be a thousand guys like his cellmate. He mewled, "Please, I can't go to prison."

"That's not up to me, but what are the odds? Ever heard of anyone going to chokey for something like that? Not in our lifetimes."

Rhys was right. They wouldn't send him up for that. Especially since he hadn't sold the plans. Anyway, a good solicitor could argue that his confession was coerced. He might not be convicted at all. A sly look began to seep over his face, which he quickly sponged away.

Owen made it worse by pressing his luck. "You must want to help Thomas pretty badly. That's got to be worth getting my job back," he said tentatively.

Rhys rose to leave and said, "I didn't come here to haggle."

"Wait!"

Rhys halted, burning to leave but forcing himself to stay for Thomas's sake.

Owen said, "I'll tell them."

Rhys walked to the locked visitor's room door, feeling like he needed a shower. He buzzed to signal the guard, then looked back at Owen's face. He couldn't help taking some pleasure in the distress he saw.

"I'll go post bail. You wait here." It was a stupid joke and he knew it, but he couldn't resist twisting the icepick in Owen's eye a little. The guard opened the door and Rhys walked down the hall toward the bail clerk's office.

When the door clicked shut again Owen smiled, smugly pleased at his own flawless technique.

It was nearing nightfall and Arwel's car wasn't in his driveway, so Thomas felt safe in knocking on his door. He couldn't be sure Terri was there but her car was parked on the street; it was a good bet. He looked around to check for neighbors; the street was dead quiet. He felt more relieved already.

He needed a safe place to hide and think. Arwel's home was the last place he should feel secure. But when he was with Terri, he felt he could deal with anything, even her father.

He stowed away his rambling thoughts to focus on the present. He knocked medium hard, anxious for her to answer the door right away but worried about alerting the neighbors. There was no one visible but one old woman peeking through her curtains. He knocked again, harder, and waited an eternity.

When there was still no answer, he checked to make sure the woman wasn't watching and then skulked to the back of the house. He spied into the window and saw Terri chiseling away furiously at a sculpture as if nothing had happened the past two days.

He tapped on the glass.

She looked up. She cast a broad smile his way and rushed to open the window. She squeezed his face and kissed him as if they were lovers parted by war. When she let him go, she whispered, "Come in before someone sees you."

He crawled in, then shut the window. Inside he had a better view of the room. It was practically bare. There was a bed, but it appeared not to have been used for years. The windows were all curtainless. The tables held tools and sculpting clay but nothing else, nothing for comfort or even decoration.

As he turned to finish his survey, he stumbled and clomped a step in the direction of her sculpture to steady himself. He stopped cold.

The piece was not half done, but he could already make out what it was intended to be. The contours of his own face were etched into the rock. He turned to her and smiled, feeling fifteen years of loneliness evaporate with a blink. "You've made my nose too small," he said, smiling.

She launched herself into his arms and he kissed her, their bodies blending like a plaster mold of two pieces.

He drew her in, working his hand down to the small of her back. His stomach clenched when she moaned. Then he stopped abruptly and held her away just far enough to look at her face. "Your father could come home at any minute and I'm a fugitive from the law."

"Da never comes in my studio without permission." She pulled his head toward hers, then bit his earlobe and whispered, "Just don't make any loud sounds."

He thought that might be harder than waiting for another chance. A second later he thought he might not get another chance. A second after that he was beyond thinking. He pulled her hips to his.

An hour later, Arwel was still not home and they lay on the cot in Terri's studio, looking up at the ceiling. It was fully dark outside now and the moonlight shone in through the window.

He turned toward her, leaning his head on the heel of his palm. He wanted to talk to her about amiable things, but he found himself able to think only of the barriers to a future with her.

"Terri, I'm in real trouble now. They had no hard evidence to connect me with that man's death at the cave. But I escaped from the immigration authorities, so now I'm cooked."

"The worst they can do is deport you. It's not like you'd have to go to the glasshouse," she said, using her father's Army slang.

"You say that as if being an ocean away from you wouldn't be worse than jail." He pulled her in closer and brushed her neck with his lips. "Unless you came, too."

She eased away from him, shaking her head. "I can't, Thomas. Not yet." She sat up, wrapping the sheet around her top. "I'm building a network here. The gallery thinks my work is about to get noticed. It would mean starting over from scratch."

Thomas nodded stiffly. It took every ounce of his self-control not to argue with her. He couldn't blame her. He'd have said the same. "I understand."

He leaned in and began kissing her again, starting at her ear and working his way down one kiss at a time toward Dante's Inferno. If he couldn't have her with him right away, he'd have as much of her as he could now.

Terri put her hand behind his head and forced it down, too inflamed to let him reach his destination on his own timetable.

Carl's killer sat at a desk in Owen's apartment, programming a computer virus. He had nothing to gain by planting it in the server at Thomas's lab. He wasn't eager to help Owen destroy the logs that could be used to convict him. He just wanted to keep in practice.

The Mynah, standing on a bar in his cage, squawked at random moments. It had been returned only an hour earlier by a messenger from Chief Inspector Mawr's home.

Owen watched over his ex-roommate's shoulder as code filled the screen. He was fascinated. For once, he didn't resent someone's superior expertise. He felt a vicarious thrill at the carnage about to be wrought.

Owen said, his voice high-pitched from nerves, "I need to get away for a while." He sat on the edge of the couch.

The hacker ignored him, still in a frenzy of typing.

Owen said, "The solicitor says he can get the whole thing delayed for at least four months." He flipped onto its face a magazine lying on the coffee table. The cover reminded him of Terri and he didn't want to be tempted to stick around Cardiff. "By that time, Thomas will be out of the country — or in jail with his own problems — and it won't matter so much."

Indifferent to Owen's problem, his ex-roommate didn't bother to point out that Inspector Mawr was now a bigger danger than Thomas. Still, with Owen facing prison he might be willing to cut a deal. Keeping Owen grateful could be useful.

He stopped typing and looked up. "A trip *is* a good idea. You should go up to Bushmills in Northern Ireland. The Marble Arch caves are nearby."

Owen didn't really care much for caving. He only went because he thought he could ingratiate himself with his co-workers. There was no point in that now. "Yeah, that would be interesting" he said, his voice lackluster. "Can you loan me some money?"

The hacker hid his annoyance. He tried to think of some way to get Owen safely tucked in prison without himself becoming a plea-bargain chip. Nothing came to mind. Best to get him out of the way. He might have an accident on the journey, after all.

He held out a hundred pounds and said, "Spend it slowly. I'm short myself for a while."

Owen packed his bag. He was about to open the front door when he delayed to ask, "Do you think the police will decide Carl just fell?"

He was about to fabricate a response when there was a soft knock at the door.

Owen stood near it but dithered, reluctant to see who was there. When his mate lowered the lid of the laptop and nodded okay, he pulled it open a crack, wedging his foot behind the metal strip at the bottom.

James Paine stood on the stoop.

Owen wanted to shove the door closed and bolt it, but ruled against it. James would see that as an insult, and offending this schizo was not wise. He stepped aside to let him enter.

James glided in, his head weaving to and fro like a panther sniffing his surroundings. He sat down on the couch without being invited. He eyed Owen but spoke to his roommate, saying, "The Owen lad here has let me down."

The roommate stifled a barb. "What do you want?" he asked.

"I want you to send a message to Thomas to meet you somewhere. Somewhere he'll go and not suspect anything."

Owen didn't have to ask why. The roommate did. He said, "Because?"

"The lad promised to help me with a little plan, but he got nicked instead. I have an alternati—"

Owen protested, "I'm still working on it! I'm leaving now." He pointed to his duffel bag on the floor.

James hissed, "Never interrupt me, boy!" When Owen froze with a look of panic, it placated him for the moment. He coughed several times and waved his hand, "Sit down, lad. It's all right. I've changed my plan."

Owen looked crestfallen, thinking this meant James wouldn't bring Terri to him now. He rubbed his jaw. He was especially eager to carry through with the plan after those hammer blows. "But, I can still—"

James waved him quiet with a hand.

Owen slumped onto the couch, as far from James as he could manage.

James handed the roommate a piece of paper with a map drawn in ink made from the farm woman's menstrual blood. He smiled, remembering how he had concocted it. "You get Thomas to meet me there."

He had no idea why, but he didn't care. From his perspective, it was a no-risk way to get rid of Thomas.

He looked at the map and its markings. "I know this place." He picked up his phone and navigated to the email app. He composed a short message to Thomas, letting James review it before hitting send.

Seeing that the note sounded natural, James nodded his approval.

Then, before pressing send, the roommate quickly pasted in added text that read: "Your father wants to meet you on Staffa in Scotland. He knows the identity of Carl's killer."

He sent the note, delighting in the irony that for once the truth would serve him better than a lie. He had no doubt Thomas would show up now.

Thomas received an email on his cell phone just as he and Terri finished their fourth round. He was going to ignore it, but Terri reached over to pick the phone off the table. She handed it to him, saying, "With everything going on, it might be important."

Thomas took the phone reluctantly and skimmed the message. His face went pale. It was a suggestion to meet his father.

He said only, "It's an invitation to go caving on Staffa, in Scotland."

He was horrified at the prospect. Even if the anonymous sender were telling the truth, James Paine was still the last man in the world he wanted help from. He'd rather take his chances in court, if it came to that. His finger hovered near the delete key.

Leaning on his shoulder, Terri said, "You should go. It will be good for you to get away from everything for a day."

He watched her cross the room, thinking she was just going to use the bathroom. She stopped midway and started pulling clothes out of a dresser, then threw them into a suitcase. "What are you doing? Did you decide you want to go to Staffa with me?" he asked, his tone hopeful. Then he remembered who was to be there and tensed up again.

"I'm not going anywhere with you, Thomas, because you're going back to America and I have to stay here. But I'm going away for a while so you won't be tempted to stick around."

Thomas was about to argue with her when she went into the bathroom and shut the door with a bang. He saw a small jade piece on a shelf start to wobble. He rushed to rescue it before it fell off, arriving just in time. He tapped his bare foot onto the floor beneath the shelf and felt the board vibrate in response.

"Amazing how vibrations flow through this old wood."

He stood there for a moment, trying to think what to do, when he heard the shower start. He gave up and decamped to the cot.

Idly, he picked up his cell phone and re-read the message, carefully this time. Maybe it wasn't such a bad idea after all, to hide out in the Hebrides. The authorities would never find him there, and he wasn't eager to return home without Terri.

A few minutes later she stepped out of the bathroom naked, drying her hair with a towel. "So, who was the Staffa invitation from?"

Thomas stalled, then said, "It was anonymous." He saw her expression and knew then he could never tell her anything less than the full truth, ever again. "It said my father would be there, and that he knew the identity of Carl's killer."

"And you don't want to go because you don't want to see your father."

He smiled. *Of course she would sense that,* he thought. That's what he felt at the jail, that somehow she would always know things like that.

"Why not?" she asked.

He told her briefly about his childhood. He kept his face as impassive as possible, wanting to convey only the facts and leave his feelings about it aside for the time being. He had discarded much of his upbringing, but he still valued the Quaker distaste for dramatizing his own life.

He finished with, "Once, my mother told me that, when she was pregnant, she asked my father whether he was 'Praying for a boy or girl?' He told her, 'It'll be trouble either way.'"

"I'll go in your place," she offered, aware of what she was suggesting.

He shook his head a firm no.

She asked, "Then what are you going to do?"

Before Thomas could answer, the studio door slammed against the wall hard enough to knock the jade sculpture off the shelf. It crashed onto the floor like an exploding light bulb.

Arwel stood in the doorway with Arthur Pancost-Swinton right behind him. Arwel said, "That's for us to decide."

12

$\mathcal{T}$HE next morning, in jail again, Thomas paced the room like a caged tiger gone mad from claustrophobia. He checked his watch for the tenth time in as many minutes since being put in Interrogation, desperate for Arwel to enter right away, yet hoping he'd never come.

He checked his face in the mirror of the one-way glass. After a fitful night, it was not a pretty sight. He'd had a dream about having different parents, older and kinder. When he woke, he couldn't shake the feeling that his dream was true. Then he remembered he had wished that very thing many times as a child, but wishing did not make it so.

Thoughts of parents brought him back to Terri's father. He would never forget the look on Arwel's face when he saw Terri near the bathroom and him on the bed, both naked. It was as if Thomas had raped her, though anyone could see at a glance that wasn't so.

It made no difference. He hauled Thomas off the bed and into Arthur's car without even letting him get dressed, tossing his clothing in as an afterthought. The immigration officer hit the gas before he could get his pants on.

They didn't go to the airport, or the immigration offices, as Thomas thought they might. Arthur drove straight to the main Cardiff Police Station. Apparently, he was more interested in revenge than doing his duty, and he was satisfied to let others mete it out. That, or Arwel's murder investigation took precedence and the scum just wanted to watch.

The room smelled as if it held many fear-crazed animals over the years. Their dried sweat stained the walls, the table surface, even the floor. The look of the room matched the odor, a dismal gray-green that resembled day-old puke.

He didn't know if that was all part of some psychological game to make suspects uneasy, or the simple indifference of men who dealt with vermin day in, day out. All he knew for sure was his situation had just gone from bad to worse.

Still, he refused to give hyena Arthur the final victory. He sat down and sat up straight, folding his hands on the table, his face bland. If he was going to a Welsh prison, there'd be Venus heat on Earth before he showed them any sweat.

He looked up at the corner of the room and wondered if the camera was recording him. Then he focused at the glass where there were no doubt men — probably Arthur and Arwel — waiting for the right moment to begin grilling him.

His total experience with any legal system to date was an hour in the Brecon jail and another four in a cell in this station. But sitting in this room he knew now what his father had known many times. *Let them come,* he thought. *I'm not my father, and I won't let them make me feel like I am.*

Arwel entered the room shadowed by Arthur and a man Thomas didn't recognize. He talked to the third man briefly, thanking him for the courtesy of allowing the Brecon police to perform the interrogation. The third man nodded and left.

It was all an act. The detective would be on the other side of the glass, watching live as video recorded every minute of the proceedings. If he wanted Inspector Mawr to ask a specific question it was easy enough to relay it to the earplug receiver that had replaced one of Arwel's hearing aids.

Arwel sat down at the table opposite Thomas and slid a folder, containing who knew what, to his immediate right. Actually, it was empty, a prop filled with blank paper. But it was a useful item to make the suspect nervous. He could tap the top at helpful moments while referring ominously to "testimony" or "evidence."

Arthur stood in the corner behind Thomas's right shoulder where he could see Arwel's face. He didn't need to see Thomas's, since his immigration case was open and shut. He enjoyed the thought of making a prisoner sweat by lurking behind him, unseen but not unfelt.

Arwel began, "Mister, you're in a lot of trouble. You know that, right?"

His voice was so perfectly modulated Thomas couldn't tell whether it was a technique or complete sincerity. Either way, Arwel had stated an undeniable fact. Thomas nodded his acceptance of it.

"Running away from the immigration authorities is not just a separate crime. It makes you look all the more suspect for the murder."

So, Arwel had concluded — or pretended flawlessly — that Carl's death was murder and he the guilty party. So be it. It was a relief to hear the shoe finally drop.

Thomas kept his voice even and said, "Inspector Mawr. With respect, is there any reason we can't condense Interrogation 101 to summer school length? What exactly are we here for?"

Arwel rose, his face flush, looking as if he were about to lean over and smack Thomas for impudence. Instead, he walked to the door, which opened as if on cue, and accepted a cup of coffee. He turned back, not offering any to Arthur or Thomas.

Arwel walked back to the table and set the cup down, making sure to place it far enough away that the prisoner couldn't use it as a weapon. He knew having it in the room was against regulations and hoped Thomas did, too. It would encourage the fear there were no rules here, that his will was absolute.

"Rest assured, before you leave this room you're going to tell me everything I want to know."

It was all Thomas could do not to burst out laughing at the cliché. He masked his reaction and said, "I'd be happy to, sir, if I knew what that was." He paused for effect. "Provided, of course, that what you want to know is the truth."

Arwel reached over and smacked him with a huge, heavy paw. Thomas fell sideways onto the floor. "This isn't America, smart arse! Here, you speak to the police with respect, or you regret it straight off."

Even Arthur was shocked by the violence. All the bloke did was shag his daughter and run from immigration, so far as was proved. Not exactly original, and not notably serious crimes.

Thomas picked himself off the floor. He straightened his chair without a sound and sat back down, then folded his hands in front of him. He looked at Arwel intently but without malice, waiting patiently for whatever came next. It wasn't the first time a father had slapped his face.

A few hours later at the Mawr home in Brecon, Terri glared at her father sitting calmly in his chair at the dining table, lighting his pipe. He looked very concentrated, probably thinking over what Thomas had told him.

Terri stood in front of him, a clean wet dish in her hand, drying it furiously. She looked down until he looked up. "I thought you were going to help him," she spat at him, a charge rather than a question.

"I don't know what made you think that. I told you I was only interested in solving the case. And then, when I saw you—"

Terri flipped up a traffic-cop hand. "Don't even say it, Da. It's none of your business."

He waved her aside from blocking his view of his car sitting in the driveway.

Terri glowered across the table between them, half-daring him with a look to speak. When it became clear he wasn't going to take the bait, she returned to the kitchen. She put away the dish, folded the towel neatly over the rack, and went into her bedroom. She changed her clothes, putting on a business suit she reserved for gallery openings, and walked back to the dining room.

Arwel had left it and was sitting in his chair in the living room, smoking his pipe, pensive. Thomas had told him nothing damning, making him either innocent or a more clever criminal than expected.

He began to think possibly he was innocent. Few could stand up to one of his interrogations. But he was still the key to solving the case, he'd bet his Bath stars. His gaze fell on those pips on the epaulettes of his jacket.

The passport didn't wind up on that body by accident. If it didn't belong to the victim, either Thomas put it there or the killer did. Discovering which, and why, was central to filing this case away.

What to do?

Just then a text message appeared on his phone. It set his thinking in a new direction.

He decided if he brought Thomas and Owen Caldicott together, some sparks might fly. Despite his failure to get anything out of the Mynah, he was convinced that bird knew something. And it was a sure bet Caldicott was the source of whatever it was.

Arwel's thoughts were interrupted when Terri came into the living room dressed up to the nines, her hair coiffed to perfection. "Where are you going?" he asked, trying to keep his voice from sounding tart.

"Rhys made an appointment with a solicitor to get Thomas out of jail. I'm meeting him there."

She was obviously prepared for him to object. When he said nothing beyond a low grunt, she nodded and left.

It took just over an hour to reach the solicitor's office in Cardiff. When she arrived, Rhys was waiting for her on the stoop. He smiled, trying to appear more chipper than he felt. He took her hand. "Don't worry. We'll get him free."

"Knowing how my father thinks, and that Thomas's father is roaming around, he might be safer in jail."

Rhys drifted down to the sidewalk wearing a puzzled look. "His father? In Wales? I thought he was dead. And how'd you know he was here?"

Terri told him what she knew. She finished with, "...so it wouldn't make any sense unless James had been in Owen's apartment, would it?"

"True." He had the look of concentration Terri had seen on Thomas's face in jail the first day. "What do you suppose he wants after 15 years?"

They started up the steps to the solicitor's office. On Terri's way through the door she said, "I don't know. But Thomas is pretty touchy on the subject. He tried to hide an email from me that mentioned him."

Rhys followed her in. "That said what?"

Terri told him the message. "I suppose that's off, though. There's no chance for Thomas to meet anyone if he's stuck in jail." She looked downcast.

He touched her arm. "He won't be for long."

At the elevator door, Rhys said, "Advocates are paid to give advice." He stabbed the button three times. "Maybe he'll have some worth the price."

A passing janitor told them the elevator was out of order and they took the stairs up one flight. The paint in the stairwell was new but the rest of the place looked like it hadn't seen maintenance for a decade. Rhys tapped on a door that seemed it might rupture from his moderate knock.

"Not first class, is it?" she said, her voice low and worried.

"No, but I'm reliably told that Mr. Hefin is." He wanted to chuck her chin but thought better of it before his hand rose halfway to her face.

The door opened and an elderly man, slightly stooped, smiled and gestured them inside. The frizz on his head was thinner than the beard on his face, making his head look upside down at a casual glimpse.

Hefin said, "Mr. Anarawd?"

He didn't ask who was with him. Rhys would be eager to tell him soon enough. No man could keep the identity of a pretty girl at his side unspoken for long.

Hefin sat again behind an antique desk older than he was, though such a thing seemed impossible. He rested his elbows on the Victorian chair arms and put his fingers together into a little tent, obscuring the lower half of his face. His eyes showed an intelligence as rich as the furniture, if equally worn by age.

"How may I help your friend?"

Rhys outlined the facts, repeating most of what he'd said on the phone and adding what

Terri had told him. After the summary, he asked, "What do you think are his chances?"

"Of what?"

Terri was annoyed. So like a lawyer. "Of freeing him, of course."

"On bail? That's probably not too difficult. Permanently? That we will have to see. The difficulty is chiefly with immigration, of course. The passport, you know."

Terri said spontaneously, "Not the murder?"

He noted their surprised looks as he laid his hands flat on the arms of the chair. He tried to pull himself up a little straighter, only half succeeding. "You haven't quite seen it yet, have you?" he asked, his tone gentle but patronizing.

"Seen what?" Rhys asked.

"Well, I don't suppose there's any reason you should." He smiled, enjoying a brief moment alone of superior insight. "Why would the police allow immigration to deport him if they truly thought he were guilty?"

Rhys was stunned.

Terri felt anger and relief at the same instant, relieved that her father had thought him innocent after all, angry that he pretended otherwise. Then she thought back. He had never actually said one way or the other what he thought. The anger grew stronger; that meant he was willing to use Thomas as bait to solve the case.

She grilled Hefin with a few questions, then asked, "So how soon can we get him freed?"

Hefin said, "I called a bail bondsman before you arrived." He rang him again now and arranged to go to the Cardiff Police Station in Cathays Park. "Now, if it isn't too delicate a matter, who will be paying the bail bondsman's fees?"

Terri thought it interesting that he hadn't mentioned his own. "I will. And yours, as well." It would take working civic commissions for a year, which she loathed. But better her in an artist's jail than Thomas in a real one.

The trip to the station took just a few minutes. Hefin explained during the taxi ride what to expect.

Terri was on edge the entire way. She remarked it was good to have a competent solicitor on her side in rough seas. "I just wish you could bail the bilge water faster."

Hefin said, "Ah, my girl, the wheels of the law move exceedingly slow, but grind exceedingly fine." He crowed, "Somewhat like Hefin himself, I've heard it said."

Terri and Rhys waited in the visitors' area while Hefin met with the clerk. They stood up when the lawyer hop-skipped into the area, his aging gait modified by his mood.

He grinned. "Dr. Payne should be released in a few minutes. You should prepare to meet him outside. Bring him to my office first thing tomorrow."

As the trio relocated a constable took Thomas into the interrogation room. There, a detective waited for Inspector Mawr, who had followed Terri the minute she told him where she was headed. The constable left. Arwel arrived just as the pair were being seated.

The DI asked Thomas a number of leading questions containing carefully formulated lies, aiming to make Thomas look like a lunatic. On the fifth lie — he suggested Thomas slept with Terri to get Inspector Mawr's sympathy — Thomas leaped at his throat.

Arwel separated them and called for a guard to take Thomas back to his cell. While he waited for him to arrive, he turned to Thomas and said, "That doesn't help you, son."

"Stop calling me son, you conniving bastard." He plunked down onto his chair and breathed deep to get control of his emotions. "Typical cop behavior, just like my father always said."

"You're right, I shouldn't call you son. And maybe your father was right. You could ask him. Do you want me to call him and let him know you're here?"

"What the hell are you talking about?"

"If your father is James Paine, he's in Wales. At least, he was a couple of days ago when he met with Owen Caldicott in his apartment."

Thomas cocked his head, wondering if this was another trick. He searched Arwel's expression for any sign of dissembling, just as he had so often his father's.

"So, the email was legit," he remarked, surprised.

Arwel held up a hand with his thumb folded inward to signal a request to leave them alone for four minutes. "Tell me about it."

Thomas didn't see any reason to trust Terri's father. But he had nothing to lose at this stage. He related the timing and content of the email, leaving out the time and location of the intended meeting place.

Arwel asked, "Where? When?"

"No, no." Thomas wagged an index finger. "I get out of here and you call off the immigration dogs."

"I can do the first, Thomas, not the second."

"How do you propose we get to James without Arthur picking me up?"

"We?"

"I want to see his face when you arrest him."

"I have no jurisdiction here. The Cardiff fellows are just doing me a professional favor. So, unless your father planned to meet you in Brecon, he'll be taken by someone else."

Thomas smiled and said, "Never try to con a man raised by a man like James Paine, Mr. Mawr."

Arwel's best poker face could not have fooled Thomas at that moment.

Arwel wasn't entirely through lying, though. This time it was partly in Thomas's favor, partly his own. When Thomas had lunged at the detective, he had cause to get bail denied. He used it to get him released into his custody instead, still technically under arrest.

Thomas stood at the south exit of the Cardiff Police Station ten minutes later.

"I'll be nearby if you need me." He gave Thomas his mobile phone number and sent him on his way.

Thomas wasn't falling for any of it. There was no chance Arwel would have him released into his custody then set him free to wander at will. He didn't mind, actually. If his father really did meet him at Staffa, having Mawr close-by could help.

He set off for the train to the Hebrides.

Arwel lingered, watching from the top of the steps as Thomas walked in the direction of the station.

He noticed Terri and Rhys standing on the corner, engaged in intense discussion. He rushed down the steps, circling around slyly to make them face away from the departing Thomas. He said to Terri, "Why are you still here? Didn't they tell you Thomas's bail had been denied?"

She glared at him, angry at his presence yet not surprised he was there. "Something you arranged, no doubt," she shot back.

Despite all his training, Arwel finally snapped. "Fine, my girl, if that's what you think of me. I'll tell you: Thomas is not actually in that jail at this moment."

"Where is he?"

He recovered himself quickly enough to respond, "Somewhere you won't find him, I'll lay odds. Best you just go home." With that, he marched off toward his car.

"What do you think?" Terri asked Rhys. "Is he lying to get us to give up?"

Rhys shrugged. He thought for a moment, then called Hefin. The lawyer told him to wait a few minutes, that he would call him back. Two minutes after, he confirmed that Thomas had been released into DCI Mawr's custody, pending his deportation hearing. Rhys tapped the phone off.

He is out. In your father's custody."

Terri looked in the direction her father, puzzled. She had seen him drive off as he circled Alexandra Gardens. Unless Thomas hid, Arwel was alone.

Then it hit her. "Jeebus, I know where he's gone."

"Where?"

"Staffa. To meet his father."

"How do you know that?"

"I'll tell you on the way."

She took off running, her heels clacking on the stone pavement.

Arwel idled his car at the corner of the park. He knew Terri would have to pass it, whether she went home or toward Mr. Hefin's office. He was surprised when he saw her head instead for the train station, north.

He reasoned at once where she must be going. She must know about Thomas' email and its contents. He should have anticipated that. "Damn. I'm just not thinking straight today."

He bolted out of the car, stabbing his phone as he ran. He breathed hard for the few seconds it took to connect with Thomas's phone. The call went to voice mail. As he raced down the steps to the train, hoping to prevent her from leaving, he left a message for Thomas in case he failed. "Catch her at the first stop and hold her there!"

He reached the bottom step and whipped his view left and right. She was nowhere in sight and the train was preparing to leave. Had she decided to take a later one? He ran back up the steps to the ticket counter, skimming the schedule at top speed. There was no other train until the next day.

"Did a young woman buy a ticket for Oban just now?" he asked the clerk.

The young man nodded and Arwel dashed down the steps again. He reached the bottom in time to see the train pulling away. Terri catapulted from behind a pillar near the far end of the station.

She sprinted across the platform alongside the train and lunged for the handle, short by an inch. She put on a burst of speed and stretched enough to imperil a shoulder tendon. She ran straight toward the final awning pillar, then seized the car handle just in time to step on.

She turned and blew a kiss to her father. She winked and waved as the train sped out of the station.

13

THOMAS didn't stop Terri at the next station. He wasn't on the train. He'd been delayed by an overwhelming desire to take a shower and change his clothes after the grueling episode at the station. He'd gone to his apartment in Cardiff and stayed under the water for a full fifteen minutes, then toweled off.

When he finally listened to Arwel's message, he panicked. He rushed to dress, then checked the same train schedule, finding the same depressing result as Arwel had. Tomorrow would be too late.

He took a taxi to the airport and boarded the first available flight to Glasgow, using a fake ID Rhys had cooked up for him.

He was fortunate to catch a train in Glasgow with only a short delay. He estimated whether his route would reach Oban before Terri's did. It was touch and go, but with luck he'd get there by six o'clock, ten minutes before her train was scheduled to arrive.

If he missed her, it would be another hour until he could reach Staffa, a tiny island off the west coast. That is, *if* he was lucky enough to get a boat.

Luck was not with him; his train was delayed by twenty minutes. The moment he stepped out of the car he rushed to take one of the tourist boats, but the last one had left at six o'clock.

He hoped at least one of the captains dotting the shoreline wouldn't be rigid about sailing with such a narrow window to return before dark. He wandered down the line, searching for one who might care more about money than rules.

He checked the time again, then the position of the sun in a cloudless sky. Scanning the sky, he was reminded of one of the odder aspects of the email. The sender had waxed eloquent about seeing the cave in just the right light, assuring him "the weather would be perfect."

It seemed a paltry error, but anyone who confidently predicted the fickle weather in the Hebrides certainly didn't know the area. He struggled to use that clue to deduce the sender's identity, or at least eliminate his father, but it was too little to go on. He had no way of knowing if James was familiar with the island or not.

He studied the dock, seeing men standing near their boats and chatting. No great judge of character, he nonetheless tried to spot one that looked like he would ask few questions. He saw a sailor that resembled his father, not so much in appearance as expressions and body language, and decided he'd found his man.

Four minutes later he was on a small sloop, his sizable overpayment outweighing the owner's concern over the time of day. "From the crazy American tourist," he overheard the captain say to his crewman as he fanned out a series of bills.

Thomas didn't care what the man thought of him so long as he was an able pilot. Crashing on the basalt rocks of Staffa would not suit his plans. He hoped the captain was like James in at least one respect: evil his father was, for sure, but he accomplished with skill anything he tackled. A look at the pilot's hands gave him some comfort. This was no pretend sailor who toted tourists for his living.

They stopped at the tip of land off Dunollie so the captain could repair the halyard. The bay looked desolate, half the blue sky now muddied by fog. Thomas chafed at the delay, but to chastise the captain struck him as unwise, so he kept silent. He cooled his impatience by a slow perusal of Dunollie Castle, a 15th century ruin at the top of the hill.

Walking up, the view matched his mood. The castle was interesting enough but it was decaying, set on a somber mound. There were few flowers to liven the place up, and everything around said that it had never been more than a place to inflict destruction.

The captain finished his business and announced to his crewman he was about to take off again. The man signaled to Thomas to come back down the hill. Thomas took a last look at the arch over the castle entrance and started his descent back to the boat. He made his way quickly through the thicket. As he neared the bottom, he stopped cold.

James Paine stood fifteen feet away.

Under any other circumstances, Thomas would've preferred it be fifteen million at least. As it was, he couldn't believe his luck. He wouldn't have to go to Staffa at all, and if Terri was there already, she'd certainly be safe now. He guessed that James had been on a similar journey, and coincidence had brought them to the same spot at the same time.

He took a path winding away from his father toward the boat, knowing he would have only a few seconds before James caught up with him at the water's edge. He wanted to send the boat away to ensure there were no witnesses to their meeting. Afterward, he could walk back to Oban then continue on to Staffa by train.

He whispered to the captain of his rented vessel, slipped him an extra 20 pounds, and told him he could shove off without his passenger. The sea dog was happy to oblige the mad American since he'd already been paid for a round trip. "You can't do better than that," he said to his crewman, and set sail for home.

Thomas walked cautiously closer to where James was kneeling. His father was untethering his sailboat from a stone. The man looked as gray and weathered as the ancient rock, carved for some long-forgotten purpose, like his father's life.

Thomas had seen him just once in the past fifteen years, a frantic figure swooping past his boyhood hiding spot. He'd been searching for Thomas during his teenage escape from his home town. He hadn't been afraid. He knew well how to hide. He had been forced to practice many times.

Yet even after the passage of all those years, he could never forget that demonic face. It presented a blend of wind-roughened features and a fixed expression of cold rage, just as it had in his youth.

He had no clue as a young boy what James could have against his own son, why he should resent and detest him. He recalled a time when he was six and sat down near his father's footstool, admiring his father's face as he watched a British crime drama on television. Thomas reached over and hugged his leg, flashing up a son's idolizing smile. In return, James kicked him away, hard.

Later, he had hints that his father's resentment grew in proportion to his son's intellect, but he found the idea hard to accept. Still, the son never tried to get close to the father again. Eventually, he stopped thinking of him as his father entirely. He was just a man his mother knew, one he'd been forced to live with the first half of his life, a half he tried to forget.

From that day, he had avoided meeting him. He ran as far as he could, eventually ending up near a university town in Virginia. After that he hid in plain sight, thinking that keeping his name, only slightly altered, would throw James off the trail. It had worked. James had not unearthed him in fifteen years.

Thomas was about to confront him in the present when he saw Rhys step onto James's boat. His colleague had appeared unexpectedly from behind a boulder and was carrying bags of what looked like lunch food. Thomas was too bewildered to think straight.

Rhys couldn't be part of a plot against him; he knew him too well to believe that. He had never shown a moment's resentment over being second-in-command at the lab, despite Thomas being offsite. In fact, he had never behaved dishonorably in any way in all the months they'd worked together. But what else could explain his presence here at just this moment?

Thomas was actually relieved when James jumped onto the deck and bounded toward Rhys, ready to eject him. If they were partners, there'd be no reason for his father to shove him off.

Rhys stood his ground and said, "Mr. Paine, I presume. I recognize you from your mug shot." His assistant's face was a mix of hate and hope.

As James drew closer, the difference in their builds grew more obvious. James was strong, but wiry. Rhys was a foot taller, twice as broad, and solid as a rock column from years of caving. Rhys smiled, as if daring James to sling it, suggesting he'd love nothing more than to see him try.

Thomas stumbled toward the boat almost in a daze. He was two feet away from the gunwale when Rhys set down the bags and noticed him there.

Rhys knelt on the deck and said, his voice low, "Everything's going to be all right, friend. Every magnet has a north and south pole, you know." He winked. "And they're inseparable."

Thomas walked forward, stiff-legged, not steady enough yet to hop onto the bobbing boat. "What are you doing here?"

Rhys grinned and said in a normal voice, "Terri's father thought you could use something to eat. He was worried about you." He pointed to the bags, then reached a hand down to help Thomas onto the boat. He whispered as Thomas came aboard, "He can't be far away."

"But how did you find *him*?" he asked, pointing to James.

"I'll tell you later."

"Anyway, there's no reason to go now," Thomas murmured. "Terri is safe, so long as James stays here. All we have to do is alert Arwel to come pick him up."

Rhys was about to ask him, "On what charge?"

He hadn't the chance. Unawares, James had crept close enough to hear. He said, "Not gonna happen, git. If he tries, I'll just off him." He bore down on Thomas and said, "And you know I can."

Rhys said, laughing, "I've known Inspector Mawr all my life. Worth a big ticket price to see you try."

James ignored him.

Unable to hold off confronting him any longer, Thomas said, "What do you want? Why are you here? In the UK, I mean."

"Why, I came to see your future wife, son," he said jovially, like Beelzebub announcing the arrival of ice cream at a party of little girls. "Isn't that a father's natural desire?" His expression said he didn't expect him to believe such a transparent lie.

At the possible reference to Terri, Thomas tensed even more. The feeling induced by James' presence was amplified by the thought of them meeting, the hell of his past touching his present heaven.

"You'll never get close to her," he insisted. His face assumed a younger version of his father's cross-eyed look of rage. "Except," he added, "maybe staring up sightless from a pine box."

James smiled, a grisly sight. "Be careful, son. You're sounding like me now."

Thomas spat into the water. "We're nothing alike."

"I don't know. Getting slapped around by police captains is a pretty good start." He walked over to a hatch and flipped it open. "Breathe easy, though. I took care of him for you." He gestured for him to look in the hold.

Thomas crossed the deck, followed swiftly by Rhys. The pair looked down. Arwel was lying on the floor in a bunch, trussed up with his mouth taped over and his eyes bandaged.

Thomas said smoothly, "It's nothing to me. He's been trouble since I arrived in Wales."

James knew he was bluffing. James said, "Let's test that theory, eh?" He pulled a Ruger from behind his back and ratcheted the slide to put a round in the chamber. He aimed down, then looked over at Thomas. "You can save him with a word."

Rhys screamed, "No!"

James said, not looking at him, "Not you, fairy dust. My son."

Thomas swiveled his view down mechanically at Arwel. He was no more fond of policemen than his father was, and the inspector had given him plenty of reason to favor his demise. But he could never let an innocent man suffer for his sake.

He turned to James and said, "You win. What do you want?"

James lowered the weapon and slammed the hatch shut with a sweep of his foot. "Like I said, son. I just want to meet your future bride."

"Nothing like that's been discussed, but I won't argue the point." He sat down on the hatch and leaned back on his arms. "I'll tell you one thing, though. If you think you can get me to Staffa to watch you kill her in my presence, forget it." He sat up, his arms relaxed on his thighs. "You can just shoot me now."

Rhys compressed the space between them, ready to lunge if James raised the pistol.

"So, she's going to Staffa is she." James said. "I didn't know that."

Thomas felt his chest clench. He wished at that moment that James *would* shoot him for such a stupid blunder. But that wouldn't help Terri.

James stuffed the weapon into his waistband at the small of his back. "I didn't come here to shoot anyone, young fool. If I wanted to do that, I'd have done it and gone." He slid a smug look at Rhys and added, "You don't think this one could stop me, do you?"

In a lightning thrust, he punched Rhys in the diaphragm and the giant went down, airless, like a punctured blimp.

Thomas was about to react when Rhys put up a hand and waved him off. They stayed where they were as James sauntered off to prepare the sails. The pair agreed it might be best to see what he really had in mind.

"At least until we can free Arwel safely," Rhys puffed, rubbing his stomach.

James loosened the restraining ropes one at a time. "And, by the by, Tom. I've no interest in shooting your fiancée, either," he said over the rushing wind. "I could've done that when she passed through Oban an hour ago."

For once, Staffa was bathed in sunlight. Despite the yellow disc dipping ever nearer the horizon, its rays were still ample and hot. Terri leaned back on her hands and soaked up the heat, granting herself a few moments of peace. She opened her eyes again and searched discreetly for the man who had invited Thomas to the island.

She was determined to appear casual, to keep her potential observer off guard. But the strain of waiting was taking its toll. With every muscle taut, she was beginning to tire.

Relax, girl, she told herself. *He'll get here. And his face will tell you if he's the one who framed Thomas.*

She was glad now she'd stopped at a shop in Glasgow to pick up a change of clothing. The bikini top and shorts suited her purpose much better than her business suit. She flicked a look at the lowering sun and hoped she would still be glad in a little while. The weather in the Hebrides could change from bright to stormy on a whim.

She tipped her head back and slowly moved her face from one shoulder to the other, like a delphinium following the sun. But she took no pleasure in it this time. It was a feint so she could look around again without seeming obvious. She was sure she would know the man who sent the email, though she could not have explained why. She saw no one nearby.

Even during the summer, in late evening there were but a dozen people on the island that held Fingal's Cave. This day, two were sunning themselves, but far from her. Most of the rest were clambering over the rocks, leaving the cave, trying to avoid slipping off the basalt columns and into the sea. A couple were already waiting at the shore. There was now less than ten minutes before the last boat left.

Terri debated whether she should check inside the cave. If she stayed where she was much longer, she'd miss the ferry, and camping on Staffa overnight could be suicide. She looked at the dark clouds in the distance and judged that trouble was on the way. Then she measured again how low the sun was. She'd give her quarry another few minutes to show.

When he didn't, she looked at the boat anxiously, checking her phone's clock for the fourth time.

The minutes slipped by, soon passing the deadline.

To avoid being reported by the tour boat captain, she watched from behind a boulder as the boat left. Once gone, she ambled back to her previous spot and lay down again.

Unseen, a man lying on his stomach watched her from the tan bluff atop Fingal's Cave. He'd have preferred to use binoculars. They'd give him a better look at her bikinied chest. But he didn't want to be conspicuous.

He canvassed the sea for approaching boats. It was too late for any ferries to arrive, and the last one left without him. He laughed to himself, remembering how annoyed its captain had been at his refusal to leave.

He eased back from the edge and lifted his binoculars to take another visual sweep of the the island. He couldn't imagine Thomas would come from any direction but Black Crofts or Connel or Achnacloich – all within a narrow cone to the south – but he was taking no chances.

Anyway, it hardly mattered. He'd have plenty of time to react, no matter where the boat landed. It was barely fifty feet from his perch to the mouth of the cave.

He looked satisfied a second later when he spotted a sailboat approaching, well illuminated by the setting sun. He scrambled down from the bluff to avoid being silhouetted against the sky.

As the boat neared Staffa, the man watched from a lower vantage point, growing more excited the closer it came.

James piloted the boat to within a few hundred yards from the southeast point of the island. He looked at Thomas and said with a sneer, "I see you've got your seasickness under control." He could see him shaking from the effort to master it. He cackled. "That's right, son. Confront your fears head on. The more you fear something, the more you should invite it."

Thomas was more ill at the reminder of his father's favorite homily than from the bobbing of the boat. He'd worked half his life to reverse the teachings he'd absorbed, but it was like moving to a higher plateau while standing on air.

James snorted, as if reading his thoughts. "Here, take over the helm."

Thomas took control of the ship and instantly tacked hard to port to reach the other side of the island.

"Where are you going? You can't get onto the island at the mouth of Fingal's Cave."

Thomas ignored him. If his father wanted him to go to one place, the opposite spot was the wiser choice.

In any case, the man he spotted watching them surely meant them no good. No telling who the man was — James' partner, he guessed — but his best bet lay in being unpredictable.

James shrugged and went to check on Arwel.

Rhys sidled up to Thomas. He looked at the sky ahead, darkening fast from a series of rain-filled clouds gathering not far off. "That course really ain't a very good idea, mate."

"You're right. But I can't think of a better one, can you?"

Rhys shook his head. He assayed the sky again and said, "You've got about ten more minutes. After that, the seas will get rough. You'll wreck the boat coming in."

Thomas nodded without looking at him, busy steering the craft. Rhys prepared for the shift of the boom by side-stepping to the bow, waiting to duck.

At two hundred yards out, Thomas tacked for the final approach to the cave mouth. Suddenly, the boat hit a swell, tipping them at a steep angle. Rhys reached for the rail to steady himself too late; a gust of wind knocked him overboard.

Thomas shouted, "James! Man overboard!"

James returned a blank look, as if to say: "Why tell me?"

Thomas looked behind but the boat was already a dozen yards away from his friend, too far to throw a life preserver. He knew it would be impossible for him to turn around in this wind. He looked again at James, who just crossed his arms and leaned back against the rail, grinning maliciously.

Rhys waved from the water to signal he was fine, then pointed to the darkening sky, then his watch. He cupped his hand to his mouth and said, "Keep going. I'll swim the rest."

Thomas looked skyward, seeing good reason to agree with Rhys. He waved, then resumed piloting the boat around the cigar-shaped island.

A minute later, he could see he was making poor progress. He checked his watch again, then the sky. Getting into the cove without beaching would be chancy under normal circumstances. In choppy seas with fading light, it was a sure shipwreck without a better pilot.

Terri was alone on the island with James' partner. He could afford no mistakes and no delays. Swallowing his disgust, he said, "Friend, you'd better take over."

James caught the sarcasm in the reference to his Quaker past, but he also sensed the real concern — and an admission of inadequacy. He flashed a victory smirk and took over the helm. He swung the boat parallel to the line of wet rocks, still a few dozen yards outside the cave mouth. He checked to see what Thomas was doing and noticed him pulling off his shoes. "If you fancy swimming, forget it."

"There's no other way. You'll never be able to dock here."

His competence challenged, James was about to argue when the boat slammed into a basalt column under the surface, running the ship aground. The force of the sudden stop bowled him over and he banged his head against the tiller on his way down to the deck.

Thomas rushed over, then reached down to corral James' gun. Stuck atop the rocks and with no pilot, the boat lurched like a whirling circus plate on a rod, and he had to try three times before he could get close to the waistband. Finally succeeding, he tucked the weapon into his own belt then rushed to the hatch, threw it open, and jumped down into the cabin.

Arwel was still groggy, drugged he guessed. He whisked off his bonds and took the rope from Arwel's hands to use on James. He tied the lengthy portion freed from his legs around his own waist, intending to use it as a safety line on his swim. The swells could drag a man out to sea in minutes.

He squinted at the waning light and the rising sea as spray splashed his eyes. He had five minutes to get ashore or face certain drowning in the attempt. He hesitated, weighing if he should wait 'til Arwel recovered, sure he couldn't swim to shore with the big man. But that would leave Terri alone on the island with a storm coming on — and James' partner with her.

He went topside, then dragged James into the cabin and tied him to a metal bar. He lay Arwel on the berth next to him and stuffed cushions all around his trunk. The hull was just stuck, not punctured, so he'd be safe and dry until he woke up fully. That is, he would be if the waves didn't push the boat off the rocks and swamp it when the storm rose. He had to risk it.

He started to leave, then held back again, imagining how Terri would feel if he let her father die to save her. He looked at the sky one last time, then at the position of the ship. He looked carefully at Arwel's position and said aloud, "Damn it all. I don't even like the man."

He went topside again, untied the rope from his waist, tied it to a gunwale cleat, then jumped overboard. He landed on one of the basalt columns. Balancing precariously, it was all he could do to resist the push of the waves as he wound the rope around a low pyramid jutting above the water. He prayed it would hold if the boat floated loose from its undersea shelf.

He jumped into the water, swimming as hard as he could for a point fifty feet away, where he could climb up to the island. From there, he'd bear little risk of being seen.

He was a good swimmer, and in calm water the trip would've taken at most a few seconds. Now he struggled just to hold his position and not be washed out to sea. With every stroke forward, the waves pulled him back an equal amount.

His arms were already beginning to tire. A few more minutes of this and the oncoming dark would be the least of his problems. His mind went instinctively to a quiz question from his calculus course. He estimated the optimal angle at which to swim to reach the shore in the shortest time.

He kept himself as rigid as he could at that angle by focusing on a rock seventy feet away.

He thought, "Now, if that rock will just stay visible 'til I reach it."

Eternal seconds ticked off as he forced his limbs into a robotic rhythm, ignoring how they ached. He thrust his feet with all his might to give his arms the maximum help as water pushed into his nose.

A spot of dull sunlight the size of a serving platter shone on his stony lighthouse. Soon it shrank to a teacup saucer, then the bowl of a spoon. He was still twenty feet away when the light vanished entirely, as if swallowed.

Ten feet from shore his arms gave out for the final time. He rolled over onto his back and carried on by demanding his legs do all the work, giving his arms precious time to recover. If he lasted, he would still need them to haul himself ashore.

At five feet away he no longer controlled his legs. They just reacted impulsively to nerve signals, a memory of his will to push on. He could hold his head up so weakly he wasn't sure he still swam toward the rock. Equal odds he was floating out to sea.

He'd accounted for side drift in his initial calculation, but that was a lifetime ago, when he was still a conscious being with mastery of his body. Now he was just a machine with an unknown reserve of dwindling fuel.

Then he saw the rock.

Eighteen inches from it, he reached up for a handhold, hoping his arms were long enough. He was a finger-length short. He flopped his other arm into the air and down to the water, fighting to gain a precious four inches. He succeeded only in falling back another six.

Then, the light on the rock long gone, the light in his mind winked out, too.

14

*T*ERRI reached down to tug Thomas up to the shore by his collar. Her first attempt dragged her more into the water than him out of it. She didn't dare let go of him, so she dug her heel into the slippery moss and mud at the shoreline, then roped a boulder with her free arm.

She couldn't exert enough pull to get him completely out with one hand. His lower half floated in the water while he lay face down in the moss, the storm clouds looming ever closer. Terri spiked her other heel into the earth near his shoulder. She let go of her handhold on the rock and raked him up as hard as she could.

His collar ripped.

As he started to slide back into the water, she reached down, bending at the waist as far as she could without tipping over. She curled her hands under his armpits and pulled, bringing him back up to his previous position. A series of short, sharp jerks brought him all the way out of the water and she turned him over.

She wiped the moss and mud off his face, making him look worse for all the smears. She reached down and cupped some water and tried again. Just as she had him cleaned up, he woke up. He smiled up at her.

Terri smiled ruefully back at him. She said, "I see you didn't go back to America like I said you should."

He coughed, disgorging water. When he could speak, he said, "Did you really hope for that?"

"No. Not without me." She bent down and kissed his forehead then raised her head again. "We'd better get to higher ground," she warned. "The storm's near."

He looked past her shoulder at the sky and jumped up. He would have fallen back but Terri steadied his legs, then stood up herself. With one arm around his waist, she led him away from the water and onto a small bluff near the cave mouth.

He surveyed the flat landscape, seeing nothing to serve as shelter. The wind against his chest grew stronger until he could barely stand, even with her help. "We should find a cave," he said.

"Fingal's is all there is. And we can't go in there."

"We have to. Exposed, we'll be blown right off the island."

"Inside, the sea will drown us."

He had studied the cave online during the plane ride and knew better. "There's an area inside where we can hunker down. It's a small nook at the end of the walkway, well above the sea level. At worst, we'll get some spray."

He started to lead her by the hand toward the basalt columns lining the cave, but she held firm at the length of their two arms. "No," she insisted, her head bowed, her back arched like a turtle. "I can't."

He circled behind her, using his body to shield her from the squall. "Why not?" he said in her ear, above the howl.

"I don't want to say. Just accept it." She looked over her shoulder and could see he wanted a reason. "Please."

The last of the light was fading in time with the rising wind. Soon there would be an avalanche of rain as well. "Terri, we have to get out of this storm and we have to do it now."

"I'm claustrophobic," she blurted.

He blinked at her for a moment. His teeth started to chatter, cold from the soaking rain and the chilling gusts. He wanted to laugh, noting one more thing they had in common and thinking how ironic it was. But this was not the time.

He unfolded one arm and tacked to her side, urging her forward. "Force yourself, because otherwise we're going to die." He walked ahead, feigning more confidence than he felt. Now was not the time to confess.

The thought of making him suffer for her phobia apparently dissolved her resistance and she marched behind him, doing her best to keep from quivering.

They reached the opening and Thomas went inside first, keeping a tight hold on her hand. The waves splashed them more and more often as they scurried deeper into the cave, a combined effect of shrinking columns and waves swelling with the rising gale.

He'd never been to Fingal's before but the description on the caving website proved accurate. Even in the dark he could feel his way without a misstep. He counted the columns until they reached the nook, a dugout barely big enough for two bodies. He urged her in first, then settled in front of her.

"You're crushing me," she complained. "I'd feel less shut in if I were nearer the opening."

"And more likely to lunge out in a panic. Stay put." He edged over to keep her from being pinned, but stayed on guard in case she should bolt.

He was off the mark on the sheltering effect of the dugout, though. The waves splashed higher and the small space gave less protection than he'd forecast. But there was no shelter on the outside they could reach in time. He put his arm around her, covering her head as much as possible.

He looked above his own head and discerned a small rock formation, one that could tumble down with the right blow. If he could pile a few small boulders in front of them, to make the dugout its own mini-cave, it might be enough.

But what tool to use? Thornier still, how to do it without crushing them in the process? He didn't know, and time was running out.

He leaned back against the rock and felt something poke him in the spine. Miraculously, the gun he'd put in his waistband was still there.

He couldn't know whether he could dislodge the rocks. That required experiment and he'd have but a short trial. Worst of all, if the rocks fell wrong they could kill them.

He looked at the waves below, surging to within a foot of them. In another minute, the sea level would reach their ledge with enough force to wash them both into the water.

He elbowed in front of Terri and pressed her backward, ignoring her complaints. Any debris would have to hit him to get to her. He raised the gun butt, aiming at the crack he hoped was the weak spot in the rocks.

"Terri, cover your head with your arms," he hollered over the wind. In a normal voice he said to himself, "This is nuts."

Then he struck.

One whack and the dugout became a prison. It had no opening and only whatever oxygen was trapped inside when the rocks fell. There were a few feet of vertical space in front of them and a foot above, but apart from that they might as well have been in a stone coffin.

"Well, that should put me on the short list for a Darwin Award," Thomas said. "Now let's see if I can avoid winning it."

He felt for broken bones, finding none. He turned to assess Terri. "You okay?" he asked. When there was no answer, he tapped her face. "Terri. Terri, are you alright?" Still no answer.

He quelled his rising panic. She would need him to be calm and able to think clearly now. He felt behind her head, thinking she might have instinctively thrust back with the bang. He could feel a warm, wet ooze on the back of her head.

"Not good. If we get out of this, I promise to give you the biggest apology you've ever had." He ripped off a piece of shirt and pressed it to her head wound.

Talking kept up his spirits but it did nothing to revive her. He shifted around to face the front of their tomb, seeking a way to rise from the dead.

He felt the wall that held them in. He tapped it with his palm from the floor to above his head, then left to right. Wet silicate had filled every crevice between the boulders. There was no gap between the rocks big enough for air to move through. He tried pushing some of the natural cement loose with no luck.

"What are the odds?" he wondered aloud. They had, he estimated, an hour's worth of oxygen.

If he put his back to the rear wall and pressed outward with his feet, he might be able to create a hole. The trick was shoving a single rock into the sea without causing an avalanche toward them or, almost as bad, tumbling the whole structure down and defeating his original purpose.

He quickly worked out a method, then abandoned it right away as hopeless. It required climbing up at an impossible angle, given the space available and the topography of the rear wall.

He considered climbing up the front wall and shoving with his feet on the rear. That would topple the barrier outward, but he'd fly into the sea after it. If it would save Terri, he was willing, but he wasn't sure she'd be better off without him in this storm.

In the end, he opted for stepping up the stones on either side and trying to push one off from the top. If he was careful, and very lucky, he could unseat it and not have the whole front wall collapse. He could open a hole for air, then wait out the storm to remove the rest.

He tried one more time to rouse Terri, to let her know what he had in mind. He thought it would be much safer if she were alert so she could dodge any stone that fell inward. He finally decided it didn't make much difference. In the dark, she couldn't tell which way to duck anyway.

He climbed halfway up the wall, muttering softly to himself, "Please, please, don't let me bring a rock down on her. I just found her." His voice echoed off the walls. He chuckled. "Well, at least I can hear now."

"What are you yammering about?" came Terri's weak voice.

He turned, almost launching himself off his precarious perch. "Are you all right?"

"My head hurts like hell." She felt the back of it. "And I'm bleeding."

"I know. But you're conscious. That's a good sign. No shock, no coma."

"Very comforting. Tell that to my pounding skull." She noticed his voice came from above her. "What are you doing? And what the hell happened anyway?"

"Just what I'd hoped. Sort of."

"Then you need some guidance on what to hope for."

He couldn't argue. "We're sealed in. I'm going to try to shove the top boulder into the sea."

"Shouldn't you wait 'til the storm passes? It's pretty cozy in here," she lied. "And there's no druggist around to get some aspirin anyway."

"I'm glad you can make jokes, but no. We don't have enough air to last."

"Then I guess I'd better stop making jokes. They take more oxygen, you know."

He was glad she felt well enough to wisecrack, but he knew their odds of escaping. They were not good. Wet silicate and heavy boulders made for a sturdy barrier. He had seen something similar during a caving expedition his third time out. They had worked for hours to free two men trapped after a cave-in, behind a barrier not much thicker than this one. The two never came home.

He continued his slow climb, reaching the top in a few seconds. "Cover your head with your arms in case some rocks fall inward."

"Okay. Go."

He shoved, feeling the rock budge a hair, then fall back perfectly into place. He knew he could get the maximum force by pounding the rock with his palm, but that might break a bone. They had troubles enough without him getting handicapped. Still, that the rock moved at all was a hopeful sign. Even if he couldn't remove it, he might nudge it far enough to leave a gap.

He pressed his palm against the cold stone and readied his shoulder for one more push. He rested an extra minute, trying to regain some of the strength lost during his long swim. Then he thrust forward with what was left of his power.

The boulder moved. It tilted forward and Thomas gave it a second shove before it could fall back to the equilibrium point. It tumbled down, making a splash in the sea that he couldn't hear over the wind whistling through the cave.

"Hey, watch it!" a voice cried out.

"Rhys?" Thomas ventured in a gleeful voice.

"Yeah. But not for long if you break my head with pumpkin-sized rocks." His face appeared in the hole. "Haven't we been here before?"

"How'd you find us?" Thomas asked.

"I saw you from the shoreline."

"You'd better join us until the winds die down. It wouldn't do for you to wind up in the sea."

"Again, you mean."

"Never mind that." Thomas edged aside. "You'll need to make the hole bigger. Try to avoid everything coming down. I built this for shelter." Thomas thought it best not to explain how. "Ok, try to pull the next rock out as I push. On three." He readied himself.

Together, they removed the rock and Rhys slid in, taking up every spare inch of space.

In two hours, the worst of the storm had passed and Rhys and Thomas began removing more boulders. Twenty minutes later they were both soaked, but the two of them had cleared all but a knee-high garden wall of stones from in front of the nook. They were each so cramped they all felt claustrophobic.

Unable to keep herself from shaking, Terri insisted on leaving, no matter what conditions were like outside the cave.

Afraid she would leap out to her death, Thomas relented and tapped Rhys to climb out first. He stepped aside to let Terri go next. "Rhys, move over. But keep watch to make sure she doesn't tumble off the walkway."

"She'll get just about as wet either way," he said.

Terri stepped up to the wall and pushed herself onto the ledge then thrust a leg over, in the meantime letting go of the cloth covering her scalp. She felt the back of her head; the blood had congealed. "Well, that's something to be thankful for, anyway."

"What?" Rhys asked.

"Never mind. I'm coming out."

Rhys readied himself to catch her in case she slipped off the narrow ledge. "Be careful. The wind is really howling."

In a few seconds they were all standing on the basalt walkway, Rhys in front. He led them toward the entrance, feeling his way out of the cave.

The storm was now at half-force, a gale by normal standards, a moderate blow in the Hebrides. Rhys squinted around the corner, seeing the sparse vegetation bent sideways.

"We should go back until it blows over," he said.

"Not a chance," Terri said over the howl and shoved past him onto the wider platform above. She looked back at the two men, their disapproval obvious. "We'll either find some shelter or ride it out in the open by huddling in a three-bodied tent. Either way, there's no way I'm going back down there."

The two men followed her onto the open plain, squinting against the horizontal rain whipping into their faces. Thomas said, "I was once at a convention in Chicago a lot like this."

Rhys said, "To a Welshman, this is just a summer breeze."

"We should head back to the boat," Thomas suggested, dreading what they might face when they arrived.

Rhys shook his head. "Gone. I saw it pulling out to sea as I reached the shore."

Thomas nodded, his expression morose. He wondered if his father had worked loose his bonds before Arwel recovered.

More familiar with the terrain than the men, Terri led them off on a grim search for shelter.

Her experience soon proved useless. It was impossible to see more than a few feet in any direction. Pitch black would've been better than the all-engulfing gray that dissolved every landmark. The wind made it impossible to keep their eyes open for long anyway.

The trio slowly scoured the island, staggering forward at a steep angle. Walking upright was a guarantee of being blown over backwards. Bits of wet moss flew in their faces, carrying with them pebbles that pelted them without end. The moisture made the tiny rocks sting all the more.

There had never been a human settlement on Staffa. There was no way to survive off the small island's meager store of life, and no reason to use it as a defensive fort. So, unlike other spots in the Hebrides, it was devoid of the usual ancient stone huts and earthen mounds that might have served as shelter.

The longer they searched, the weaker they grew. Both Rhys and Thomas had endured long, hard swims. Terri was still shaky from carrying Thomas and the blow to her head. They would find a spot soon or exhaustion would force them onto the ground as surely as the storm.

Going too near the shore threatened to blow them into the sea. Trudging back to the cave was sure suicide now.

After searching for half an hour, Terri stopped them in the middle of the island, unable to move another step.

"Well, guys," she said, her voice making a wink her eyes couldn't manage, "here's your one chance for a threesome. Kneel down."

They squatted and formed a tent by wrapping their arms around one another's shoulders. They huddled there as the rain beat down on their backs, the wind-driven pellets bruising their bodies to form constellations of pain.

15

*I*n the morning, the wind and rain were gone as if they had never materialized. The sole evidence of their passing was a few dozen small ponds here and there. The sun shone through a cloudless blue sky of the sort that made the Scottish Hebrides a paradise on these rare days.

The trio unlocked their arms and stood up to walk around, working out stiff backs and sore knees. Terri's bare back looked like a negative of the night sky, with purple stars and white space, but she seemed not to notice. She'd refused to let the two men cover her more than they did each other.

"How's your head?" Thomas asked her.

"Sore. Fine. But I'm hungry."

Rhys said, "Too early for the first ferry so you'll have to bear up a bit longer."

Thomas recalled Rhys saying the sailboat had gone away. But how could Arwel have taken it safely back to Oban in that storm? "Terri, does your father have any sailing experience?" he asked, keeping his voice neutral.

"Not a jot. He's a forest man, not a sailor. Won't even go on the water if he can avoid it." She blinked at him, waiting to hear the reason he asked. When he didn't volunteer it, she said, "Why?"

"He was on the boat that brought me here. Piloted by my father." He explained what had happened.

Terri waited, holding her questions until he'd finished. When he had, she looked out to sea. She said what both men were thinking. "You think he died, trying to get back to the mainland." She shook her head. "You don't know my father."

Thomas said, "I hope you're right." He didn't think she could be. Even a man with extraordinary skills like James couldn't sail in that storm.

Watching Thomas' face, Terri said, "My father's not so easy to kill."

He droned, "We should make for the ferry."

They all walked in silence to the docking point.

They were equally mute on the trip back to the mainland. They simply ignored anyone who asked questions on the boat. When they arrived at Oban, Terri invited Thomas to her house.

Thomas hung his head. "I'd better not. I'm still wanted by the authorities, and they might show up at your house." That wasn't his reason and he couldn't mask a lie, not from her.

"Thomas, tell the truth."

He was surprised at her vehemence, but he didn't respond. Telling her what was really in his mind wouldn't make her any less angry.

If he admitted he was relieved the boat went down, she'd be outraged. If he said he was sorry, she'd know he was lying.

Feeling guilty over the relief wouldn't change her reaction. And pretending her father might have made it, while his died, went against his nature.

Faced with the choice to deceive her or deceive himself, he opted for the first, though the dilemma grated his nerves.

Terri misinterpreted his expression and said, "Fine. Pout. I'm going home." With that, she stormed off toward the train station without looking back.

Thomas watched her go.

Rhys said, "She's right, you know. You need to show some grit here, Thomas. Otherwise, you're going to lose a lot more than her."

"There's no such a thing as 'a lot more than her'."

"Then go after her, fool."

Thomas shook his head, downcast.

Rhys shook his head, baffled. "I can tell you this, man: if she felt about me like she does you, nothing would stop me." He stomped off in Terri's direction.

Thomas looked around the lush green hills. He couldn't explain why, but it felt like home, though he'd never been there before. The three-story stone houses looked familiar. Even the tall, red brick chimney jutting from a tall building seemed like something he'd seen before.

He wrote it off to seeing so many classic films.

Walking to the station the clack of his heels on the cobblestones echoed off the close-set stone walls of the houses lining the narrow streets.

He delayed a few minutes to give Rhys and Terri time to get their tickets and board, then started for the ticket counter. He stepped onto the train, choosing a car far from the one he'd seen them enter.

Seated, he stared out the window, thinking. There seemed no way out of the mess except surrender to immigration.

Remember, though, you didn't put yourself in it. Someone arranged things that way. But, who?

It made no sense for Father to be guilty. What motive could he have? Kill a complete stranger to pin the crime on you, after an absence of fifteen years? Not credible.

Owen was hardly a likely suspect, either. Too passive, and it would draw attention to him just as he planned to steal the designs.

He mulled the insane hash over his university records. How could they get so fouled up?

Wrong. Not hash. Hack.

The guy who fled from Owen's apartment on the bike? The roommate. Yes. Find him.

Otherwise, you'll go back to America a fugitive, just like Father.

"Just like Father," he murmured. That, he could not tolerate.

By the time he detrained near the airport he had worked out a plan.

Owen's roommate had his own plan.

He finished tightening the jib on his sloop as it floated idly at the Atlantic shoreline a few miles north of the Cliffs of Moher. He jumped off the deck onto the dock and looked at the fine teak planks of the hull, shining like a dark mirror. He smiled at two girls who walked by admiring his boat. Too bad his plans meant he wouldn't have time to nail them today.

Owen had told him he'd never persuade Thomas to come on board, that his seasickness would make him refuse, but he knew better. He'd always been able to convince the twit to do pretty much anything. The man was just plain naïve.

Pure-hearted people gave him a pain, and Thomas was at the top of the list. He was proving to be even more so than normal, lately. The man had more lives than a Hindu. This time, though, he'd finish the job.

He checked the engine to ensure it was in perfect working order. He tested all four life vests, first tugging on the straps, then floating each one for a few minutes. The sails were all flawless, and he had performed thorough maintenance on the gear the day before.

As he performed each test, he made a big show of it. That way someone from one of the nearby boats could testify later, if need be. They would say he had taken every normal precaution.

When he finished with the safety checklist, he went to the store to stock up on supplies. The trip he planned would take no more than twenty minutes, but the bus ride from Shannon took an hour. He wanted to make sure his passengers were fresh, relaxed, and well fed. Fatigue caused more than one sailor to fall overboard. He might be blamed for any accident on board.

He strutted down the street, smiling at his ability to cover every contingency.

Once he had Thomas atop the castle near the cliff, it would be a different story.

His boss might be wary at first, despite his naïve nature. The putz was unpredictable. Thomas had asked him to adjust a coil setting in the lab one day. He made a trivial mistake. You'd have thought he punched in a nuclear attack code by the way he reacted.

He knew how to relax him, though. Thomas had a weak spot for seaside geology and he was fascinated by sea life.

Owen would guide him around the castle for a while, waiting until he dropped his guard. They would approach the edge that looked out over the Atlantic Ocean. Owen would offer him binoculars to get a better look at the puffins at Hag's Head. Then, with one heave, it'd be into the drink with the giant sharks a hundred feet below.

Terri arrived home in a bout of black thoughts more gloomy than Thomas'. Da was gone, for always. Despite what she had said, in her heart she knew that. There was no way he could've sailed through that storm alone, and he would never let a criminal loose to help him. He'd die first.

She moped into the bathroom, feeling guilty for scolding Thomas for the same attitude. She pulled her shoulders back to fight it and turned on the shower, then soaked under the spray for a long time. She emerged feeling at least semi-human again. Unable to think, feel, or walk another step, she plopped down on the bed for a long nap.

She woke up hours later when the front door opened and closed. She rushed out of the bedroom, heedless of her partial state of dress, a T-shirt and underwear.

Arwel stood before her, bedraggled but looking uninjured. She rushed into his arms and stayed there until her tears forced a choice between a tissue and her sleeve.

She sat at the foot of his favorite chair and patted the seat with her hand. When he sat, she hugged his leg for a moment, then looked up to ask, "Can I fix you some tea, Da? Are you hungry? Then you can tell me how you made it home."

He shook his head. "I had something on the way. I just want a shower and to rest a while." Then he turned all business. "Do you know where I might find Thomas?"

In truth, she didn't; still, the question rankled. She couldn't believe he would still be after Thomas after he had, in effect, saved his life against James. But she was too happy to start a row. She shook her head. "How did you get off the island?"

His face grew dark, half-ashamed at the memory. "To tell the truth, I'm not sure. I'd planned to weather it." He lit his pipe, then went on. "Then I was struck from behind and that's the last thing I knew until I woke up in the cabin with the boat docked at Oban."

"Thomas's father, do you suppose?"

He shook his head. "He was trussed up pretty well when the storm started, as I hazily recall." He puffed with the expression he bore when confronted by a puzzle. "Nice ship she was, too. Teak hull. DI Bedwyr is tracing the registration."

Her own expression grew as dark as his. "So James didn't kill that boy at the cave."

Arwel laughed, feeling himself return to normal. "That's quite a leap, daughter. What brought that to mind? And why do you think so?"

"Da, please don't question me now. Just this once, let me slide."

Arwel was about to bray that no one slides in his home. Looking at her wet face, tears sliding from cheek to jowl, he didn't have the heart. "All right, my little cactus."

He held her in his lap and they stayed still for a long time, not talking. Then he eased her onto the seat and went into the bathroom to shower and shave.

"Little cactus," she echoed softly, smiling and wiping her tears on her T-shirt sleeve. He hadn't called her that in many years. She dried her face, then pulled her hair back in a ponytail and tied it. She thought about what had happened on Staffa.

Despite her father's gentle mockery, she was convinced the man on the hill was the one who'd started all of Thomas's troubles. She had no hard proof, but it stood to reason.

Someone sent Thomas the message and he was the last man on the island, still there a half-hour after the final ferry left. He was almost surely waiting for Thomas. She'd caught a glimpse of him checking out his boat through binoculars. And who else was around to bash her father over the head? But why had he left the island before Thomas arrived? Not least, who was he?

She was still struggling with questions when she heard Arwel leave his bedroom. She padded down the hallway to her own. She slipped on fresh clothes, then walked into the kitchen to find him preparing her favorite dish: shepherd's pie.

When he looked up from the stove, she said, "Da, I've got some things to tell you."

Thomas arrived in Shannon and prepared to board the bus to Doolin a few minutes later, to be followed by a short trip south to the Cliffs of Moher. He looked around at the Irish landscape, wishing he had time for a holiday. His purpose now was considerably grimmer.

He'd sent an email in care of Owen addressed to his roommate. He hadn't worked out all the details, but he was sure now the man was responsible for Carl's death.

The note hadn't been from his father. The style didn't match, and he could always tell when James lied.

That left someone else as responsible for his troubles. The list was short. The only other people in the UK who knew him were members of the Four-C. That narrowed the field to five men and one woman. Owen's roommate floated again to the top of the list.

To confirm his theory, he'd asked Rhys to find the origin of the email inviting him to meet on Staffa. The data put it within Owen's apartment. Thomas thought he knew now who shared it with him. A face-to-face meeting seemed the best way to flush him out.

Thomas boarded the bus to the Irish coast and sat behind a woman who acted as if she recognized him. He wished he had a magazine to hide his face. It seemed counterproductive to ask for the one sitting on the empty space beside her.

After she stared at him briefly for the second time, not smiling, he wondered if his photo was in it. When she did it again, he got the idea to check some websites.

He snooped over her seat again to find out which magazine was beside her, but it was now firmly squished between her thigh and the side of the bus. He dropped a coin in the aisle, hoping she would move aside and pick it up. A young boy in the seat ahead turned at the noise and glommed onto it in a flash.

Thomas swiveled to see if anyone could be solicited to get it for him. Seeing their faces, he gave up the idea. It would make him look odd, raising their curiosity. Finally, he thought to get the attention of the elderly woman across the aisle from her. "Excuse me, but aren't you Siobhan McKenna?" he asked, naming the only Irish actress he knew.

"Doubtful, young man," the woman said stiffly. "She died years ago."

Thomas nodded sheepishly. "My mistake," he said to her. "Beg your pardon." He leaned back in his seat, dejected.

It worked anyway. The woman in front of him turned toward her out of curiosity. She tilted left just enough to free up the paper. He reached over the seat back quickly and flipped it open, exposing the table of contents. He sat back down before she knew what was happening.

He looked up the publication's website. He found no mention of him and no picture, as he should've expected. There was little reason for an Irish zine to carry a story about a common incident in Wales, and he hadn't been indicted anyway.

That left him wondering why this woman continued to take such an interest in him. She certainly didn't look like an undercover policewoman. That might be exactly why she was chosen for the assignment, though. If so, she was being oddly obvious. Or, was that another clever police tactic?

"Stop it," he muttered to himself. "You're being paranoid."

"Pardon me?" the woman said, swiveling around for a fourth time. She stayed facing him this time.

"Nothing. Sorry." He tried to ignore her as he searched several other online papers for news of the murder, out of curiosity. Odd it didn't appear in any of them.

He could feel the woman continuing to stare at him. He glanced up uneasily then down again, increasingly uncomfortable at her relentless attention.

The woman finally smiled, showing big buck teeth. "Excuse me," she said breathlessly, "aren't you Dr. Thomas Payne, professor of physics at the University of Virginia?"

He froze with a deer-in-the-headlights look. Should he lie? She seemed very sure, and lying would raise suspicion. He pretended to look at the view out the window for a few seconds, stalling for time. "Y-Y-Yes," he stammered finally. He tried to swallow but his mouth was dry.

She expanded her toothy smile. "I was sure of it. I saw you at a magnet design conference at Dartmouth two years ago. You were working then on something very interesting involving wireless power transfer, if I recall rightly. How did that work out?"

Whew. A physics groupie. "Great, great. I've made a lot of progress." He didn't want to tell her he'd solved the problem completely and was poised to become bloody rich as a result. She would pepper him with questions.

"First rate. Perhaps you'd be kind enough to provide me a reference to your latest paper. I'd love to read up."

Thomas smiled, relieved. "Certainly."

He emailed her a link to a year-old journal paper, before he had stopped publishing on the subject. She became engrossed and he felt relieved.

A few minutes later, she interrupted her reading long enough to invite him to supper. Noting her expression, he declined in a rude tone. She turned sour and left him alone the rest of the trip.

He stepped off the bus in Doolin ten minutes later, hoping to see Owen's roommate on his motorcycle. Instead, he saw Owen himself, waiting for him with no transportation in sight. He frowned. "Where's your roommate?"

"He'll meet us a him few miles south of here, at the shore."

Owen walked ahead toward the Moped rental shop.

Arrangements made, Thomas said, "Well, shall we go? I'm eager to meet your roommate. He promised me some information about the accident at Dan-yr-Ogof."

Owen reacted too slowly to fully mask his surprise. He had wondered what pretext was used to lure Thomas to the Cliffs.

Owen led him on a long ride across the southwestern edge of The Burren in County Clare, an unearthly environment in places, half-moonscape, half-lush greenery. He dipped into his backpack from time to time and pulled out a bottle that Thomas suspected held Ouzo. It was as clear as water but showed an oily swirl around the surface.

It didn't bother him. He couldn't think of any faster way for Owen to kill himself in this blast-furnace heat.

Arriving at the shoreline, Owen jumped onto a boat, grabbed a piece of paper off the side of the cabin and said, "We're to meet him at Hag's Head," He leaned over the gunwale and handed the paper to Thomas.

Just then, Terri and Rhys drove up in Arwel's car. They bounded up and Terri kissed Thomas on the cheek. Owen looked afraid and angry at once. Rhys smirked at him.

Thomas said, "What the he–"

Terri interrupted, "My father, of course. You didn't think you could go anywhere without him knowing did you?" When he started to object she added, "We're here to help. Just accept it."

Thomas sighed. "Fine. Let's go."

They all boarded. Thomas strode into the wheel house and flipped on the engine. He was too impatient to bother with unfurling the canvas for a trip of scarcely a mile.

Terri soon joined him. "Are you alright? You look green." He bobbed a curt nod and she went on. "What do you think we'll find at Hag's Head?"

He looked at her with a determined expression. "Some answers."

Shortly, they neared their destination and Thomas cut the engine, looking for a place to drop anchor. A few yards farther out, where the water went deep very quickly, he could see the dorsal fins of two giant sharks.

Thomas drew the board at close to the shore as possible then jumped into the water. The others followed, reaching the sand in a few seconds, Owen bringing up the rear.

Owen assessed the area, seeing clumps of tourists here and there. He looked for Moher Tower and led them in its direction.

If he could get Thomas to hike to the top alone the rest would be easy. The crowd concentrated on the view, the Cliffs, and the Atlantic Ocean beyond. Whether anyone discovered the body didn't matter.

If this worked out, his roommate would owe him big time. It didn't hurt that Thomas wouldn't be able to give evidence about the theft, either. Rhys, he could deal with later. The trick was, how to get that myrmidon away from Thomas at the crucial moment.

He looked behind, seeing him chatting up that frigid growler — a small iceberg — Terri. He smiled when the idea came to him how to accomplish the deed.

Terri caught up to Thomas and asked, "So now what?"

He said, his voice low, "Can't even guess. I just hope the trip hasn't been wasted."

They soon reached the bottom of the tower near the main cliff. It rose several dozen yards above the ground, straight and severe and crumbling.

Owen said, "Thomas, follow me." He slunk through the entrance and mounted the first stone step to the top. As he expected, Rhys was right behind them.

Owen stepped aside, and let Thomas continue on a few steps ahead. He whispered to Rhys, "You should stay here."

"Nothing doing."

Prepared for the response, Owen wagged his double chin in Terri's direction, standing a few feet away. He whispered, "If you stay here with her, you can feel her up while Thomas is chatting with my roommate."

It was a laughably transparent ploy to separate them. So obvious, in fact, it would be useful to find out what he planned.

Rhys looked over at Terri and said in a low voice, "Yeah, that idea is kind of appealing." He said loudly to her, "We have to wait down here. Owen's roommate doesn't feel comfortable talking around a cop's daughter."

Thomas heard the last two words and turned around. His expression mirrored hers: a mixture of outrage, contempt, and disbelief. Owen's roommate must think him incredibly stupid. An instant's thought told him it *would* be best if she were out of harm's way.

Terri started to say something when Thomas interrupted, his voice impatient, "Fine. Let's go Owen. I want to get this over with."

Owen and Thomas mounted the flights of steps as fast as the first could carry his bulk up them. Thomas's curiosity sped him onward. As he rose, he tried to guess what they had in mind.

They couldn't believe they could overpower him and toss him off a rampart. One of them must have a weapon. But they wouldn't risk the noise of a gunshot, and he felt confident he could handle anything else. Ironic that there turned out to be one advantage to being James Paine's son.

He peered furtively around every turn before committing himself to rise onto the next flight of steps. He kept Owen in his peripheral vision every second.

They were one flight from the top when the first open window appeared in the Napoleonic-era structure. If it had ever held glass, it was long gone, not even a trace of shards at the base. He could see the bay not far away, far below.

He hugged the inner wall, bracing himself, trying to see ahead and hear behind. He kept two steps ahead of Owen to give himself time to react, ready for anything. A few strides later, he could see open sky at the top of the stairs.

Thomas emerged from the stairwell and swept his view at top speed around the entire 360 degrees. The roof was vacant and there wasn't so much as a piece of gravel to hide behind.

He said, "What gives?"

He turned to see a tire iron swooping down, aimed at his skull. He ducked, just in time.

Owen advanced on him as he backed away at a fast clip. Thomas soon ran out of room to retreat. Owen swished the tire iron back and forth like the Black Knight birring a mace in a duel. The sound was like a swarm of hornets, the sight just as menacing.

Off to one side, Thomas could see the ocean below. It seemed his only escape from the flashing piece of iron. With luck he could make the plunge and still come out alive.

He prepared to hop backwards onto the knee-high ledge, ready to turn and jump the instant the slashing metal rod reached its lowest point.

Thomas jumped onto the stone and at the same time heard Terri scream, "No!"

Owen froze and she rushed forward, making it halfway to the pair before he could raise the weapon again. Thomas used the pause to jump down and clamp his wrist.

Terri reached them, hot to scratch Owen's eyes out, then smash his face onto the stone ledge.

Owen wrenched his hand free to strike Thomas, sure he could take care of her right after. It caused him to bump Terri with his arm.

She fell past him and tripped on the ledge, then hurtled into space, a powder blue sky above, the inky ocean below.

16

*T*HOMAS looked down in horror for one compressed instant, then whirled back to Owen and smashed his face so hard the crack of his jawbone could be heard at the base of the tower.

Owen wilted like a bag of liquid shit.

Rhys rushed forward from the top step. He peered over the edge and saw Terri floating in the water below. "Look, she's waving. She's alive!"

Thomas' gaze followed Rhys' finger. Seeing her move was such a relief he had to support himself with the wall. Then he shoved himself upright, planning to rush down the steps and plunge into the water.

Rhys held him back by the shoulders, urging him to look again. "What's that in the water?"

Thomas looked down again, squinting. He thought he could make out the gray hump of a shark ten feet from Terri's swirling form. He tore free from Rhys's grip and rocketed down the steps, touching only every third stone. He reached the bottom and sprinted to the water's edge, dodging tourists frozen in shock.

"Where is she? Where is she?" he shouted to the crowd.

"It took her under," a young boy said, his face a cartoonish mask of disbelief. He had never seen anyone die before, much less that way. "That's the biggest shark I've ever seen, even in the movies. It's gotta be 30 feet!"

Thomas plunged into the water anyway, but two men near the shore rushed after him and dragged him back. "That's starkers, mate," one of them wailed. "You'll just get yourself killed as well, and for nothin'."

Thomas struggled to break free, but they were determined not to let him try again. It took the help of a third man pushing from behind to force him away from the waterline. They shoved him down onto a bench at the base of the tower and stood in a semi-circle in front of him, watching intently should he try to bolt again for the ocean.

After a minute, Rhys joined them. "Let me through. I'm his friend," he said, urging them aside. He put his arm around Thomas' shoulder as his friend wept. He looked up at the three men. "It's okay, mates, thanks. He won't try it again. I'll see to that."

Rhys looked fixedly at the water, wishing without hope that Terri would reappear like Venus reborn from the waves.

Thomas slumped, his eyes lifeless gray pearls, hearing none of the talk around him. His hands rested limply on the bench, palms up. He couldn't even muster the will to hate the men who had held him back. That would come later.

A sea bird landed on his hand and pecked at bits of insect-covered seaweed stuck to his finger, drawing blood. He made no effort to shoo it away, unaware it was even there.

The sun's rays had tilted into his eyes, his sightless stare still directed seaward. Some time later he could feel a tap on his shoulder. It might have been the first tap or the tenth, he didn't know. His eyes swiveled up to find Arwel staring down at him.

"Thomas, come with me," Arwel said.

Thomas made an effort to recognize the face. "Owen Caldicott killed Terri. His roommate helped him. Just like he killed the man at the cave."

"I know Mr. Caldicott's roommate did not kill Thomas Payne at Dan-yr-Ogof."

So, he still doesn't believe I am who I say. Well, what does it matter. What did he say? Wait. It could be taken two different ways. "What do you mean?"

"Please come with me." Arwel moped off in the direction of his car without looking behind, trusting Thomas to follow.

Thomas stood up and shuffled behind Arwel like an autistic puppy. He didn't know where he was headed — home, jail, or back to Arwel's house — and could not have cared less which it was.

Arwel deposited Thomas in the Brecon jail that evening for his own safety.

Terri had convinced him there was more to the case than he'd originally thought. But releasing the man on his own recognizance just now might result in his suicide. He couldn't have that, no matter how much sympathy he felt.

As Arwel looked down at the hunched figure, it was hard even for a callous old warhorse like him to leave Thomas there. But the staff could watch him much better, and he had things to do. James Paine was still on the loose.

"Not for long," he swore aloud, and walked out without a word to anybody. It took an effort greater than he'd ever exerted not to lapse into passivity by the thought of his daughter's death. But he had his duty to perform, and doing it was the best way he knew to avenge her.

The next morning, he entered the cell area and saw Thomas in the same position as when he'd left. "Are you ready to talk to me, yet, son?" Arwel asked him, his voice gentle.

For once, he felt Thomas and he had something in common. Thinking of what it was, he fought back a tear. Failing, he turned his face aside for a moment, wiped it off, and turned back to his prisoner.

Thomas looked at him glassy-eyed for a long time, then eked out, "About what, sir? She's gone." There didn't seem to be anything worth discussing.

Arwel shook his head, irked. "Look, man, can you pull yourself out of it long enough to imagine how I must feel?" He dropped his hands limply to his sides, as if the loss made them too heavy to lift. "You knew her a few days. I loved her all her life." His voice was as heavy as his hands.

That worked. The glassy eyes focused to polished lenses. "I'm very sorry. Ask me anything you want. I'll answer as best I can."

Arwel pulled a chair up in front of the cell and unlocked the door to make Thomas feel less a prisoner. He plopped down on the backwards-facing chair, all discipline gone. Coatless, he rolled up his sleeves and leaned in, looking like a detective from one of the old films Thomas enjoyed. "First, tell me who led you to Moher."

"Owen Caldicott, the computer technician who worked for me until a few days ago."

"I'm familiar. Quit or fired?"

"Suspended, pending a review. He got sticky fingered with some important designs of mine."

"Of yours — if it turns out you really are Dr. Thomas Payne."

"Sir, if you don't believe that by now, I can't think what would convince you."

"There's been no new evidence to change my view one way or the other on that subject." He paused to let Thomas offer some. When he didn't, he prompted him. "Has there?"

That attitude, Thomas understood. He was equally stubborn about facts, not speculation. But he also understood the need to make a hypothesis to knit all the facts together. None other fit. If he could just think clearly enough to put it all together for the detective.

He forced himself to clarity. "Inspector Mawr, I went to Ireland for the express purpose of getting that evidence. Terri told me you sent her to Shannon. Why would you do that if you didn't already half-believe me?"

At the mention of her name, Arwel's expression became unsympathetic and Thomas knew he'd made a mistake. He rushed on. "Even without that, there's been plenty to make even you wonder." Arwel's expression grew softer.

Thomas weighed what to do next. He was oh-for-three, and it was now clear he couldn't do this without Arwel's help. He laid out in detail what had happened to him the several days past.

Arwel listened patiently, storing each fact away to fit into his own version of events. It was consistent with what Terri had told him, and Thomas offered several points she hadn't. He'd heard enough to instill reasonable doubt about the murder.

He wasn't yet sure who this man really was, though. Children needn't be like their fathers; Terri, rest her soul, was proof enough of that. But his every instinct told him this fellow simply couldn't be James Paine's son.

Turning him over to the immigration authorities would not help his investigation. He would have to find a way to stall them. That raised the question of where to stash him. Keeping him at the Brecon jail upped the odds of immigration finding him.

"You're coming home with me," he said, an order, not an offer.

Thomas started to protest.

Arwel put up a hand to silence him. "If you're going to grieve, you might as well do it where I can keep an eye on you." He rolled down his sleeves and slipped on his jacket. "Anyway, it wasn't an invitation. You're still legally in my custody."

Thomas wasn't fooled by the gruff tone. He knew generosity when he saw it.

He rose and trundled after Arwel, making an effort to keep his shoulders from stooping. On the way out, he remembered something. He said, "You never did tell me why you thought Owen's roommate was not the killer."

Arwel hid his smile. It was the first sign that Thomas was coming back to life. As the younger man passed through the station exit ahead of him, he said, "Now, that's not exactly what I said, is it?"

Terri crawled ashore a quarter mile from where she fell into the water. She was tired, but not harmed. She was used to making even higher dives in competition. Still, she was lucky the cliffs at that point were much lower than Moher's maximum; her knees hurt like mad. After dodging the giant basking shark, she'd swum to the surface following a strong riptide. She'd emerged far from all the shouting.

She rolled over on the sand and closed her eyes against the sun, resting for several minutes while she caught her breath, her chest heaving up and down. When she opened her eyes again, she wondered for a moment if it might not have been better had she drowned.

Owen loomed over her, eyes wide, riveted by the rising and falling of her rib cage.

She was about to kick him in the groin when he pulled out a gun. It seemed such a cliché she had to laugh. Then, seeing his glassy-eyed expression, she grew sober. "How did you find me?"

His jaw was massively sore from Thomas's punch and he didn't answer. He pointed at the bluff above them where his bicycle stood on the ridge.

Terri rolled over, ready to hurl herself at him when he stepped back.

"Unh, unh," he grunted and looked around at the deserted strip of beach. He waved the gun, gesturing for her to stand up.

Terri pulled herself upright, trying covertly to unglue her wet shirt from her skin. She shimmied up to sit on her knees and said, "You'll *have* to shoot me to get what you want, duffer." She added mockingly, "You'd be just as happy porking me after I was dead anyway, no?"

He kicked her temple hard and she went out like a light clicked off in a darkroom. Dull red faded to deep black before her head hit the sand.

When she woke up again, she was in a small cabin, lying on a bed with one wrist handcuffed to a sturdy wooden post. She could hear seabirds chirping outside as morning light streamed in through the window.

It made no sense. She couldn't have been knocked out that long from any kick that didn't kill her. She felt groggy and checked her arm. A brief search revealed a small red puncture wound, no doubt from a syringe's needle.

She checked herself, relieved her insult about screwing her dead body hadn't been accurate. But it made her wonder what he was waiting for. She stiffened, trying not to lose her clarity to disabling fear. She would need her wits.

She canvassed the cabin, searching for the fastest way out once she conned him into removing the handcuffs. There was a small window, but still large enough to jump out. It was closed, so she'd have to take her chances with the glass. There wouldn't be time to open it.

She heard sizzling sounds emanating from the kitchenette and the smell made her hungry against her will. She watched as Owen put a plate filled with ham and eggs onto a table near her cot. She studied his expression; it said she was his next meal.

"Eat," he grunted, scooting her plate closer.

She was about to refuse on general principle, but quickly changed her mind. If she was eating, he wouldn't try any funny business. She dragged the cot toward the table, finding that she'd sprained an ankle. Luckily, her knees felt much better.

She remembered how the sprain happened as she dug into the food. She had entered the water a few feet from a huge basking shark, a typical 30-footer. She hadn't been afraid. They were harmless, unless they swallowed you by accident as they filtered the water for plankton.

She had pushed off the face of the gentle monster just to get out of its way. Her foot hit it at a bad angle and she almost swallowed water yelping. The pain made one leg much less efficient for swimming. By the time she reached the shoreline, she was exhausted.

Onshore, bad luck changed to worse.

The worse luck returned to the dining area with his plate, the pistol in his waistband. He wasn't taking any chances. He sat at the other end of the table, too far away to grab the gun before he could react. He kept his grisly eyes on her while he shoveled his food.

The pain in his jaw had subsided enough to mumble, thanks in part to the vodka he swigged every few minutes. He said, his voice like nails on a chalkboard, "Cooperate and it'll go easy for you. Fight and you won't be able to sit down for days."

She looked mocking. "Wouldn't a little boy be more your speed?"

"Vexing me won't work, bitch," he said.

"Owen, I promise you, one of us will be dead long before you get truly pissed off."

He tittered, dribbling some food down his chin. He wiped it off by brushing his jaw over a shoulder. He winced. "Spunky. Super. Best eat your breakfast and figure how to cosh me before the fun starts."

Terri turned to her food and proceeded to do just that.

Thomas and Arwel sat across from one another at the dining table. Arwel had just downed a small portion of re-heated shepherd's pie, trying hard to keep his eyes from misting up. It was the leftovers of what he had made for Terri only a few days earlier. Thomas hadn't touched his food at all.

"Man, you've got to eat. You can't afford to get ill now."

Eating seemed like too much trouble, but he could never brush aside a gesture kindly meant. He forced himself to put a bite into his mouth and chewed languidly, then put the fork down.

He didn't pick it up again for several silent minutes. Arwel was about to encourage him some more when there was a knock at the door. He rose to answer it. Rhys stood on the porch, a sheepish look on his face. "Can I see Thomas, Inspector Mawr?"

"Come in." He wasn't happy to see Rhys and showed it. It brought home how the boy failed to keep his daughter from harm, like he promised. But there was still a job to do and this young man was part of the solution, he felt sure.

Rhys stepped in and before making his way to Thomas said, "I'm terribly, terribly sorry, sir, about Terri. If there was anything I could've done—"

Arwel stopped him, not in the mood to forgive. "Thomas is in the dining room," he said, pointing in that direction. He stuffed his feelings down and waited for Rhys to move.

Rhys preceded Arwel through the living room, cluttered with clothes and papers for the first time ever. He sat down and reached across the table to rest his hand on his friend's forearm.

They sat without talking for a long time as Arwel watched them from the other end of the table. Scientists had always been a mystery to him, and he disliked a puzzle he couldn't solve. But he understood deep friendship. At that moment, he envied them, having someone to share their grief with.

He held out the bowl of shepherd's pie and said, "Mr. Anarawd, would you care for some supper?"

Rhys wasn't hungry but he took it anyway, grateful for the gesture. He ate a few bites, then said what he'd come to say. "You've got a job to finish, Thomas."

"You can do that. The prototype is done."

Rhys looked confused for a moment, then said, "I didn't mean the power system. I meant finding Terri's killer."

Arwel changed in a blink from sympathizer to police inspector. "Here, here, boy, don't get carried away. Finding killers is no work for amateurs." He leaned in, his expression threatening. "You have information, pony it up. Otherwise, keep your nose out of police business."

Thomas was roused. "Sir, I appreciate your hospitality, but you have to know that we can't let it rest with the authorities."

"And why not?" he asked, clanking down his spoon. "I ask only to satisfy my curiosity." He picked up his pipe and lit it. "You able to do something I can't, young man?"

Thomas wasn't about to get tangled up with Inspector Mawr's professional pride. Arwel was interested in doing his job. He, by contrast, had to avenge Terri and recapture his identity. He was convinced the same man had taken both from him.

He looked at Arwel straight on and said, "No sir, there's nothing you can't do that I can, I'm sure. But there are things I *will* do that you won't."

Arwel rose from his chair and towered over Thomas, tapping his pipe on a plate. "That sounds ominous, lad. Say more and I'll be duty-bound to put you back in lock-up."

Rhys put an arm between them and said, "Please, Mr. Mawr, let me talk to him alone. I'll get him to see reason."

Arwel looked at Rhys, guessing what he had in mind, and snuffed a smile. Did the man really think someone with his experience would be that naïve?

Still, it would get him off the hook with the Council. They were pressuring him to lock Thomas away and call immigration. "Charge him or deport him," the Mayor had said. "With this fellow on the loose, there's too much angst about town to suit me."

Arwel picked up the dishes and went into the kitchen, closing the dining room door behind him, pretending to give them privacy. He turned on the tap, hoping they'd believe he was washing up. He crept to the dining room door and listened to the two men talk in low voices. Through the crack, he could see some papers in front of Rhys.

"Aren't you at all curious about your past?" Rhys asked.

"No, my present is who I am. Your identity is whoever you choose to be, not who your parents were."

"But as a scientist, you know that prior events influence it, and the future."

"In physics, yes. In people, not necessarily."

"Thomas, you can use this to convince them of your real identity."

Thomas shook his head. "You know they wouldn't even convince *him*." He wiggled a thumb toward the kitchen.

Rhys paced alongside the table. After a few cycles he stopped and leaned over the table, his face close to Thomas's. "We drive to London tonight. You know where the Friends congregate. We talk to the clerk at the library. He asks the elders to testify. Persuade them, they persuade the police."

"How could they do that?"

"Who but you would know *this*," he pointed to a paragraph, "about James Paine?"

Arwel saw Rhys shove the sheaf of papers across the table to Thomas.

Thomas didn't pick them up, but he did dip his chin and skim the text. Unable to help himself, he flipped to the next page. "Where did you get this?"

"From Terri. She gave it to me when she came over to ask me to go to Moher."

Thomas read it over again, then huffed, "It's all nonsense. How could they know any of this?"

"You know the Quakers. Devoted to historical truth in every detail."

Arwel saw Thomas rivet Rhys with his eyes for a long moment, then get up from the table, fold the papers, and tuck them into his pocket.

Thomas quietly put on his coat as he headed for the door. He looked back and said, his voice soft and devoid of any pleading, "Are you coming?"

Rhys smiled and said, "Try to stop me."

After they left, Arwel smiled while clearing the rest of the dishes. He washed and dried them, then ambled to the phone. He pressed the number for Sergeant Bevan and said, "I may be gone from the station for a day or two. Don't tell anyone unless you have to."

On the evening of Terri's captivity, Owen received two visitors. She could hear the annoyance in his voice as he spoke to them at the door, which obscured their bodies.

Whoever they were, the men had interrupted his plan to wait for dark to rape her. It amused him to have a nice long nap following a leisurely supper before getting started. But the pair had wakened him early, and he was grumpy.

They stepped just inside the door. One stood in shadow near the front door. She was still cuffed to the bed and denied a better look at him. She didn't dare drag it closer.

When he saw someone with Owen in the cabin, he was careful to stay turned away. He was tall, that she could tell.

The companion was James Paine, whom she recognized from the photo in the Quaker family tree album. He had aged by, she guessed, about thirty years, but there was no mistaking that dybbuk's face.

She strained to overhear what they were saying, with partial success. "Roommate" stuck out, along with "Staffa." She heard enough to suspect he was the man she was looking for. When she heard the tall one chortle, "the jerk smashed into jelly at Dan-yr-Ogof," she was certain.

Her heart pounded, and she wrapped the thin blanket covering her nakedness around her tighter. She tried again to slip her hand out of the cuff.

On his way out, the tall man said clearly, as if he wanted her to hear, "I'll be back there day after tomorrow. You be done with your sport by then. I expect you to meet me."

Then they both left, James glancing in her direction for the briefest of moments.

Owen moved to stand near her and said, "I guess you can't expect to leave here now. Can't have you telling your Da 'bout us, can we?"

She inched as close to him as she could. She whispered, "Owen, it's very satisfying to have you here, right where I want you." She smiled at his mystified look, her eyes bright and maniacal. "If you leave, your roommate would have help hurting Thomas. Can't have that, can we?"

He leaned over and tugged playfully at her blanket, ready to begin his evil, his teeth reminding her of the shark she had escaped. She kicked at his face with her good foot, but he dodged and she made contact with his shoulder instead.

The blow knocked him back against the wall He rubbed his shoulder blade for a moment, then advanced toward her, unzipping his fly.

Suddenly, the cabin door slammed open and James Paine stepped into the room.

17

THOMAS was driving Terri's car toward London when Rhys received a text message. He read it, then angled his phone so Thomas could see the screen without taking his eyes off the road. Thomas skimmed it and said, "You've got to be kidding. Does he seriously think we'll go there?"

"I think we should," Rhys insisted.

"Why? It's a big detour."

"He doesn't just make a vague promise of information, like Staffa. He gives the exact position of Carl, the killer, and you at the time of Carl's death."

"How is that any use?"

The road signs whisked past as Thomas pressed the gas pedal even farther, exceeding the speed limit by 20 miles per hour. He checked the side of the road, then the rearview mirror, for anything resembling a police car.

Rhys had had to persuade him to go to London. After accepting his reasoning, now he was in a hurry to get there. He noted the time. The only place he was likely to find a group of Friends at this hour would probably be closed, unless he could reach it in twenty minutes. Even at this speed, it would take eighteen.

Rhys scrolled down the text on his screen. "He goes on to describe the sequence of events in detail." The glow from the display showed his animated face. "If we can validate who this came from, it might constitute a confession."

Thomas removed his hand from the gearshift knob and took the phone from Rhys. He looked ahead at the road to check for any upcoming stops, then slowed down enough to study the message. His face grew grim when he saw that the note was allegedly from his father.

He tossed the phone back to Rhys. "Been there, done that. There's no way to know if it's really him. And he doesn't really say who killed Carl. Useless." He punched the gas pedal again.

"There's one way to find out. Go to Sherkin Friary and meet him. He says he'll have the killer with him."

Thomas's first impulse was to hang his father rather than take help from him. He waited long enough to let the feeling pass, to gain some objectivity, then said, "Even assuming it's him, I have no reason to trust him."

Rhys said, "What if he really does want you alive and wed and producing babies?"

Thomas huffed. "Why should he care after all this time?" The last time his father had helped him was when he gave him the ancient science kit.

He had never understood why his father had been so eager for him to have it. He never before or after showed any interest in encouraging him.

Rhys read the postscript. "He says he's dying. He wants to see his line continue. That's a pretty powerful impulse, even for the devil."

Thomas burst out laughing, a dark, ugly sound. "The devil doesn't reproduce, Rhys. He just captures new souls. Looks like he's about to rope yours with another one of his lies."

He tried to remember if James had ever told him the truth on anything important. He came up blank. He did remember his father had insisted family was the only thing you could trust, that in the end it was the tie that never burst.

Rhys pressed the point. "Your soul isn't at any risk. You can afford a detour to find out. To put all this behind you. Can't you?"

He debated the choice, his temples deeply creased with thought: London to establish his identity, or Sherkin Island to catch the thief who stole it? He waffled only seconds, then whipped the Austin around on the two-lane road. "Bring up a map and point me toward the nearest ferry embarkation point to Cork."

Rhys brought up the map without arguing, then said, "I'd better drive."

Thomas clutched the wheel and shook his head in a definite "No."

Rhys shook his own head, adding an audible snort. "Fine. Head southwest, then take the M4 toward Swansea."

James approached Owen, who let go at once of Terri's blanket and backed up toward the cabin wall.

"What have you in mind here, friend?" James asked, his voice low and menacing. Events had changed his mind about Terri's fate. With Owen poised to obscure his future grandchild's paternity, James's face lost its usual cool blankness. It was replaced by a terrifying sneer. The ambiance of violence in his posture was unmistakable.

Owen was frightened. James had agreed to help him arrange this long before. Why didn't he object then? "Would you like a piece first?" he said, trying to smile casually.

James reached a hand toward her and she shrunk back. He chuckled as she scooted away, amused by her failed efforts to keep the coverlet over her top. He reached toward the blanket, as if to pull it off entirely, then moved past, to the bedpost. His granite hand busted the knob off the top, freeing her. The freed handcuff dangled off the chain.

Terri looked at it, then back at him, mystified.

Owen looked at what he'd done and cried, "Hey, what's up?"

James said, "Well, you weren't contemplating taking her that way, were you, boy? No fun if she can't squirm." He whirled around behind her and clasped her hair, yanking her head backward, as if to restrain her while Owen took his degenerate pleasure. Then he leaned down and whispered in her ear, "When I move, run."

Terri chanced a glance at the window and readied herself to spring up.

James moved in front of her. "You know, Owen, I've changed my mind. I don't think I'll let you have her after all."

"Eff off, plonker," Owen barked with pretended gusto.

James wagged a crusty finger. "I'm not fond of a gent who's got to take a woman by force. Makes me think he's not a real man."

Owen ran for his gun on the dining room table. James was right behind him.

Terri watched for a split-second as the older but fitter man caught up. Then she grabbed the blanket, ran to the cabin window and crashed through, rolling as she hit the ground, scraping her arms and face before coming up on one knee.

Before running, she paused just long enough to flip a look over her shoulder. She could see the two struggling over the gun. She fantasized for an instant they would kill each other and she could retrieve her clothes. Then reality set in. She ran.

Within ten strides she heard the loud crack of a pistol shot. There were no more. One of them had won on the first round. She heard shouts of her name through the window, but she was already too far away to make out the voice.

She ran blindly, with no idea where she was or where she was headed. She flashed a look at the stars, hoping to get a quick fix on a general direction at least. Too many clouds. She could smell sea air, but it was too diffuse to judge whether it came from her left or right or straight ahead.

After fleeing for a solid minute, she slacked off long enough to see if she was being followed. No longer masked by adrenalin, the pain in her ankle shocked her like the jolt in Thomas' lab. She collapsed on the spot, clutching her foot, her eyes pinched shut.

She took several deep breaths, then opened them to check for any pursuer. She could see little, but heard no one. The sound of a faint breeze brushed her ears; cool air grazed her bare arms. She shivered. She warmed them with her hands while she tried to work out her location.

She couldn't hear waves, putting her at least a mile inland. She heard no cars, so no highway was nearby. Beyond that, she was utterly lost. She could be in Ireland still, or Scotland, or outside the UK entirely for all she knew. The sandy ground and sparse vegetation could belong to any of several countries. She needed more evidence.

The pain subsided enough for her to stand, still clutching the blanket. She limped toward a tree and broke off a branch to use as a walking stick, then moved in a larger circle, trying to orient herself. The clouds parted enough for her to see some familiar constellations and get a direction.

Good, she thought. *Still in the UK.*

She headed north, hoping the cabin was not far from a major road. Even with the walking stick it was slow going. The clouds cleared, helping her steer a course. The moon shone full, helping even more.

Twenty minutes of hobbling brought her to the seashore and an unearthly landscape of basaltic columns: the Giant's Causeway near Bushmills in Northern Ireland. The moonlight made them glow red like Hades' bedchamber. She recognized the place at once and exhaled a sigh of relief.

It would take her about an hour by car to reach Belfast, where she could hop a plane home. She was sure she could find a kind person to loan her a phone to book a flight. If she caught a ride.

A few minutes limping brought her to a familiar motorway, the B17 at Dunluce Manor. She tucked the white coverlet tightly around her, making it look as much as possible like a toga-style gown. It was filthy from the tumble but that couldn't be helped.

To her chagrin, she found it impossible to hitch a ride. In her bedraggled state, her face as dirty as her dress and almost as torn, she was a frightening sight. It was a new experience having men reject her for her appearance. Oddly, it made her feel safe.

She looked around then down at the cuts on her arms, the burn on her knee, and felt the pain in her ankle... and burst out laughing. "Safe" didn't seem to describe her present state. Still, she was out of the worst of it.

She shuffled on down the road, whistling an old Scottish folk tune.

She soon reached a rest station off to the side and stopped in. She clumsily washed the mixture of mud and blood off her face and arms, then straightened her 'gown' as best she could. She brushed her fingers through her hair, then tied it back into a ponytail. Then she hobbled back to the motorway to try again.

Twenty minutes later, she got lucky. An American couple were driving to Belfast for a flight.

Surprising her, they recognized her name, a fond memory from one of her gallery shows. The husband was an art dealer in Philadelphia. She got into the car, full of gratitude.

The woman even insisted she take some of her clothes from a suitcase. She misted up when they forced enough cash on her to get her home.

On the way, they chatted for an hour about her work before arriving at the airport.

Before she boarded the plane, she tried to call Thomas using their phone, but failed. There was no voicemail, not even a recording saying the number wasn't in service. Just ring after ring into dead air.

She was frantic to tell him about the plan Owen's friend had to harm him.

She tried again the minute the plane landed, with the same result. Now she was really beginning to worry. It was a few hours before daybreak, but whatever that guy had in mind would start to take shape before long.

She reluctantly phoned her father and got an equally depressing result. There was a message on the home phone that he would be away for a couple of days. As usual, he didn't answer a strange number to his mobile. She wouldn't call the Brecon police station. One of the men would exaggerate her condition.

As a final resort she called Rhys, but got no answer. He didn't respond to email either. She gave up and boarded the bus.

At home, she tried the front door only to find it locked. No surprise, that. Da was security conscious even in little Brecon, despite the fact that home invasion was about as likely as murder. Then she remembered the incident at Dan-yr-Ogof and chuckled grimly.

She *was* surprised when the hidden key wasn't under the topsoil of the flower pot they kept near the back door. She could see by the pre-dawn light that the earth had been disturbed. Why would Da remove the key?

"Work that out when he comes home," she said with a sigh. Shower, rest, find out where the hell everyone went. In that order.

She looked through the window into her studio. All her sculpture were covered with individual small cloths, like shrouds. What the hell? She went to the tool shed to get a screwdriver to jimmy the window lock.

She had it open in under a minute. She hauled herself through and plopped onto the wood floor. It was immaculate, not a speck of stone dust anywhere. Her father had never before asked Clara to clean her studio. Why now?

She tried to call Thomas and Rhys again, still getting no answer. After a shower and a short meal, she went to bed.

She dozed, but two hours later she was up again, too restless to sleep well. She tried calling Thomas one more time, getting the same mystifying unanswered ring.

She dug out the home phone number of the Brecknock Gallery owner in Brecon, her one remaining friend after four years away in London.

A voice answered on the third ring and replied to her hello with an excited, "Terri! Everyone in town thinks you're dead! Your father, of course, wanted to keep it to himself, but you know Sgt. Bevan."

Terri was stunned. When it wore off a bit, it made sense. Why would they think otherwise? She understood now about the state of her studio. She waited for Becky's babbling to die down, then asked, "Any idea where my father is right now? He's not answering his phone."

"Call the station. They might know."

Terri thanked her and hung up.

She called the police station, getting much the same reaction from Bevan as from Becky. He'd torn the phone away from the duty sergeant when he heard her voice.

After calming down, he answered her thrice-repeated question. "He wouldn't tell me where he was going. Said I should contact him only in emergency. This qualifying, I tried on the other line just now. But he ain't picking up, the blighter."

"So you don't know where he went?"

"Didn't say that, girl. Said he didn't tell me. But I figured it out."

The chest-pounding tone came clearly through the receiver. He described how he ferreted out DCI Mawr's intended route. "Anyway, when he gets back to me, I'll relay the happy news. Tell him to call home."

"Right. Thanks." Making a snap decision, she added, "But I don't know where I'll be either. Just ask him to call my mobile."

She hung up in the middle of his insisting she should stay home. A second later she realized she no longer had a mobile. It was at the bottom of the ocean near Moher. She would pick up a temporary on the way and phone Bevan back later with the number.

She went outside to find her car missing, something she hadn't noticed in her exhaustion when she first arrived. "He couldn't have sold it already." She pondered that a moment, to no avail.

She walked to Thomas's hotel in Brecon, hoping but not really expecting to find him. She used the lobby phone to call his apartment in Cardiff, then the lab. Another washout. She tried his cell phone again. Nothing. She called Rhys again. Zilch. She returned home, more worried than ever.

She sat in her father's big chair, trying to work out where the men in her life, old and new, had gone.

Bevan's blathering was absurd, since her father had absolutely no reason to go to Ireland. Thomas and Rhys both remained unreachable after repeated attempts.

Unable to bear the anxiety any longer, she called the one man who might know where they went: Owen's roommate.

18

"*T*ERRI Mawr," Owen's ex-roommate said, hanging up the phone.

He sat in Owen's apartment swilling a cheap beer mixed with Red Bull. The combined effect made him even more twitchy than usual.

He looked at the Mynah and, when it squawked, he threw a pillow at the cage, knocking it over. He laughed and tossed another at James when he objected.

James said, annoyed, "I got that. Why did you tell her where to find Thomas?"

"Why did you let her go free from the cabin?"

"You don't need to know," James replied hotly. When he didn't get any argument, he added, "You don't really care either way."

He nodded. "Not quite true. Better for me that she did escape. Now I can use her against Thomas."

James flipped his finger back and forth like a metronome. "Best not. She's coming back to the States with me and Thomas."

He laughed and went to sit on the couch. "Too funny. You think Thomas will go anywhere with you? You really think he'll mate with her because you want him to?"

"No. Because *he* wants to. The result is the same. And all I care about."

He listened as James told him his goal. *Bone-chilling daft this git*, the roommate thought. But he already knew better than to say so.

James crept up and stole his phone out of his back pocket. Before he could do more than complain, James was already typing in a message. "Who are you sending that to?" he asked, suspecting the answer and not happy about it.

James scowled. "Thomas." He turned the phone outward, mocking him for being unable to stop him.

He tried to retrieve the phone before James could press send. A backhand like a flying anvil knocked him sideways and down.

He started to rebound off the floor when James wagged his finger again. He thought it best to stay down.

James said, "Never try to put your hands on a man who likes to hurt people. It just gives him leave to indulge his pastime."

The ex-roommate snail-crawled toward the coffee table, pretending to grovel. He was after his Bowie knife inside the drawer.

He watched as James turned away and pressed "Send" on the phone. He slid closer to the coffee table. James swiveled back to see what he was doing. He yanked open the drawer and snatched the knife before James could react.

James launched a kick at his hand and missed. On the second kick, he connected. The blade went flying and the two men flew after it.

On the drive to Pembroke to catch the ferry to Ireland, Thomas and Rhys both remained silent. Trees flew past their vision but neither saw them. The ruins at Carmarthen normally would've engaged Rhys's attention. Now they didn't register at all. Thomas, equally buried in his thoughts, ignored the cable-stayed bridge at the halfway mark on the trip. On a happier day, it would've prompted an excited comment.

Thomas refocused on the road as the first rays of the new day bled over the mountains.

He drove on while Rhys slept. He looked down from time to time at the innocent face of his newfound best friend. He decided he couldn't let Rhys risk himself any further.

A few hours later. he nudged him and said, "We're nearing Baltimore."

He pointed to the distant ferry waiting at the southern tip of Ireland, preparing to leave for Sherkin Island. The beach was within sight across the water, its sands sparkling in the morning sun.

Minutes later, Thomas pulled into a restaurant near the dock. The pair stretched outside the car for a moment then went into the diner.

The odor of frying cod reminded Thomas of the rancid fish sticks his father forced him to eat as a child. It didn't help his mood. After finding a table he said, "I'll be back in a minute," and fled for the restroom.

Rhys ordered for both of them and waited. Several minutes passed and Thomas didn't emerge from the loo. His food arrived with still no sign of him.

Just as he was about to check on him, he glimpsed a woman outside that could've been Terri's twin.

"Wishful thinking, for sure, mate," he grumbled to himself. He rubbed the sleep out of his eyes and looked again. "Impossible," he said. But he couldn't resist his feeling and went outside to check her out.

Seconds later, Thomas peeped out of the restroom at his table. No Rhys in sight. He scoped the room, still not seeing him. *Must've popped outside for a smoke*, he thought.

Good time to ditch him. He darted out of the loo and headed for the kitchen, trying to leave the restaurant unseen.

"Is there a back door?" he asked the cook.

The man just grunted, wiping a hand through his greasy hair. A bemused waitress pointed and Thomas ducked out the rear exit.

Hiding at the corner of the building, Thomas checked for any sign of Rhys as he eyed a private boat anchored a dozen yards away. Seeing no sign of his friend, he sped toward a man stooping on its deck and coiling a rope.

"I'm Thomas Payne. Are you the man I spoke to on the phone a little while ago about a trip to Sherkin Island?"

The captain plodded down the deck with his hand cupped to his ear. His white pants were worn but clean, like his blue and white-striped shirt. His face was as lean and leathery as his hands. He reminded Thomas of his father for a moment, but his expression was entirely different. This man enjoyed life.

The captain said, "Why'd you want to hire a private boat? The ferry's only a few coins."

Thomas thought fast. "It doesn't leave for an hour. I need to get there right away."

"What's that, sir?" the man asked, leaning down closer.

"Nothing. Will you take me to the island?" He held out a wad of cash.

The captain nodded and held out his gnarled hand. He stuffed the bills into his pocket and reached down to help Thomas up.

Thomas was about to board when Rhys came into view outside the restaurant, looking in his direction. Thomas ducked behind the ferry boat ticket booth a yard to his right.

He searched the deck for a place to hide that wouldn't raise the captain's curiosity. Seeing none, he checked his watch and whispered up to the man, "Wait a minute, please."

Rhys and Terri entered the restaurant, then he dragged her by the elbow to their table. "How did you find us?"

She waved his question away. "Is he here?"

"Stay here," he said excitedly, his eyes shining. "I'll get him out of the bathroom."

Terri started to sit, then changed her mind and followed Rhys, unable to bear a wait of even a few extra seconds.

Rhys came out from the loo five seconds later and said, astonished, "He's not there."

Terri moaned.

Rhys scanned the restaurant, then the parking lot outside. "I can't understand it."

Terri looked out the window anxiously. "Maybe he went outside to get some fresh air. He hates the smell of cooking fish." She fidgeted, looking around anxiously.

Rhys said, "He must have." He joined Terri in looking through the restaurant window.

Thomas could see Rhys through the glass from his hiding place but the sun's reflection obscured any view of Terri. He could see that

Rhys had a clear line of sight to the rental boat. He waited impatiently for his chance to board unseen, but Rhys never looked away.

After two minutes, Terri walked toward the door. "I can't stand it. I have to go look for him." She started to elbow past the people entering the diner when she felt a sudden urge. "I'm going to use the loo. I'll join you outside in a minute."

Outside, Rhys thought, *"He must be deliberately avoiding me."* He scanned the parking area once more. *"But why?"*

From behind the ticket booth, Thomas shifted his gaze between Rhys and the captain. The old sailor had gone about his preparations. He took a rubber band from his pocket, wrapped the bills, and handed them to a mate lounging on the dock.

"Give this to the daft American... if he ever shows up." After a final canvassing of the car park, the captain started to set sail.

Thomas could see the wind start to fill the sheets of the sloop. In a few seconds, he would lose his ride to Sherkin. He daren't risk taking the ferry and meeting Rhys. He'd never shake him a second time.

Just as the ship separated from the dock, the restaurant door opened. Rhys turned around at the sound. Thomas made a mad leap for the boat, his back to the restaurant, just as Terri emerged from the shadow of the awning over the entrance.

Thomas arrived at the private pier on Sherkin a few minutes later, grateful for the short trip. He thanked the captain again and scrutinized the dock, searching for anyone whose face he might recognize.

The sun was fully up now and he could see clearly for a hundred yards in every direction. He saw no familiar face. He nervously stepped off. He might be killed at once. Or Owen's roommate might have something more cat-and-mouse in mind.

There were a few locals in the area but no tourists yet. He checked his watch. He had beaten the ferry by a comfortable margin, at least half an hour. He had that long to meet the man who would free him or kill him.

He asked directions to the Mainster Inis friary and then walked toward it on high alert.

A few of the island's citizens looked at him askance. There were only roughly a hundred who owned property or worked there. Any new face stuck out when it arrived before the ferry.

Thomas avoided their eyes, then thought that might attract their attention even more. He didn't know if there was anything like a constable on the island, and he didn't want to find out.

A few minutes later he arrived at the friary. On one side, the low vegetation allowed him to see anyone coming from any direction. The other side stood close to a hill where he could see nothing. He walked up it to get a downward view from the rise.

He could see small, scattered clumps of people moving around in the distance. None of them appeared to be moving toward the friary.

He waited there, sitting like a cocked crossbow on the cool grass at the top of the hill, ready to bolt. He looked seaward but there were no boats visible from that point.

He checked the time again. The ferry would dock soon. Five minutes to meeting time, still with no idea what to say to Owen's roommate to make him confess.

He tapped the mossy earth impatiently. He took a deep whiff of sea air to calm himself. It didn't help. He tried to think of something to say that would at least start the conversation in a helpful direction. Nothing came. *Think like Dr. Faustus. There must be some way to make a deal with the devil without losing your soul.*

His vision was again sweeping the grounds around the friary when he spotted Rhys approaching the 15th century ruins.

His friend was still a hundred yards away. "Damn!" he moaned aloud. What to do? He searched frantically for an idea. *Leave a message to meet elsewhere.*

He scribbled a note and scrambled down the hill to search out one of the two friars, in reality tourist guides for the defunct abbey. He invented a story on the fly and begged the man to pass on the note.

Thomas had distanced himself a scant fifty feet when Rhys spotted him. Rhys waved to Terri to stay at the abbey and ran to close the gap. Terri ignored his wishes and rushed ahead, reaching the corner before Rhys that Thomas had ducked around.

She paused a split second to see which way he'd fled. Rhys caught up and railed at her to stay put. She said, already on the run again, "You're wasting breath." She raced off, but her ankle was still sore, making it difficult to reach top speed.

The pair spotted Thomas again a few feet from the old schoolhouse sitting atop a low hill and standing only a few feet from the water. The high bushes surrounding it would make it easy for him to hide, and they put on a burst of speed.

Terri said, "He can't go anywhere now. That's the edge of the island."

Rhys saw him immediately take a sharp left turn and run toward the medieval Celtic fort. "So much for being cornered."

Terri frowned. Thomas was receding so she picked up the pace, ignoring the pain in her ankle. A few seconds later she slammed full on into a middle-aged woman who went down like a flour sack. Dust puffed up into the woman's face. Terri apologized and kept on running.

Rhys bent down to help the woman up, apologizing profusely. "Forgive her, ma'am. Love makes people crazy sometimes."

The woman smiled, looking at Terri shambling at the highest speed she could manage after her prey. "But it's a great motivator equal times."

Thomas put all his effort into running and none to looking back, desperate to get away from Rhys and join Owen's roommate at the new meeting place. He reached the promontory fort fifty yards ahead of his pursuer. He hid behind an Iron Age wall and risked a pause to scan the area.

His quick once-over showed only a few tourists, but he knew Rhys couldn't be far behind. He looked at one man who seemed to be a local. The man glared back and trotted off, looking as he were going to get help.

Thomas glanced to his rear. He had nowhere to go but off a cliff ten feet away that looked over Baltimore Harbour. He ran to it, peered down, then scrambled down the cliff face and took off running.

Soon he was racing across the sands of the Silver Strand at the north edge of the island. From there he could see a figure standing at the top of a cliff, waving, but the angle of the sun made it impossible to make out who it was.

From the silhouette, it was certainly not Rhys, he concluded. Too short and too curvy. Could Owen's roommate be a woman? He tried to remember Brenda's body style. From where he stood, he couldn't tell whether or not it was a match.

He picked out a spot forty yards ahead. There were no obstructions to hide any mischief but a boulder would give him some cover.

If Owen's roommate had a gun, all his precautions might mean nothing, but Thomas didn't think he'd risk a shot in the clear. Not with so many tourists around. The beach was the most heavily populated area on Sherkin. He rushed to the boulder.

Terri partly stumbled, partly scraped down the cliff face, trying to get to Thomas before he could disappear again. She gained a few yards, only to have the gap widen as he sprinted ahead.

"Thomas my love, in the name of Venus, slow down!" She was shouting into the wind and the sound waves damped to nothing before they reached halfway to his ears.

She half-ran, half-hopped down the beach until she thought her ankle would collapse.

She threw her hands up in despair when she saw Thomas climb into a small motor boat with a large man. The engine sped them off before she could get close enough to be recognized.

19

$\mathcal{T}$ERRI raced back toward the public square to get a cell phone signal again. She anxiously watched the bars rise on the display as she wended her way through the crowd. When the signal strength grew to half height, she pressed "Brecon Station."

An eon later, the phone connected. "Sergeant Bevan, speaking."

His voice came across scratchy. Terri angled the phone, trying to get a clearer signal. "Bevan, this is Terri. It's an emergency and I want you to make every effort to contact my father right away." She explained where she was and why she wanted him.

"But, Terri, you know it's out of his jurisdiction."

"When did that ever stop him? Anyway, just tell him my future husband is about to be killed. He'll come."

She listened for a few seconds to his barking about her "future husband" then cut him off. She gave him details about where her father should meet her and hung up. "Now, if he can just get here in time," she muttered, knowing how unlikely it was.

Just then, Rhys joined up with her. "Who?"

"Da."

He motioned for her to follow him and they walked toward the dock. He pointed to Silver Strand beach, down the shoreline. "Your father's already here, Terri." He smiled at the surprised look on her face. "That was him in the boat with Thomas. I saw them with a borrowed pair of binoculars from the top of the cliff."

She leaned back on a wall, too stunned for a long moment to speak. Her ankle hurt. She hobbled to the shoreline and rubbed it with salt water. "Why in hell did they run away from me?"

"They don't know yet you're alive. Thomas must've thought you were Owen's roommate."

"That's who he was meeting? Why didn't you tell me earlier?"

Rhys ignored her second question, embarrassed. He'd been too excited to see her alive to mention it. He put his arm around her waist to take the pressure off her ankle and led her to an isolated spot on the sand. "Do you know who the roommate is?"

She looked grim as she remembered the last time she'd seen him. "If it's who think, yes and no. The whoreson showed up at the cabin in Bushmills, but I never saw him before."

She looked at her ankle, puffy and turning purple. Rhys noticed and said, "What happened in Bushmills?"

She explained.

Rhys sat heavily, not knowing how to respond. "You never did tell me how you found us."

"I phoned Owen's apartment thinking he might—no, I can't really say I was thinking. I was desperate to find Thomas, and I couldn't reach him or you. I recognized his voice. Strangely, he told me where I could reach you."

"Why would he do that?"

"I offered him a trade."

"For what? Or should I not ask?"

She shook her head, unwilling to say.

A young man in yachting attire caught her eye, and she surveyed the sailboats lining the dock a hundred yards off. A covey of men was preparing for the annual Regatta, some ashore, many more onboard.

She noticed the name on one of the ships. "That's his," she said, pointing, her heart suddenly racing. Without warning, she jumped up and marched toward the craft.

Rhys followed her. "What's his? What's whose?" He followed her gaze. "The racing sloop?"

"I recognize the name from our trip to Moher." She was halfway to it before he caught on what she was about to do. He hooked her elbow. "You can't go on there, Terri."

"Why not?"

He went silent a moment, stumped, just as he did whenever a student questioned something plainly obvious. "Uh, because he's a killer and you never know what might happen?"

"Well, how else can we find out?" She clawed her arm free and forged ahead. She waited a few minutes by the side of the sloop to see if anyone would come out on his own.

There were dozens of people milling about, looking over the ships and chatting with the crew. She said, "He's not around. Anyway, what can happen with so many people nearby?"

"There were lots of people at Moher, too," he objected.

She wasn't listening. When no one appeared on the boat after another minute, she padded closer. She stood on tiptoe to spy into the cabin. "I don't see anyone."

She hopped aboard and landed on her good foot as softly as a leaf on snow. Rhys leapt on right behind her, making a loud thunk. She glared at him angrily a second, then limped ahead.

They stepped quietly around the deck, exhausting in a few seconds any places he could be and not be seen.

"There's no one aboard," she said. "Let's take it."

"Take what?"

"His boat. Before he comes back."

"Uh, you know that's grand larceny, right? And that you're a policeman's daughter?"

"What do I care? The lowlife just walked away when I was held prisoner by his roommate."

Rhys could think of no good argument. The image of Terri in the cabin lingered in his mind. "Fine, let's do it."

She pivoted to enter the bridge, noted something in the corner, then saw the keys sitting in the ignition.

She wouldn't need any help sailing it. She could leave the canvas furled and just motor to the mainland after picking up Thomas and Da. Then all would wait together for Owen's roommate to reveal himself. She hoped. But she couldn't let Rhys take the risk with her.

"Come take a look at this," she said, pulling him by the arm. She walked resolutely toward the stern. He followed, suspecting nothing. She

cobra. "I wondered when you were going to come out of your little pit."

Thomas and Arwel stepped out of the motor boat at Baltimore Pier and continued their argument.

"That really wasn't necessary," Thomas insisted. "I had the situation under control."

"Sure, son, sure," Arwel said patronizingly. "That's why you were running away at top speed. To lure the killer into a trap."

"I was running away from..." He drifted off. "Never mind." He said instead, "How'd you find me?"

"Professional secret."

"And why are you here, anyway?"

"You didn't think I'd let my linchpin in this case get killed, did you?" He tried to lighten the mood. "Isn't once enough this vacation?"

Thomas frowned. "I was about to get the evidence we both want. I was meeting the man I think killed Carl."

"Killed Thomas Payne, you mean." Arwel said it only to needle him. He was persuaded by this time that Thomas was who he said he was. Still, he was sure he knew more than he was telling. He poked the needle in again. "At that lonely spot?" Arwel scoffed. "He'd have buried you right there and no one the wiser."

"If you think he was about to kill me, why didn't you let him and then just arrest him?"

Arwel clucked his tongue. "Is that a serious question, or an offer?"

Thomas didn't want to argue any more. He looked out to sea again, noting that one regatta ship had already left the Sherkin shoreline. He looked puzzled for a moment. He was about to point it out to Arwel but, seeing that the boat still had its sheets tied, dropped it.

They reached the car park. Thomas was about to lean up against the Bentley when he thought better of it. He said, "I'm not so sure Owen's roommate is a he."

He explained.

At first, Arwel said nothing. He was busy working the information into his jigsaw puzzle. After a long moment, he said, "Doubtful. Remember the motorcycle rider who knocked you over? Wasn't he a big fellow?"

Thomas nodded. The sun blinded him for a moment and he shaded his eyes. Across the water, he saw the ship speed up, then take an erratic course.

He pointed it out to Arwel, who ignored it. He gave Thomas instructions about what to do next. Thomas started to object and he cut him off. "No matter. Don't go back to that island." He eased into the Bentley. "The man'll be gone anyway."

Arwel started to fire up the motor then hesitated, debating whether to order Thomas into the car. He decided the rat he was after wouldn't nibble his bait if they stayed too close together.

He started the motor, then lowered the sun visor. He gave Thomas a useless warning to be cautious, and put the car into gear. "Call me before nightfall," he growled, then pressed the accelerator.

Thomas watched him speed off then checked his watch. That gave him about twelve hours. He jangled the car keys, trying to decide whether to follow orders as he walked toward Terri's car. If he went along, Arwel might beg, in to consider him more ally than suspect. On the other hand, he was a policeman and no good ever came from cooperating with one.

He was deep in thought and looked up only when he heard a scuffing sound near him. He was surprised to find Rhys standing there, looking like a field mouse after a tussle with a goshawk.

Rhys said, his voice angry and excited, "Thomas, I've got a bone to pick with you. But first I have to tell—"

"How in hell did you get across the bay?" He scanned down to the shore. The ferry was still disembarking passengers.

"EarthQuaker! Terr—"

Thomas interrupted, not in the mood for explanations. "Never mind. Get in. Arwel made me promise to go to Terri's funeral tomorrow and there are—"

"Listen to me!" Rhys screeched, shaking him by the shirtsleeve. "Terri's alive!"

Thomas wilted against the car. After a lifetime, he was reborn. "Tell me everything you know."

"Later. She's on the sailboat we rode to Moher." Thomas' looked fearful. "Yes, the one owned by Owen's roommate." He pointed at the ocean. "She's out there. Going to meet him, I think."

Thomas swiveled his head. There were now dozens of sailboats in the water. The annual Regatta had begun. "How in hell are we going to find her among all those?"

"She was headed for Silver Strand beach."

"Christ on a stick! And you didn't stop her?"

"I tried." Rhys' mouth curled downward as he shook his wet shirt. "How do you think I got like this?"

Thomas put a hand on Rhys' shoulder as a gesture of apology. He looked out to sea again and scanned the water, hoping to catch sight of her or the sloop. There were too many in the water to get a clear view. He unlocked Terri's car and pulled binoculars out of the glovebox.

The ships were in a tight knot, racing toward Baltimore. Then suddenly he realized he wasn't thinking clearly. "There'd be no reason for her to be among them. She'd try to separate from the group."

He scanned Silver Strand for the man he was to meet on Sherkin. No sign. He put the binoculars back into the glovebox. "Decamped, I'll bet."

Now what?

A second later, he flung open the car door without warning and jumped in. He fired up the engine. Rhys made it in just as he was slamming the Austin into first gear. Both flipped down their visors to block the glaring sun as Thomas sped off.

"Where are you going?" Rhys asked, holding tight onto the dashboard.

"Owen's apartment. I'm betting that's where the roommate will be."

"Why? Won't he try to get his boat back?"

"It's not his. It's my father's." He noticed Rhys' skeptical expression. "The message arranging the meeting at Sherkin. It wasn't from Owen's roommate, it was from my father."

"You're nuts. I checked the IP address. It belonged to a computer at Owen's apartment." Rhys looked thoughtful for a moment. In truth, that only pinned it down to a place, not a person.

Thomas said, "The email had a phrase, something he said often when I was a kid. 'The devil mixes lies with the truth to keep you guessing.' Only he'd have used that."

"That's weak. Lots of people might have picked that up somewhere."

"I thought he was referring to himself. He meant Owen's roommate. That means they've met."

Thomas steered the car onto the N71 motorway, headed for Cork. This time they would have to take a plane to Cardiff. He must waste no time getting back. He borrowed Rhys' phone and sent Terri an email, telling her to pick up the car in Cork and where to meet them.

Rhys asked, "And you think they're going to meet again at his apartment? Now? Why?"

"At the end of the message. Something he used when he wanted to meet secretly at a certain time and place."

Rhys gave him the look that said he was making wild leaps again. "That's a stretch. Even for you."

Thomas checked the time on the dashboard clock, then had Rhys check the flight schedules. A little more than an hour to Cork, then a couple of hours to reach Cardiff — if they caught a plane right away. Then, it would take hours to get through security, board, fly. He thought for a moment. "Look up if there are any private planes to charter."

While he was checking, Rhys said, "You don't know he'll be there."

"I have to gamble."

"Being wrong isn't worth gambling Terri's life. Isn't that what you're doing, rushing off and leaving her?"

"She'll be alright by herself on the boat."

20

*T*ERRI drew back instinctively when the hulking man began to mount the steps to the bridge.

She had known he was onboard since before taking the ship from shore. She dumped Rhys to keep him out of trouble.

So this is Owen's roommate, she thought, glowering. For the first time, she got a clear look at him. He was big, bigger than she remembered from the cabin, broad-shouldered and muscular all over, but with a small head that made him look like a cartoon.

Obviously, he was much too strong to overcome in a straight struggle. She scoured the bridge for a weapon; there was nothing at hand.

Damn, she thought.

There wasn't time for other thoughts. He was already reaching for her. She clawed his face hard then fled the bridge to the sound of his scream.

On deck she could evade him, but only so long. She would have seconds at most before he recovered and gave chase. With her weakened ankle, it wouldn't take long for him to catch her.

She could jump overboard. She snapped her view to Baltimore harbor. They were still minutes from shore, too far to swim. She hobbled toward the stern. Halfway there, she tripped over the rope hastily jerked off the dock cleat.

The wounded boar chasing her watched her go down and laughed, then lunged.

Terri started to scramble to her feet, but he was already above her. She leaned back on her elbows, sneaking her hand around the rope.

"Oh, well. They say if it's inevitable, relax and enjoy it, no?"

She used one hand to flick the edge of her blouse playfully, hoping to distract his view from the other. She smiled fetchingly.

He was surprised by the switch, but couldn't guess at once if she was playing him or playing with him. He paused a second.

It was enough. She whipped the rope around his ankles and tugged, hauling him off his feet. She jumped up and kicked him in the side with her good leg, knocking him further down onto the deck. Down, but not over the side, as she'd hoped.

She leaned her back against the wall below the bridge. In a flash, she put both feet on his ribcage and slid down 'til her butt touched the deck, then shoved as hard as possible.

It hurt like hell; her ankle was on fire. But it worked.

He rolled off the deck under the railing and into the air, tumbling toward the water. He never got there. Terri grabbed the end of the rope and twirled it around the deck cleat before his head hit the surface.

She headed up to the bridge while he dangled upside down an inch above the wake from the sloop's hull. His body caromed off it multiple times, like a pig on a hook repeatedly smacked by a meat packer's club.

She grabbed the wheel and gave it several jerks left and right. She could hear him bounce off the wood.

He struggled to right himself, folding at theh waist to fumble for the rope that clamped his ankles together. It was no use, even for someone with his strength. Every time he got close the boat plowed through another wave and he was thrown back down.

If he made progress, Terri slacked off speed then wrenched the throttle wide open, bouncing him again and again off the side of the boat.

He thrashed for a solid five seconds after every smack, weakening with each attempt. Her technique was working, and each repetition brought them half a minute closer to shore.

But there were still too many halves to go and, despite his fatigue, he was inching up. He'd worked out a method to compensate for Terri's trick. Eventually, he reached the low wooden rail around the deck.

His hand slipped off a couple of times, but his fingers were so strong the third attempt secured a solid grip. He locked onto the rail above with his other hand and ratcheted his body onto the deck. He rested just long enough for one deep breath, in and out, then reached up to untie his legs.

Terri heard a scraping movement and glanced to port. She realized he would soon be free again and full of vengeance.

She snapped the throttle all the way down, revving the engine more than it could safely take. If it burst, they would slow down and drift. She looked ahead. They were ten yards from shore, moving at top speed.

They were racing too fast, too close to the sand for safety, but she kept it up. To slacken would give him more time to reach her. She tried a couple of quick twists of the wheel to knock him off his feet but it didn't work.

He reached the bridge and stretched out an arm to nab her just as the boat hit something. The jar against a sandbar beneath the waterline flung his hands aside at the last second. They sped forward as he reached for her again.

An instant before the final impact, Terri noticed a cell phone lying on the radio. She filched it then jumped out of the bridge at the moment his hands touched her hair.

They slammed the beach. The boat shot straight ahead, she at an angle, both flying.

She sailed into a huge rock, her flight stopped dead with a dull *whump*, too stunned to note her attacker's fate.

Terri regained her focus within seconds and could see her attacker flopped onto the foredeck. The lower half of his body still hung into the bridge.

For a brief, shining moment, she thought he was dead. Then he raised his head, shook it, and dragged himself the rest of the way through the broken window. As he rose, he dripped blood from a cut near the elbow. He didn't seem to notice or care.

Terri did.

She watched him as he rested on the foredeck with his legs dangling over the edge.

In a moment, he would be recovered enough to walk.

She had to get out of there.

She tried to move but the space around her was hot and cloistered, and surprisingly dark for mid-morning. It had been clear only a minute before on the water, but now there wasn't enough light to see if she had any wounds. She was fuzzy-headed, and it took her a moment to realize why it was so dim.

A small pool of people congealed around her, asking if she was alright. She was grateful, then grew alarmed when she looked through their legs; a cop was jogging her way. Still on the ground, she tried to nudge everyone away.

As she crawled toward the back of the crowd, she snuck the cell phone out of her pocket, hoping it would tell her the owner's identity. She glanced up to see the constable getting close. The phone would have to wait. She was poised to rise and run when two burly young men leaned close to her face.

One asked if she was injured, and before she could answer, they were helping her up. She tried to tuck the phone into her pocket. With her forearms restrained, she was able to secure it only halfway.

The two men pulled her up the rest of the way and she tested her ankle. It was surprisingly sound so she edged away from them, using the crowd to obscure the approaching policeman's view of her. Then she turned and ran.

In two strides, she lost the phone as her leg motion pushed it out of her pocket and into the sand. She halted at once and went down on her knees. The hive started to waft toward her again, some thinking she had collapsed as a result of her injuries.

She shouted, "Please stand back! I've lost my phone!"

Terri combed the sand in a state of panic. She dug her hands down and through the hot grains, muttering, "How do things get so bugger all lost, so quick?"

She stopped long enough to shift her head left and right, trying to peer through a dozen legs. The cop was almost on them and her attacker would not be far behind.

She felt around frenetically as he drew near the outer edge of the bystanders. Just as he started to shove his way through the cluster of people, her hand *whapped* the phone.

She salvaged it then brushed it off, already rising to her feet. She fled up the hill and melted into the crowd milling around the buildings at the north edge of town.

She saw a two-story yellow building at the top of the rise, a popular hotel, and walked quickly toward it. Reaching the summit, she entered. She tapped the phone to send Thomas a text message. She stood near a pillar, away from the entrance, and waited.

Two minutes later, there was no still answer.

She wanted to call but couldn't remember his number, and she could find no listing. She sent an email, wondering if he was still in the area. She couldn't know it went straight to his junk folder, since it came from the roommate's phone.

She sat in a chair in the lobby and examined its contents.

She warily scanned the street from time to time for any sign of its owner. She felt reasonably safe inside the hotel, but he would only have to wait for her to leave to start all over again.

She worked her way first through the email section. A number of them were exchanges with Owen. No doubt her father would find them very interesting. She read the list back to the day of the murder, then exited out.

She navigated next to a section that held some of his personal documents. There were notes about an unexplored section of the Dan-yr-Ogof complex, complete with a miniature, stylus-drawn map.

She pondered their implications for a few minutes, wondering if there was any connection to the murder. She could think of none. They were all about the interior, nowhere near where the crime took place.

She made her way to the moped rental business at the north end of Baltimore. A few minutes later, she checked the route to Cork.

She sent another email message to Thomas, asking him to meet her at the cave, but there was no response. After a ten minute wait, there was still no reply.

She started the scooter and made her way to the N71 motorway.

As she rode to the airport listening to the soothing purr of the bike, she tried to work out the significance of the notes and the map, getting cracked clay for her efforts – dry, useless, unable to be formed into anything coherent.

Her instincts told her that somehow it would answer why Carl was murdered, and prove *this* man had killed him, but the solution eluded her.

"Not so much my father's daughter as you'd like, eh Da?" she said to the wind. "So, what would *you* do?"

With one hand on the handlebar, she used the other to pull up the National Showcaves website to double check the closing time for Dan-yr-Ogof.

Thomas and Rhys arrived at Owen's apartment four hours before sundown. The long shadows on the face of the building were not enough to obscure the two men but they elected to brave the chance of being seen. There was no time left for subterfuge.

Thomas mounted the steps to the front door and buzzed the upstairs apartment, hoping the landlady would let them into the building without question. Two seconds later, there was an answering buzz. She didn't bother to come onto the landing to see who it was.

Rhys stepped in right behind Thomas and immediately noted the odor. It didn't smell exactly like scum, more like a blend of seaweed and dead rat. It was impossible to tell the source, though. It might have come from the hallway or inside one of the apartments. The pair hastened to Owen's door two strides down the corridor.

Rhys stared at the door and said as a joke, "I suppose you expect me to pick the lock?"

Thomas had no reserves of patience and ignored him. He pulled a screwdriver gleaned from Terri's glove compartment out of his pocket, then smacked it into the wood at the door latch. He snapped it sideways and the door opened with a crunch.

They zipped inside and wedged the door shut with a rubber stop, hoping no one would notice the damage until they were long gone. Now was no time to be stopped by the police.

This time they were more systematic in searching for laptops, folders, notepads – anything that would give them clues about the identity of Owen's roommate. It didn't take long to convince themselves there simply were none.

Thomas said, "I shouldn't be surprised. The police already went over the place after Owen's arrest, no doubt. Probably confiscated all the equipment."

Even so, he couldn't casually accept defeat. He continued to pour over the room. "The guy probably wasn't the sort to put his initials on his shirts," he said in an exasperated tone, "but there must be something."

Rhys sighed and plopped onto the couch. "Isn't it weird? It's like the git never existed. Maybe—"

He broke off when a cabinet door beneath the kitchenette sink flew open and a human arm flopped out. "Haysous Christo, what is that?" he bellowed, pointing.

"Keep your voice down. What's the mat—" Thomas sucked in a short, sharp breath. He opened both doors and dragged the folded body out of the space. Rhys, unable to see the corpse, aimed a questioning look at Thomas, who said, "My father."

He shook his head and sighed. "Somebody has ruined my hope of doing this myself someday. He's been shot through the—"

A staccato burst of knocks rattled the door.

"Owen? Owen Caldicott are you in there?" The voice was more than harsh; it had the sound of a wood saw scraping a metal helmet. "It's rent time, you know. Can't put it off forever, lad. Open up!"

"Shite," Rhys whispered harshly. He jumped off the couch and went to the door to prevent her pushing it in.

The buzzsaw said, "No cursing me, either, you ill-mannered lout. I can hear you breathing. Open the door." The landlady unleashed another salvo of knuckle gunfire on the frame.

Leaning against the edge of the door, Rhys gave his best imitation of Owen's whine. "I'm sick. Please come back tomorrow." He hoped she was the sort to be neurotic about germs. Then he remembered the general condition of the building, and the hallway in particular, and abandoned the hope. He whispered harshly to Thomas, "What should we do?"

Thomas meanwhile was trying to stuff James's body back under the sink, aiming to leave it for the police where he'd found it.

"Nice try," the woman said, "but you're already ten days overdue. You and that no account who stays with you on the sly." She heard a groan from inside. "Yes, I know, don't think I don't. Your lease says one tenant. Two is double the rent."

"Please can't you come back later? I'll pay you the full amount," Rhys said. "I'm really sick. You don't want to catch what I've got." He made retching sounds.

"By heavens, you'd better not be messing up the carpet!"

Rhys said, "I swear, I'll come up in an hour and pay you everything you're owed."

There was a long pause. "You'd better. And try to sneak out, I'll phone the coppers." They heard steps, which quickly faded, as if the landlady were walking away. Then the sound stopped. "Say, what happened to this door!" The sound rose near the end, as if she were walking back.

She pushed the door in with unexpected force, making Rhys stumble backward. She stared through the open doorway. She didn't recognize the two men standing inside. One of them knelt next to a body hanging halfway out of the kitchen cabinet. She blinked twice, too shocked to scream. But not too stunned to move. She started to turn to escape.

Rhys yanked her into the apartment by the elbow before she could run away.

"Please don't kill me. Please. I won't tell—"

A loud squawk interrupted from the kitchen. "Please don't kill! Awwk! Perry no kill! Perry, no kill! Awwk!"

Thomas looked wide-eyed at Rhys. "Perry? Perry Turcotte?"

"Perry the piton! Perry the piton! Awwk! No! No! No!" The bird then let out a grisly imitation of a human laugh, like a hyena on helium. The Mynah shoved some birdseed onto the floor, which landed on James' dead skull.

Thomas bolted to the cage to find the Mynah chewing on a piece of paper.

Rhys followed him, dragging the landlady along, her face like petrified wood. He glanced past the birdcage and saw a motorcycle parked just outside the window, not there when they arrived. He was about to point it out to Thomas and suggest they leave at once.

Just then, Perry Turcotte careened through the open door, his face badly cut up, the blood dried into slashes like a Halloween mask.

21

*T*ERRI arrived at Dan-yr-Ogof with three hours of daylight left. She stepped off the bus and took in the swarm of tourists and cavers buzzing near the entrance to the huge cave complex.

It wasn't difficult for her to distinguish the two types. The amateurs weren't dressed right. Many of them were in shorts and short-sleeved shirts. They would be shivering and badly scraped within minutes if they went beyond the large cave near the mouth. The narrow, jagged passageways further in guaranteed an injury for anyone whose ambition exceeded their ability.

She saw several cavers near the entrance donning jackets despite the warm weather. She held a similar one in her hand. Many carried helmets with lamps like the one in her other hand. They were ready for the deeper, unlit tunnels. The truly dedicated had backpacking gear resembling rock-climbers tools: rope, pitons, and spring-loaded cams used for scaling vertical caves deep in the interior.

She eased the backpack off her shoulders containing her own kit and sought shade provided by the cliff wall. She strapped on chaps over her slacks, then put on the rough leather jacket. Finally, she tucked her helmet under an arm.

She shivered, despite the heat, knowing what she was headed into. If this worked out, she'd have the hard evidence needed to clear

Thomas. But if Perry noticed his phone missing, he might guess where she'd gone. He would come to kill her, just as he'd tried to kill Thomas.

What she wasn't sure of was: why? What could Perry have against Thomas worth killing over?

Thomas had no hard facts for him to fear. He wasn't a witness to the murder. He wasn't at the cabin when Perry talked to Owen. It made no sense. Why risk murdering someone who couldn't finger you for anything?

Still, she was sure Thomas was Perry's target. His presence on Staffa, luring him to Moher, to Sherkin Island… each time, it must have been to kill him. The emails were enough to convince her of that, even if they were too ambiguous to persuade a judge.

And what for? What good would getting rid of Thomas do him? Did he think he could get away with stealing Thomas's invention, especially after Owen had been arrested for trying? Ridiculous.

She felt the answer must lie in the diagrams she'd found, the ones detailing the structures she was about to explore.

She walked resolutely toward the cave entrance, hoping to find the answers to her questions inside.

She waited in a slow-moving line behind dozens of others, wishing it would clear faster. The heat was beginning to make her sweat.

She was poised to take off her jacket when a young Irishman in front of her leered and made a rude remark about removing some clothing.

Ten minutes later, she was in the cool of the large cave just inside the opening, grateful for the protection of her jacket and chaps. She paused a moment to calm her nerves and clung to a wall out of the way of meandering tourists.

She wanted to linger to marvel at the huge speleothems — giant rock formations that resembled everything from cottage cheese to mythical sea monsters. Even her claustrophobia couldn't prevent her feeling a sense of awe in their presence.

But she had no time for feeling anything. Perry was still alive and he might track her there through his phone.

She brought up the map on his mobile and tensed, knowing what was ahead. She would be traveling almost a mile, much of it through low, narrow passages. She pulled her shoulders back and loosened up her neck muscles, tilting her head left then right.

"Please, Athena," she prayed, "let this be worth it."

She tramped down the passageway. The cave roof dipped closer to her head the farther she progressed. She checked the phone and saw the bars were gone. She was on her own now.

She studied the hand-drawn map again. It was a crude graphic showing the entrance, a side tunnel, and a small route angled off of that. Beneath it were typed the words "Rock star!"

She wondered what that meant. It seemed an odd thing to call a cavern or its contents, even for an avid trog like Perry.

Terri rummaged in the contents of her backpack and pulled out a bottle of juice. She took a swig and wiped the sweat off her brow, now beading up despite the cool temperature. She watched the ceiling growing lower as she walked, and wiped off the sweat onto a sleeve.

As the walls narrowed, she took two deep breaths and held out her hand, flexing her fingers several times. She stared at them intently, extending and curling slowly.

It was her usual technique to force her focus away from fear. It barely worked in the more open caves she explored to get stone for sculpting. Here, it was useless and she knew it right away.

She took one more deep breath and hurried on toward the side tunnel. She entered it a few minutes later and sized up the rough cylinder. She saw nothing particularly interesting. *There must be*, she thought. To Perry, anyway. Something interesting enough to kill for.

Gold? Diamonds? Impossible. Even if they existed in this geology, which was absurd, Perry could never obtain the mineral rights inside a national park.

She went inside, clutching the phone, as much to keep her hand from shaking as the fear of losing the map.

The passageway narrowed substantially almost at once. It began at two feet above her head and beyond her outstretched arms. A few yards down the tube, it tapered to just above and beside her body.

The artificial light from the main tunnel was fading fast. At this rate, she would be crawling in the dark in another twenty yards. She switched on her helmet light.

She traveled half that distance and was relieved to find the space opening up again, slightly.

Water trickled beneath her feet. She paused and took two more shallow breaths, determined to avoid hyperventilating.

She trudged on, looking for the next landmark indicated on the map: a stalactite that split the small tunnel in two.

She reached it and peered around the high, thin cone. She saw that the roof on the other side lowered again. She could advance hunched over, but no better.

She took another slow breath through her nose, smelling a familiar mixture of limestone dust, mold, and sweat. She wiped her hands on her chaps and bent down to journey further inside.

She alternately crawled and loped like an ape for forty yards. She had to worm along the next forty. As she did, her hands made small splashes in the water gurgling down the tunnel floor.

She looked anxiously over her shoulder. The dim illumination from the main cave was now completely gone. She had entered a different world, one that seemed to have no route back to the ordinary one.

She stroked her hand across the moist, rocky floor, letting the slimy stone give her a sense of familiar reality to keep her heart from bursting. It felt just like smoothing out wet modeling clay.

She hoped the batteries in her helmet lamp were fresh. She tried to remember the last time she'd changed them, but her febrile mind wouldn't let her recall.

She checked the map one last time then put the phone away, fearing her shaking hand would drop it and destroy valuable evidence.

Her hands were muddy now with limestone mush. She gave up wiping them off, knowing they would just get smeared again with the next crawling step.

It too felt like moist clay between her fingers, and she used the sensation to imagine herself in the studio on a dark night. She gained another thirty yards before the feeling wore off and the fear returned, stronger than ever.

To keep her mind off the gradual contraction of the walls, she tried to ignore everything but the ooze on her hands. Useless. The tunnel squeezed ever closer to her shoulders as she panted then swallowed her panic then panted some more.

The beam from her helmet showed the slender cylinder losing girth fast as she slithered forward. Her every muscle tensed, every nerve cell screaming like a schizophrenic low on medication.

She had enough presence of mind left to ask herself for the fourth time how this insane act would free Thomas. One answer echoed back for the fourth time: *somehow*. It must.

"Please," she cried to the indifferent walls, "let me find *something!*"

Her scream echoed down the constricted tube, but it couldn't make the tunnel any larger.

There was barely enough free space now to reach over her shoulder and wriggle out her juice bottle. She took a sip, dribbling some down her chin.

She reminded herself how vital it was to keep her salt and fluid levels right. When caving alone, disorientation meant death.

She restored the bottle, her hand going spastic as she tried to cram it into the elastic holder.

She used one part of her mind to listen for sounds behind her, the other to check the tunnel ahead. It seemed impossible that Perry could sneak up on her from either end. But knowing she had the map and his notes, he would surely try.

Worrying over that kept her occupied for another twenty yards of second-by-second trudging through the gloom. In that space of time, she convinced herself he couldn't have beat her there. She was on the first plane out from Cork to Cardiff after the boat crash, and she hadn't seen him on the flight.

So she really had nothing fear. Nothing at all. Nothing but the relentless clamping down of the ever-narrowing passageway, a vise she turned tighter on herself with every yard forward.

She scooched on her stomach Army-style for another ten yards, bewildered when she saw her endpoint. It held nothing remarkable that she could see.

What could be so important about that plain-looking spot?

Yet Perry had marked it in red on the map and annotated it: "Pot of gold!" She knew her geology, and there was simply nothing rich about these ordinary mineral deposits.

There seemed no way to go past that point to anything richer, no branching tunnel to the left or right. There was nothing extraordinary about the floor-to-ceiling stone wall. Nothing, except it wasn't totally solid; it was made of small boulders piled atop one another.

She looked puzzled, then eager. She'd been in hundreds of tunnels and she had never seen nature do something quite like that all on her own.

Just before the boulders the tunnel grew wider. She was overjoyed to find she could at last stand up as it dilated before the dead end.

She put out a hand to touch the rock wall, still tortured by not knowing what about it would incite murder.

Then she took one more step and felt the floor collapse. Gravity forced her body down a shaft that yawned an untold depth below.

22

"*I* told that stupid tosser to off that bird," Perry said, shaking his head. "But he just wouldn't."

Thomas whirled at the sound of his voice.

Perry pulled a gun from his pocket and fired one round at the Mynah, missing. The bullet did ricochet off the cage, though. Miraculously, it knocked the cage through the closed window, spilling glass shards on Thomas's head.

Perry was about to fire on Thomas when he was distracted by the landlady. She was waving an iron skillet at him, snatched from the stove, and shouting about her broken window. He knew she'd use it on his skull, but he was reluctant to shoot her, so he fled.

Thomas gawked for a second at the cage outside on the ground as he brushed glass carefully from his hair. He couldn't tell if the bird was alive or dead, and his heart wouldn't pump again until he knew. That bird had vital information. Then he saw it hop a few steps. He jumped out after it.

Rhys dodged the landlady and ran after Perry himself. He bounced off the walls on his way down the stairwell. By the time he reached the bottom Perry was on his motorcycle.

Perry hopped on and fired it up before Rhys could gain a yard. He caught sight of Thomas trying to corral the Mynah, then gunned the gas and tore off, leaving Rhys to grasp at air.

Thomas caught the bird then veered sharply toward his rented car. Rhys was a stride behind after a quick roll off the ground. Both jumped into the car at the same time.

Thomas flung the Mynah into the back seat, fired up the engine, and slapped into first gear before Perry was done burning rubber thirty yards ahead of them.

Thomas shoved the gas pedal all the way down, hoping to catch up and knock him down. But it proved impossible.

Perry stayed comfortably ahead, as much by smoothly hugging the sharp turns as by sheer speed. The rental couldn't compete without tipping over.

They soon reached a long stretch where the bike's better handling couldn't help Perry keep his lead. Thomas pulled within a few feet, ready to knock him over.

Seeing what he was about to do, Rhys shrieked, "Are you nuts? You'll kill him!"

"Today, yes. Love makes you crazy, remember?"

Thomas inched up until anyone standing on the front bumper could've kicked Perry's license plate.

If he could just get one more spurt he could bump Perry's rear. But the gas pedal was already to the floor and the motor would give no more. Perry's Harley could do one-twenty at full throttle and the rental's top speed just couldn't match it.

Thomas glanced at the tachometer; the engine was near the red line at 6,000 rpm. He forced it into third gear anyway, hoping the downshift time wouldn't cost him space he couldn't make up. The distance grew to a two-foot gap then the car bolted ahead to six inches closer than before, on its way to contact with the bike.

Then, the engine burst.

A piston rod cracked with a loud bang, and there was horrendous clacking inside the engine's cylinder. The oil pressure dropped to zero and the car began to coast as the motor seized up.

Thomas let his foot off the gas. It was useless now. The car drifted as the motorcycle sped off. Thomas sighed as the bike disappeared around a curve. He pulled the car to the side of the road and stopped.

"It's not important," Rhys insisted cheerfully. "We know his license plate number. We can just call the police to pick him up."

"On what charge? Attempted murder of a Mynah bird? Sure, a couple of upstanding citizens like us with no history of trouble with the law can just make a call and—"

"Okay, okay. No need for sarcasm."

Thomas got out of the car to cool off with a walk. Rhys followed.

"Shooting a Mynah," Thomas mumbled. He stopped in the middle of the sidewalk, ignoring the gawkers looking at the dead car with a live bird inside. "Shooting a Mynah?" *Why would he do that?* No court would accept a bird's testimony.

The Mynah squawked from the backseat but otherwise made no attempt to fly away. Thomas turned and stared at him. The bird seemed to have enjoyed the episode.

Thomas returned to the car and noticed a piece of paper around his leg like a pinwheel on a pencil tip. Apparently, the Mynah had jammed his leg through some of the lining at the bottom of the cage, which clung to him as it tipped over.

Thomas reached in through the open window and tried to free it, thinking of nothing more than making the bird more comfortable.

The Mynah hopped backward automatically, out of reach. Thomas tried again and the bird flew out of the car, then settled down two feet away.

His flapping had flung the piece of paper into the air. The scrap floated down and Thomas snatched it.

Thomas stood upright and flipped it over. He noticed a drawing on it. He was studying it when Rhys leaned over him. "What's on it?"

Thomas handed him the slip of paper.

Rhys reviewed it for a moment and said, "It's a drawing of the route you and I took that morning at Dan-yr-Ogof. What the hell does it mean?"

"It means Perry knows where we went the morning Carl was killed. I've got a hunch it's the reason he's dead."

"What's the connection?"

Thomas shrugged.

"Well, call Arwel anyway. You never know. He might at least bring Perry in for questioning based on this."

Thomas pulled out his cell phone and powered it up for the first time that day. The first things he noticed were two text messages from Terri.

"She's on her way to Dan-yr-Ogof, Thomas said.

"Odd."

Thomas grew agitated. "It gets worse. She wrote this using Perry's phone. She says it held a map. Seems it's like the one in the bird cage, only more expensive." He looked down the road. "He must realize she's on her way there."

"Shite."

Thomas tried to phone her but got only voicemail. He sent a text, getting no reply. He waited two minutes — an eternity — before saying to Rhys, "She doesn't respond."

"Double shite."

Thomas said, "We have to get there *first.*"

He looked down at the busted engine and clung to the hood to keep from punching his fist through the windshield.

Terri clung to a rock ledge with one hand, six feet below where she had been standing a few seconds earlier. Her feet were dangling and the fingers in one hand were already beginning to grow numb. She couldn't lift her other arm; the blow her shoulder suffered during the tumble paralyzed her deltoid.

Several of the small boulders that had formed the barrier in the tunnel lay scattered around the ledge. The rest fell down so far that she never heard them hit.

She twisted a few inches trying to look down but, apart from a few yards lit by her lamp, all she saw was empty darkness below. Above, there was the faintest glow, the aftereffect of a brief moment when her helmet's lamp shined on some luminescent rock.

She felt desperately around for a foothold and stuck her toe in the first one she found. She paused a second then ratcheted her body up, edging the elbow of her good arm over the ledge. She rested a moment to get her wind back.

She hoped the ledge was strong enough to hold her. The crumbling pebbles spilling off the edge didn't create a lot of confidence on that score.

She had one lucky break. The rest had allowed her shoulder muscle to recover feeling, and she draped her other arm over the platform.

After another brief pause, she pulled herself up the rest of the way and sat down on the stone. Half a minute later she still felt the effects of the adrenalin rush, but was otherwise fully recovered.

She leaned over the edge and beamed the light down the shaft. There was no bottom to this cavern, none within range of her light, anyway. The powerful beam extended at least 1,000 feet.

She shone the light upward toward the rockface just below the tunnel opening, then swished it slowly left and right. There appeared to be just one spot that might afford a hold, and she needed two to reach the top.

She considered her alternatives to free climbing.

Shouting was useless. Even at full volume there was likely no one near enough to hear. If there was, the echoes would make it impossible for them to locate her. The one man who might be close enough for an accurate fix was the one man she didn't want to alert.

Jumping up was out of the question. Even assuming the fragile rock would take it, there was slim hope she could leap high enough. If she tried and fell short of a handhold she'd surely tumble into the abyss.

That left the rope and pitons as the only way up. It would be slow going, and fraught with uncertainty. There was no way to know the quality of stone softened by untold years of erosion. But it was the only safe way.

She held her hand as high as possible and pushed her fingers hard against the rock above her head. Some of the surface crumbled into her palm, but what was behind that seemed solid enough. She could only tell for sure by trying.

She reluctantly unshouldered her backpack, painfully aware that climbing was not her strong suit. She looked down at the canvas flap. One buckle had broken during the fall. She searched inside to find all but two pitons gone. At least the rope was still there. And, thank Hephaestus, the hammer too.

She estimated the distance from her head to the tunnel floor above. If everything went perfectly – if she lost none to falling out of soft rock or dropping one by accident – two spikes would be enough.

She pulled out the rope and draped it over her shoulder, then withdrew the pitons and hammer. If the stone was solid enough to bear her weight, it would take only a few minutes to rig a few feet and climb up. If.

Too many ifs. Time to find out.

She stooped and put her backpack on, then straightened. She smacked the first piton into a crack and snapped a D-ring over some rope, draping the loop down to her feet. She put her foot into the stirrup and bounced, gently at first, then a little harder.

So far, so good. She put her full weight gently on the rope then banged the second piton into the rockface. The sounds of her hammering rang down the shaft and into the tunnel.

"Please, divine Echo, don't let Perry hear me," she whispered.

She snapped another ring in place, connected the rope, and then raised her foot into the higher loop.

She eased herself up, minimizing the stress on the stirrup, then eased up carefully. Two pebbles tumbled out of the lower crack and she gasped.

She held her breath for a moment then let it out slowly.

She rose far enough to put a hand into a groove formed where the rock had collapsed beneath her.

Now, she thought, *if I can just climb the rest of the way without slipping off the mush in the 'V', all's well that end's well.*

She peered over her shoulder, looking down at the alternative to success. "Forget that," she said in a calm voice, "I'm doing this."

She looked up, this time higher, at the other end of the triangular scoop. She saw that part of it had been carved by a tool. She had sculpted enough cave rock to recognize the distinctive look of artificial wear. She didn't have to guess who had done the chiseling. *Why* was still a mystery.

Why would Perry bother? He'd been away from here since Carl's murder. Why would he have created a booby trap that morning for anyone who might come down this far?

Pass that one on to Da. Later.

She turned her attention back to climbing.

Out of pitons, she drove the claw of her hammer into the wet furrow as high up as she could reach, then looped a third length of rope on it.

She put her hand on the handle and tension on the rope, praying hard that the rock near the top was not too much softer than that below.

She could hear the hard rush of her own breathing, but it was the only sound, apart from the aural illusion of wind every cave produces.

Now for the final test, she thought, *the real one.*

She put weight on the hammer's neck, seeing the head bend a fraction. It held.

Seconds later, she'd worked herself far enough up for the lamp to shine down the tunnel — and right into Perry Turcotte's face.

23

*T*HOMAS and Rhys sped Owen's motorcycle through the main gate to the National Showcaves Center, scattering people right and left before them. They ignored the curses as the bike screeched to a halt a few yards inside the parking lot fence.

Thomas jumped off a split second after Rhys scooted off the back, then he grabbed a lug wrench out of the saddlebag. He hooked his backpack strap with the other hand and ran toward the Dan-yr-Ogof cave entrance at full gallop.

Rhys held off the guard by trying to explain their actions. The man's shouting insistence that the facility was about to close showed he wasn't interested in excuses. The guard signaled to another to chase after this one's friend and boot them both out of the park.

Thomas ran across the dirt path toward the cave entrance until he was stopped thirty yards in.

Consumed with how to go around the man, he stood there shaking from rage and fear. The fear was the residue from what happened there a week earlier, the rage from confronting Arwel just now, who was blocking the way to rescue Terri.

He scanned the area wondering how far he would get if he just ran. He was fit but his barrier was more fit still, and his legs were several inches longer.

leaned over the side and pointed down at the water. "I don't see any anchor. Isn't that odd?"

Rhys leaned over, looking where her finger pointed and thinking, "*So what?*" Before he could straighten up, he felt a hard boot to his rear and plunged head first into the water. It took him a few seconds to recover from the shock and rise to the surface.

During the interval, Terri rushed to the port cleat and flipped off the restraining rope. She hurried back to starboard in time to see Rhys bobbing on the water. "Don't try to come aboard again. Swim away as fast as you can because I'm cranking it up and taking off."

She ran to the cabin and fired up the engine, revving it to maximum a second later.

She looked out the bridge opening to see the spray splashing Rhys, thwarting his attempt to board. When he abandoned trying, she lowered the rpm to normal. She waited long enough for him to swim away another six feet then wrenched the wheel to starboard and raised the engine speed again.

She watched a wedge of water form between the boat and the dock. The triangle grew until it disappeared, blending with the water of the bay. Soon she was too far away to hear the shouts of the Regatta racers, angered by her wake.

She was about to tie off the wheel, with the tiller headed for Thomas's last position, when a man came out of the cabin closet. He mounted the wooden steps onto the bridge, making no effort to be quiet.

Terri looked around and smiled fiercely, looking like a cornered honey badger facing a

There were dozens of people still milling about the area, but not enough to get lost behind. He held up the lug wrench taken from the bike, and waved it threateningly.

"Mr. Mawr, get out of my way or I swear I'll crush your skull." He gripped the lug wrench tighter, half-sure it wouldn't take Terri's father much effort to disarm him. He wasn't wiggling it deliberately; nervous tension was doing that for him.

Arwel didn't budge and didn't feel the least threatened. He knew Thomas wasn't the bashing sort. "Son, I'm not trying to keep you from her. I want to help you."

Thomas was too impatient for puzzles. "Step aside." He raised the lug wrench, his knuckles white. "Please," he added in a desperate tone.

Arwel shook his head. "Do it smart, man. There's something you need to know before you go in there."

Thomas swished the lug wrench to force him aside, but Arwel dodged and clamped his wrist in a vice forged from years of hard labor in the Army. "Listen, damn you." He squeezed until Thomas let go of the tool. "Perry Turcotte got here before you. He went inside and to the right."

Thomas stopped struggling. "I thought as much. Why didn't you stop him?"

Arwel pointed to a thin trail of blood on his temple. "Got past me."

He let go of Thomas's arm. A crowd started to gather, two of whom were park guards. Arwel pulled out his badge and waved them all back. The tourists melted away; the guards stood a short distance off but didn't leave.

Arwel turned his attention back to Thomas, noticing that he had picked up the lug wrench again. He ignored it. He led him inside the mouth of the cave and pointed in the direction Perry had gone.

"I followed him far enough to see which way he went." He indicated a side tunnel. "But he was fast. I came out to get help. You know where he's headed?"

Thomas looked intently in the direction Arwel had pointed. It was toward the new complex he had discovered. He was about to sprint down the path but he'd been delayed too long.

An attendant started to close the large accordion gate that shut off the cave entrance at night.

Thomas objected. The man replied, "Sorry, mate. Need a special permit after hours. Got one?"

Arwel suspected that Thomas might raise the lug wrench to cosh the guard. He stifled his forearm and said to the guard, "Sir, I'm Detective Chief Inspector Mawr of the Brecon Constabulary. We're chasing a suspect."

Arwel let go of Thomas's arm to pull out his badge and saw him raise the lug wrench against the attendant. He pushed the pair apart and Thomas ran down the tunnel.

Thomas dashed along the route he'd shown Rhys that first morning. Entering the small tunnel off to the side, he was forced to slow down. He trotted, hunched over, moving as fast as he could without smashing his head against the ceiling.

Once he reached the section that forced him to crawl, he sped across the muddy surface like a spider chased by a broom.

He reached the final section in one fourth the time Terri had taken, hoping Perry couldn't be more than a minute ahead. Then he realized what could happen in sixty seconds and hurried even more.

A few feet further on, he realized what could happen if he came upon him in a rush. Perry might react without thinking and kill them both. He didn't want to think about what he might do if Terri were already dead.

He forced himself to slow down and proceed quietly in the dark. He turned off his lamp and scooted along as softly as possible.

Army-crawling forward, he listened for the scraping sounds of his own movement, voices from the end of the tunnel, sounds of struggle... anything beyond the gurgles of water wending across the floor. He heard only his own heartbeat.

A minute later, he drew within a few dozen yards of the vertical shaft. He could see nothing but the tiny flashes inside his own eyeballs.

Every nerve ending chary, now he prepared the critical part of his plan — and prayed it wouldn't ensnare Terri as well.

He eased Rhys's camera from his fanny pack without a whisper of noise and flipped the switch to ON. In the total darkness even the minuscule red glow from the power light was enough to give him away. He covered it with his finger and crept forward. When he rounded the bend, he could see the yellow haze of two helmet lamps.

Just then, his knee pinged a rock and it went shooting down the tunnel ahead of him. It bounced off Perry's shoe and settled right at the point of the tunnel where the ceiling rose to the height of a Zulu.

"Who's there?" Perry called out.

He wanted to swash his helmet lamp around to outline the intruder but he didn't dare take his eyes off his captive. She had already kicked him once before he could subdue her.

He held fast to Terri's collar with one hand, clamping her forearm in his armpit. He held a piton in the other hand, poised to strike her.

Thomas scampered forward, heedless now of the noise. He pointed his camera at the helmet light that was now combing the tunnel for his body. The instant Terri's lamp found his face, he shouted, "Terri, close your eyes!" and snapped the shutter.

The tunnel lit up like daylight.

Blinded, Perry instinctively flung his arm up to cover his eyes, releasing Terri's collar. He clamped down harder on her forearm. His vision was beginning to clear when there was another flash, this one closer to his face.

The phone Terri had been holding out of Perry's reach flew out of her hand and into the abyss. That hand now free, she snatched her hammer and whacked him in the knee. He folded back and sideways, howling.

Terri scrambled up the 'V' to the tunnel floor. She squeezed over to the side of the tube, getting as far from the cliff edge as she could.

Thomas joined her in two scoots, then drew himself up to full height, kicking Perry in the head as hard as he could.

Perry fell groundward like an overloaded wheelbarrow. He rose again feebly on one leg and blindly grappled for Terri, trying to toss her over the edge.

She jerked sideways, but he still latched onto an arm. He yanked it, driven by rage past any practical goal, consumed by the lust to hurt Thomas.

Terri peeled off two fingers with a hand made strong by years of sculpting. She bent them backward past the point of pain and he let out a squeal.

Thomas was about to lunge at him when Perry put weight on his wounded leg. The weakness tipped him askew. He curled over the precipice and slumped over into empty space.

Head now lower than his waist, he looked destined either to fall a mile or eight feet only, down the shaft or head first onto the ledge. Either meant certain death.

Instead, his foot caught in the top stirrup of Terri's makeshift ladder, snapping two ankle bones as he came to an abrupt halt above the bottomless pit.

He screamed in pain as his face bounced off the cliff wall, banging the bruises made by his fall off the boat. The cry echoed through the cavern in both directions, down the escarpment and back through the side tunnel.

He hung upside down like a beef slab tossed onto a hook in a darkened meat locker. He swayed an inch left and right three times, then settled, moaning all the while.

Terri pointed her lamp at him and asked Thomas, "Should we bring him up or leave him there to rot?" Her expression was neutral.

Thomas couldn't decide whether or not she was joking. He looked at her in a new way. "Getting to know you better is going to be very interesting, Terri Mawr."

He knelt near the edge and said, "Perry, can you hear me?" A whimper came back that he interpreted as a yes. "In a minute, I'm going to lower my hand. Reach up. Mind you, if you try to pull me down, I'll shake you loose and walk away. No one the wiser."

Thomas looked again at Terri and whispered, "Take some rope from my backpack and tie it around my waist. Then tie yourself and take a stand as far back as you can. Walk around that stalagmiteover there if you can."

With everything ready, Thomas went down on his knees and lowered his arm. "Ok Perry, let's do this." He braced himself, ready for anything.

By the time Perry was safely in the tunnel again, Arwel had arrived. Perry struggled for a moment to stand upright, wobbling, then leaned back against the tunnel wall.

He didn't feel the need to resist any longer. At most, they could try him for assault. The judge would even throw that out once he testified how he had been the one assaulted, and he had the bruises to show for it. The phone lost, there was nothing to link him to Carl's murder.

Arwel said, "Terri, are you alright?"

"Yes, Da." She squeezed his upper arm.

Arwel said, "Turcotte, can you make it out without a stretcher?" Perry nodded and Arwel said, "Good."

He looked down at his clothes with disgust. "All right, Terri, you first, then Thomas, then Perry. I'll take up the rear."

He added, his tone dead serious, "And stay well ahead of Turcotte. If I have to shoot the blighter, I don't want to risk hitting either of you."

The quartet reached the opening of the main cave and met Rhys standing there with the two constables.

Thomas turned to Perry and said, "What was it all about? What did Carl ever do to you?"

Perry refused to speak.

Thomas said, "Go on. You're already on the hook for Terri's attempted murder, after we tell what happened in there."

Rhys added, "Fess up, man. When Sergeant Bevan finds out, you'll wish you'd confessed to Carl's murder. The lesser crime in his eyes."

Perry looked pained, but stayed mum.

Arwel urged him on. "Might as well say it all now, Turcotte. If Professor Payne's testimony," he smiled over at him in the dim light from Terri's lamp, "isn't enough to convict you, we've still got the evidence from your phone."

Perry smiled at last, knowing that at least would never be recovered.

Terri said anxiously, "Da, that was lost down the shaft."

Arwel beamed, gloating. "Doesn't matter, child. Copies of everything will be on the service provider's servers."

Seeing her expression, he tucked his thumbs in his belt and chortled. "I'm not quite as old-fashioned as you might think, girl. Nor you, Dr. Payne."

Perry could now make out clearly Thomas's expression. Noting how calm he looked, Perry exploded in anger. "There it is again, that smarmy Quaker look. Just like it would look in National Geographic when you announced your discovery."

"Huh?" Thomas said. "Why would I announce my power system there?"

"Not your invention, you dolt. The new cave complex. Back there."

He jerked a thumb behind him, shaking with rage. "Why should you get credit for the biggest caving discovery in 50 years?" He spat. "You, a mere spelunker."

Something in Rhys's head clicked. He pointed to Perry and said, "You mistook Carl for Thomas that foggy morning."

Thomas grasped the more important fact a second later. His face fell. "Committed murder... put us through all this... so you could claim discovery... of a cave??"

At the entrance, with the setting sun's rays slanting into the cave, he could see Perry's malicious expression, engorged with envy. The sight made him weary and sad.

He shook his head. "You know what? You can have it," he said, walking away. He snorted, "May the fame bring you comfort in prison."

24

*T*ERRI separated from Thomas only when the police insisted she give them a statement. Sergeant Bevan held her back. Now standing atop a small retaining wall, she watched anxiously past his shoulder as her father took Thomas aside.

"Here," Arwel said, handing Thomas his passport. "James told me what he planned for the pair of you. It didn't take long to confirm who you were after that."

"Then why all the–"

"I still had a murder to solve, man. You were the key. I just didn't know how until today."

Thomas frowned, but he hoped this man would be his future father-in-law. Now seemed a good time to start overlooking some things. He asked instead, "Just what did James have in mind?"

"I'll tell you about that later."

Thomas thought it ironic that, of all people, his father should be the one responsible for persuading the police that he was innocent. The fiend turned out to be worth something, after all.

He looked around at the mountains as they reached the exit to the park. The sun had dropped just below the rim of the tallest one, and its rays put a halo over the jagged green crown.

He tapped the passport against his palm a couple of times. He slipped it into his pocket without looking inside. "I suppose Perry is the one who hacked my personnel record at the university."

Arwel said, "I expect so. Computer forensics will let me know."

Softly, to no one in particular, he said, "Going home."

Arwel said with a sly grin, "To do that you'll need to get a new passport." He watched Thomas check the expiration date on the document. "In your right name," he said with a straight face. Then he broke out in a grin at Thomas's puzzled look, enjoying a detective's moment when he knows something others don't.

Thomas sighed and sat down hard on a boulder. "You still don't believe I'm me? But then I don't understand..."

His voice faded. The day's final rays struck him full in the face, highlighting his frustrated expression. It meant he couldn't return to Wales right away, after all. He wondered how a lengthy separation from Terri might affect them.

Arwel said, "You're not the son of James Paine, Thomas."

"You've no idea how many times I wished that were true," he said. "But I have very clear memories, unfortunately."

"Do you?" Arwel continued, "I spoke to the Society of Friends in London. They kindly provided some very helpful information about a couple in Oban." He pulled a document from his coat pocket and handed it to Thomas.

"You were kidnapped from your real parents at age two. By James and Celia Paine." He waited. When Thomas stayed silent he added, "They thought they could travel safer with a child as cover. Crazy, but there it is."

Terri joined them just in time to hear this. "So Thomas is not a Quaker, after all?"

Arwel said, "It's a choice, love, not a race."

She asked, "How did you find them?"

"Your visit to the Friends' Society made me curious." He put a hand on her arm and winked. "And you say I should pay no attention to where you go."

Arwel lit up his pipe, making his face glow in the oncoming dusk. "Pity James happened through Oban on his way. He saw me talking to them at their bookstore. That's how I came to be coshed on the head and stuffed into that boat."

Terri, eager to steer the conversation to something more cheerful, said to Thomas, "You've still got a week of vacation left. Maybe you'd like to look them up."

Thomas thought it over for a moment. "I think I would." He smiled wickedly. "If I can introduce to them my fiancée."

Terri threaded her fingers through Thomas'. She hugged his arm with the other hand and leaned on his shoulder. She answered with her own wicked grin, "We'll see."

The End

Acknowledgments

I've generally not been keen on acknowledgments.

I have to break that rule this time. "Death Is Overrated" has been so immeasurably improved by the input of Frank Palmer-White it would be churlish not to express my appreciation. Beyond correcting a number of errors and providing countless tips on UK culture, his enthusiastic feedback made the whole process a joy.

About the Author

Jeffrey Perren is the author of *The Lighthouse Pylon, The Geisha Hummingbird,* and other titles forthcoming from Deep Read Press.

www.ingramcontent.com/pod-product-compliance
Lightning Source LLC
Chambersburg PA
CBHW070306260626
47160CB00003B/743